THE BATTLE

Patrick Rambaud

THE BATTLE

Translated from the French by
Will Hobson

GROVE PRESS
New York

Originally published in 1997 as La Bataille *by Editions Grasset
et Fassquelle, Paris*
Printed in the United States of America

FIRST AMERICAN EDITION

Library of Congress Cataloging-in-Publication Data

Rambaud, Patrick.
[Bataille. English]
The battle / Patrick Rambaud ; translated from the French by
Will Hobson.
p. cm.
ISBN 0-8021-1662-0
1. Aspern-Essling, Battle of, Austria, 1809—Fiction. 2.
Napoleonic Wars, 1800-1815—Campaigns—Austria—Fiction.
3. Napoleon I, Emperor of the French, 1769-1821—Fiction.
I. Hobson, Will. II. Title.

PQ2678 .A455 B3813   2000 843'.914—dc21   99-086344

Grove Press
841 Broadway
New York, NY 10003

00 01 02 03   10 9 8 7 6 5 4 3 2 1

One

VIENNA IN 1809

In the morning of Tuesday 16 May 1809, a Berline flanked by horsemen pulled out of Schönbrunn and drove at a leisurely pace along the right bank of the Danube. It was an unremarkable carriage, olive coloured, without coats of arms on its panels. As it passed, the Austrian peasants raised their black, broad-brimmed hats, out of caution, rather than respect, because they recognized the officers riding their long-maned Arabs at a trot, a panther skin under their seats, uniforms in the Hungarian style – white, scarlet, heavy with gold – a heron's feather in their shakos: these young gentlemen were the permanent escort of Berthier, Major-General of the occupying army.

A man's arm appeared through the Berline's lowered window. The Grand Equerry Caulaincourt, who had been keeping his horse abreast of the carriage door, instantly squeezed his mount with his knees, removed his cocked hat and gloves with the dexterity of a circus rider, and unbuttoned his jacket to produce a folded map of Vienna's surroundings, which he held out with a salute. A moment later, the carriage came to a halt in front of the yellow, fast-flowing river.

A Mameluke in a turban jumped off the footman's box, unfolded the step, opened the door and prostrated himself in a flurry of exaggerated bows. The Emperor emerged, putting on his beaver-skin hat, its fur scorched by years of ironing. He had slung his frock coat of grey Louviers cloth like a cape over his grenadier's uniform. His breeches were ink-stained, since it was his habit to wipe quill pens on them and there had been an armful of decrees for him to sign before the day's parade. As ever, the Emperor wanted to decide everything himself, to settle in person every one of a thousand matters – from the distribution of new boots to the Guard to the supplying of Paris's fountains with water – matters which, more often than not, bore no relevance to the war he was now waging in Austria.

Napoleon was beginning to put on weight. His kersey-mere waistcoat was stretched tight across a rounded stomach, he no longer had a neck and his shoulders sagged. His blank, indifferent expression only became passionate when he was angry. Today he was sullen, his mouth pinched. When he had heard for certain that Austria was arming herself against him, he returned from Valladolid to Saint-Cloud in five days, riding one horse after another into the ground. Having recently been sleeping ten hours a night and another two in his bath, thanks to the setbacks in Spain and now this further imbroglio, he had recovered all his strength in an instant.

Berthier had in turn climbed out of the Berline and gone to join Napoleon, who was sitting on the stump of a durmast oak. The two men were almost the same height and they wore the same type of hat; from a distance, they might have been mistaken for one another. But the Chief of Staff had thick, curly hair and a corpulent face which lacked the symmetry of Napoleon's. Together they looked at the Danube.

'Sire,' said Berthier, biting his fingernails, 'the place seems well chosen.'

'*Sulla carta militare, è evidente!*' replied the Emperor, cramming his nostrils with snuff.

'The depth still needs to be sounded from skiffs ...'

'That's your concern!'

'... the strength of the current measured ...'

'Your concern!'

Berthier's concern, as usual, was to obey. Loyal and meticulous, he always carried out his master's wishes to the letter and, as a consequence, had acquired enormous power, the self-interested devotion of others and no small amount of jealousy.

*

The section of the Danube before them was split into several branches, which slowed its current, and was further broken up by a number of islands covered in meadows, scrub and woods of elms, willows and spreading oaks. An islet between the bank and the largest of these islands, the island of Lobau, would serve as a point of support for the bridge they were going to build. On the other side of the river, at the Lobau's furthest point, they could see a small, level expanse stretching to the villages of Aspern and Essling and then, rising above the thickets of trees, the two village steeples. Beyond that, an immense plain planted with green crops and watered by a stream that dried up in May, and finally, on the left, the wooded heights of Bisamberg, where the Austrian troops had fallen back after burning the bridges.

The bridges! Four years earlier the Emperor had entered Vienna as a saviour, its inhabitants running to meet his army. This time, when he reached its poorly protected suburbs, he had been forced to lay siege to the city for three days, and even bombard it before the garrison withdrew.

An initial attempt to cross the Danube near the destroyed Spitz bridge had failed recently. Five hundred light infantrymen of Saint-Hilaire's division, under the command of chefs de bataillons Rateau and Poux, had gained a foothold on the island of Schwartze-Laken, but acting without precise orders or coordination they had neglected to station a reserve company in a large house well placed for protecting the landing of further troops. Half of their men had been killed; the others were wounded or captured by the enemy vanguard stationed on the left bank, which played the Austrian anthem by Herr Haydn every morning to rouse the spirits of the Viennese.

Now the Emperor had taken personal command. He intended to destroy the Archduke Charles's army, a strong force on its own, before it could link up with that of the Archduke John, which was arriving from Italy by forced march. For that reason, the Emperor had posted Davout and his cavalry on lookout to the west. He gazed at the vast Marchfeld plain on the other side of the river, climbing endlessly to the horizon towards the plateau of Wagram.

An ordinary sergeant-major, with a white handlebar moustache and clumsily buttoned coat, called out to him in a reproachful voice, not even bothering to stand to attention, 'You have forgotten me, my Emperor! What about my medal?'

'What medal?' asked Napoleon, smiling for the first time in eight days.

'*La croix d'officier de la Légion d'honneur*, of course! I've deserved it from the first day I fought as a soldier in your army!'

'As long as that?'

'Rivoli! Saint Jean-d'Acre! Austerlitz! Eylau!'

'Berthier . . .'

The chief of staff noted down the name of the newly promoted officer, Rousillon, with his pencil. He had hardly finished writing before the Emperor stood up, throwing aside the hatchet with which he had been hacking at the oak's trunk. '*Andiamo!* I want a bridge by the end of the week. Station some of the brigades of light cavalry in that village behind there.'

'Ebersdorf,' said Berthier, checking it on his map.

'Bredorf if you wish, and three divisions of cuirassiers. Get started immediately!'

The Emperor never gave a direct order or reprimand any more: everything went through Berthier. Before climbing into the Berline, the latter signalled to one of his theatrically dressed aides-de-camp. 'See to it, Lejeune, with the Duke of Rivoli.'

'Very good, Your Excellency,' replied the officer, a young colonel in the Engineers with tanned skin, brown hair and a striking scar, like a stripe, across the left of his forehead.

He mounted his Arab, adjusted his black and gold silk belt, brushed a speck of dust off his fur dolman and watched the imperial carriage drive off with its escort. He lingered behind, studying the Danube with a professional eye and those islands pounded by the current. Lejeune had taken part in the construction of pontoon bridges on the Po, in the driving rain, where they had used posts, anchors and rafts, but how was one to find purchase in these swirling yellow foam-flecked waters?

The main branch of the river skirted the island of Lobau on the south. Looking towards the other bank, which they had to reach, Lejeune suspected marshy ground and quagmires which the river, as it rose and fell, would reveal as tongues of sand.

He turned his highly strung horse in the direction of Vienna. Not far from the village of Ebersdorf he noticed a sheltered creek where they could float pontoons and boats; on the other side of the copse, they could stack timber, chains, piles and girders – an entire dockyard out of enemy sight. Then Lejeune headed towards the suburbs where the Duke of Rivoli's troops were encamped. Called *'mon cousin'* by Napoleon, this dashing swordsman was greedy, lawless and an inveterate braggart. But he was also a faultless strategist, and, swept along by that hothead Augereau, it was his infantry who had distinguished themselves by storming the bridge of Arcola. He was Masséna.

*

Lannes's corps, along with three divisions of cuirassiers, was quartered in the old town. Masséna's, meanwhile, had taken up position facing the suburbs, in open countryside, and the marshal had commandeered a small, turreted baroque palace which had been left abandoned when its owners, a family of Viennese aristocrats, were forced to make for safety in another province or in the Archduke's camp. When Lejeune rode into the main courtyard he didn't need to report himself, since Berthier's aides-de-camp were the only members of the Grande Armée entitled to wear red trousers and these served as their passes: their responsibility at all times was to deliver the directives of the General Staff – in other words those of Napoleon himself. This privileged position did not, however, endear them to the rank-and-file, and the dragoon to whom Lejeune handed his thoroughbred cast envious glances at the saddle holsters and the saddle braided with gold. All around him on the paving stones slovenly dressed soldiers had dragged out high-backed Gothic seats and chairs upholstered with tapestry from the ground-floor reception rooms. Some of the men were smoking long thin clay pipes, like pirates, and swaggering in front of the bivouacs, feeding the fires with violins and ebony inlay they had torn from the palace furniture. Others were drinking wine from the barrel through straws and throwing punches at each other, swearing, shouting abuse and roaring with laughter. Still others were chasing after a flock of squawking geese and trying to slit their throats with sabres the moment they took off, so that they could roast the birds without needing to draw them first. The air was thick with white feathers and they were throwing handfuls in each other's faces like children.

Inside the palace, veterans had slashed the family portraits for sport and the canvases hung pathetically from their frames in strips. At the foot of a marble staircase, a gunner dressed as a woman in a voluminous ball gown gave Lejeune directions in a falsetto, while his fellow looters spluttered with laughter. They had rigged themselves out as well, one in a powdered wig which had slipped down over his eyes, the other in a puce-coloured moiré frock coat which had split across the back when he put it on. A third was filling his undress cap with spoons and silver-plated drinking cups from a *bombé* commode which he had kicked in. With a look of disgust, Lejeune went upstairs to the

marshal's suite of apartments. Smashed porcelain crunched
under his boots. In a drawing room opening onto a balus-
traded balcony, officers, orderlies and commissaries in
civilian clothes chatted as they took their pick of the
chandeliers and vases and had their servants pack them
away in crates stuffed with straw. On a sofa, a colonel of
Hussars was pawing a local farmer's daughter who, like
her sisters, had been pressed into a squadron's service.
Perched on a rosewood console-table, a valet in white gloves
was unhooking a chandelier. Lejeune tapped him on the
leg and asked to be announced. 'That's not my job,' the
valet said, absorbed in the business of pilfering something
for himself.

Lejeune kicked over the console-table and the valet was
left hanging from the chandelier, squealing and sawing the
air with his legs, to the great amusement of the assembled
company. Applause broke out. A brigadier, suddenly noticing the uniform of the General Staff, was offering Lejeune
some German wine in a cup when one of the drawing-
room doors flung open. Masséna, dressed in a sultan's gown
and Turkish slippers, entered, shouting, 'Can't you keep
the racket down, you bloody rabble?'

One-eyed, with a hooked nose set in an otherwise full
face and thick black hair cut in a Titus crop, the marshal
had a fine, strong voice, but instead of bringing silence, his
shout only added to the confusion. Catching sight of
Lejeune, the one person behaving with any dignity in the
throng, he ordered, 'Come this way, Colonel.'

Stooping slightly, he turned to go back to his chamber,
closely followed by the Emperor's messenger. At a bend in
the corridor, Masséna stopped dead in front of a massive

gold and silver-gilt clock. It showed some sort of gong being struck by plump cherubs.

'What do you think?'

'Of the situation, Your Grace?'

'No, no, you halfwit, of this clock!'

'It looks attractive enough.'

'Julien!'

A valet in dark red livery appeared from nowhere.

'Julien,' said Masséna, 'we'll be taking that.'

The valet carefully picked up the clock, gasping at its weight. When they reached a corner room, Masséna sat on the edge of a velvet four-poster bed and at last asked, 'Well then, young man, what are my orders?'

'To build a pontoon bridge over the Danube, six kilometres south-east of Vienna.'

Masséna was utterly imperturbable, no matter what task he was set. At fifty-one years old, there was nothing he had not suffered or achieved. He was well known to be a thief and said to bear grudges, but, once again, this was an occasion when the Emperor needed his military expertise. As a rule, the marshal despised Berthier's 'dandies' or 'the popinjays', as they were called. The son of an olive-oil merchant from Nice, and, at one stage in his life, a smuggler, he was not a marshal or duke by blood, like those good-for-nothing little puppies plucked from banking houses and aristos' salons – the Marquises Flahaut, Pourtalès, Colbert, Noailles, Montesquiou, Girardin and Périgord: smug, self-satisfied types who kept pommade and toiletries in their cartridge pouches. But Masséna made an exception of Lejeune as the only bourgeois in their group – even if he had been taught to salute, like the rest of them, by Gardel, the ballet-master at the Opéra. Besides, he had a certain talent as a painter which His Majesty admired.

'Have you reconnoitred the site?' Masséna asked.

'Yes, Your Grace.'

'And? How wide is it?'

'Roughly eight hundred metres.'

'So, eighty boats to support the roadway . . .'

'I have seen a creek where we could shelter them, Your Grace.'

'And we'll need posts, let's say nine thousand . . . There's enough forests in this godforsaken country for that.'

'But also four thousand girders, or thereabouts, and at least nine thousand metres of strong rope.'

'Yes, and anchors too.'

'Or fishermen's chests, Your Grace, which we can fill with cannonballs.'

'When it comes to cannonballs, Colonel, let's try to be economical, shall we?'

'I'll do my best.'

'Very well, look sharp, then! Requisition everything that floats!'

Lejeune was about to leave when Masséna detained him with a sudden outburst. 'Lejeune, you're always ferreting about, tell me . . .'

'Your Grace?'

'People say that the Genoese have deposited a hundred million in Viennese banks. Is that true?'

'I don't know.'

'Find out. I insist.'

Someone mumbled under the sheets. Lejeune glimpsed a few strands of hair. With the collusive smile of a horse trader, Masséna tore back the embroidered bedspread and,

grasping a mane of fair hair, yanked upright a young
woman who was only half awake. 'Colonel, let me know
quickly about that Genoese money and she's yours. She's
the widow of a Corsican skirmisher who was disembowelled last week, but she's as buxom and eager to please as a
duchess!'

Lejeune had a low opinion of such wine-shop vulgarity;
his impassive expression made this obvious. Oh well, Masséna thought to himself, these young prudes will never be
real soldiers. He let the young woman fall back onto the
silk pillows and said, in a drier tone of voice, 'Go on, then!
Cut along to Daru's!'

*

Count Daru, the Intendant-General, was in charge of the
Imperial commissariat. He had set up his department in a
wing of the Schönbrunn palace, near the Emperor, half
a league from Vienna. There, with the help of his biting
tongue, he ruled over an entire population of civilians,
because it was no longer merely an army that followed in
Napoleon's train but a horde, a city on the march, with a
baggage train of five battalions to drive two thousand five
hundred wagons of supplies and equipment, and companies
of bakers, oven-builders, Bavarian masons and almost every
other trade overseen by ninety-six commissaries and deputy
commissaries. These functionaries were responsible for
quarters, forage, horses, carriages, hospitals, provisions;
for everything. Daru would know where they could dig out
the boats they needed.

Lejeune rode past the ornamental sphinx that decorated
the bridge over the River Wien, and then through a tall
gate flanked by two lead eagles on pink stone obelisks.

He entered the quadrangular courtyard of Schönbrunn, the Habsburgs' less formal summer residence. It lay in the shade of a park, home to a colony of tame squirrels. In the bustle of supply services and battalions of the Guard, he spotted a corporal with green woollen epaulettes.

'Daru?' he shouted at him.

'That way, Colonel. Past the large pond and under the colonnade on the left.'

It was a Viennese palace. In other words, it was pompous, baroque, intimate and austere all at once; an imitation of Versailles in ochre, but on a smaller scale and with less attention to symmetry. Lejeune found Daru in the middle of a group of commissaries. He was gesticulating and swearing at one who was wearing an opera hat. Lejeune's arrival was a fresh annoyance. What *further* demand was going to be made of him now? Dressed in a morning coat buttoned tight over an imposing stomach, with the coat tails hitched up, he put his hands on his hips.

'Count,' Lejeune began as he dismounted.

'Come to the point! What impossibility is His Majesty asking of me?'

He articulated each syllable, as they do in the South, and spoke with a lilting, musical intonation.

'Eighty boats, Count.'

'Hullo! That's all, is it? And I'm supposed to conjure these tubs out of thin air, am I? What, is the army going boating down the Danube?'

'They're to support a bridge.'

'I thought as much.'

Turning to his entourage, he snapped, 'Don't stand there like blockheads! Haven't you got enough work to do?'

Then, as the others moved off with grave expressions, he continued, 'Colonel, there are no more boats in Vienna. Not a single one! The Austrians are not such simpletons! They've scuppered most of them or taken them downriver out of our reach, to Pressburg. No fools, eh? They don't want a sniff of us on the left bank of their beloved Danube!'

Daru took Lejeune by the arm and led him into an office cluttered with crates and piles of furniture, put his felt cockade hat on a table, chased out with a roar two deputy commissaries who were unfortunate enough to be sitting there dozing and then, changing his tone like an actor, switched from fury to a feigned despondency.

'It's chaos, Colonel, chaos! Nothing is turning out right! *All* I have is problems! This cursed blockade is working against us, I can tell you!'

Three years earlier the Emperor had decided to isolate England by banning the sale of its goods on the Continent, but this had not put a stop to smuggling. Besides, the army's greatcoats were still made of cloth woven in Leeds and its shoes still came from Northampton. England dominated the world's commerce and it was Imperial Europe which was condemning itself to self-sufficiency, with the result that they had run out of sugar and the indigo they needed to dye the uniforms blue. Daru was complaining about this consequence in particular. 'Our soldiers dress any old how, in what they can get their hands on in the villages or after a battle. How does that make them look, eh? Like a troupe of tattered strolling players! They wear grey jackets they've thieved from the Austrians and then what happens? You don't know? I'll tell you, Colonel, I'll tell you.' He sighed heavily. 'At the first wound, even the slightest flesh wound, the blood spreads on a light material and it shows. A graze looks as if you've taken a bayonet thrust in the guts and that blood demoralizes the other men, it scares the life out of them, it paralyses them!'

Daru suddenly started speaking like a gentleman's tailor. 'Whereas on a blue, a beautiful dark blue, those terrible stains show less.'

He collapsed into a rococo armchair, which creaked loudly under his weight, and spread out a staff map.

'His Majesty wants to plant woad near Toulouse, Albi and Florence. Fine. It grew there marvellously in the past, but now we haven't the time! And then have you seen the conscripts? Compared to them, last year's draft look like veterans! We're waging war with children in fancy dress, Colonel.'

He looked at the map and, once again, changed his tone.

'Where do you want it, this bridge?'

Lejeune pointed to the island of Lobau on the outspread map. Daru gave an even heavier sigh.

'We'll see to it, Colonel.'

'Immediately?'

'As immediately as possible.'

'We also need to collect ropes, chains . . .'

'That won't be so difficult. But come now, my guess is that you haven't had a bite to eat since this morning.'

'No, I haven't.'

'Well, make use of my cooks. They've prepared a squirrel stew today, just like they did yesterday and just like they'll do tomorrow. It's not too bad, it tastes a little like rabbit, and then there's so many of them in the park! After that, well, we'll just have to tuck into the tigers and kangaroos in the palace menagerie! Our jaded appetites have got a few shocks in store . . . Go and see Commissary

Beyle, in the office just above this one; I'll leave you now, the hospitals aren't ready, the forage is poor, and your cursed boats ... Bah, as the poet Horace said, my dear Horace, a well-prepared soul hopes for contentment in the midst of adversity.'

'One last thing, Count.'

'Tell me.'

'It appears that the Genoese...'

'Oh no! Colonel! Damn it all, will I never be left in peace about these imaginary millions! You're the third person Masséna has sent to ask about them! All that I've found, apart from the guns of the Arsenal, is this...'

He tipped over a wooden chest with his buckled shoe. Austrian florins tumbled out onto the floor.

'We owe these to the fastidious work of M. Savary,' Daru explained. 'They're fakes. I use them to pay my local suppliers. Take a bundle or two.'

*

'Henri!'

'Louis-François!'

Louis-François Lejeune and Henri Beyle, who had not yet started calling himself Stendhal, had known each other for nine years. When they were stationed in Milan they had vied for the provocative charms of a local woman, but Lejeune had carried the day and Henri, secretly, had been glad. He preferred his desires to remain unfulfilled and, anyway, would that excessively beautiful Italian woman have been satisfied with him? At the time he thought of himself as extremely ugly and it made him bashful, despite his green uniform of the 6th Dragoons and his helmet bound in lizard-skin with a plume of horsehair. A few years later they had bumped into each other in a lottery booth in the Palais Royal and gone out onto the boulevards, to Vérys, to eat oysters at twelve sous a dozen under gilt candelabras. Lejeune had paid. Henri, who had left the army and hadn't a sou to his name, made the most of this treat by devouring a whole chicken. Lejeune was preparing to rejoin his regiment in Holland: Henri, meanwhile, was envisaging a future either as a planter in Louisiana, or as a banker, or, largely because of the actresses, as a successful playwright.

Now they had met again near Vienna, by the chance of active service. One was surprised, the other not. Nothing could be more natural than Lejeune's being a colonel, because he had chosen his career and applied himself to it. But Henri? At the time, he was a fat twenty-six-year-old with shiny skin, a thin mouth with almost no lips, almond-brown eyes and tousled hair which stood high over his broad forehead. Lejeune, astonished, asked him what on earth he was doing in that commissariat's office.

'Ah! Louis-François, to be happy I need to live at the heart of great events.'

'As a commissary of war?'

'Deputy, only deputy.'

'But Daru sent me to Commissary Beyle.'

'He is too kind, he must be ill.'

Count Daru had little regard for Henri. He invariably treated him as a scatterbrain, harshly ordering him about and only delegating jobs to him if they were irritating or of absolutely no interest.

'What are my orders?' he asked his friend, delighted to see him again but at the same time anxious as to what was going to be asked of him.

'Nothing too elaborate. You are to give me some squirrel stew at Count Daru's expense.'

'*My God!* Is that what you want?'

'No.'

Henri buttoned his morning coat, snatched up his hat with the tricolour cockade and seized on this chance to flee his office as if it were a godsend. Passing through the next room, he informed his secretaries and book-keepers that he would be gone for the day and seeing Lejeune's uniform, they conspicuously did not ask the reason, assuming it to be significant. Outside, Lejeune asked, 'Do you get on with those pen-pushers?'

'Oh no, Louis-François! You don't have to worry about that. They're a vulgar, scheming, imbecile, worthless lot.'

'Tell me more.'

'Where are we going?'

'I've requisitioned a house in the old town, I'm lodging there with Périgord.'

'Good, let's go there, as long as you're not ashamed of my civilian clothes and my horse. I'm warning you, it's a real carthorse.'

On the stable road they talked about their lives, particularly Henri's. No, he hadn't given up the theatre: he studied Shakespeare, Gozzi and Crébillon *fils* whenever he could, even when he was travelling, but writing comedies didn't make one a living and he didn't want to be indebted to his family any longer. In the meantime he had accepted the patronage of Daru, who was a distant relative. From the Imperial Intendance he hoped to manoeuvre himself into the post of Auditor to the State Council, which was not, in itself, a profession, but a stepping stone to all the other professions and, first and foremost, an annual income.

Henri had just spent two years in Germany where he had
divided his time between the commissariat, the opera,
hunting and young girls.

'In Brunswick,' he said, 'I learnt how not to be so shy
and how to hunt.'

'Are you a good shot?'

'On my first duck shoot, I bagged two crows!'

'No Austrians?'

'I still haven't seen real fighting, Louis-François. I
missed Jena by a few days. On the outskirts of Neuburg
I thought I heard cannon-fire; it was a thunderstorm.'

Henri had, however, crossed the Ebersberg bridge when
the town was still in flames. His coach had driven over
corpses whose faces had been burnt away. He had seen
entrails spilling out under the wheels. To prove he was
made of stern stuff, he had continued chatting nonchalantly
despite a fierce desire to vomit.

As they reached the commissariat's stables, Lejeune
exclaimed, 'So that's your horse?'

'That's the one they've given me, yes. I warned you.'

'You're right. All it's missing is a plough!'

As dissimilar in their dress and mounts as could be
imagined, but unconcerned by any ridicule this might
provoke, the two friends set off on the road to Vienna. In
the distance, they could see the city's ramparts and the tall
spire of St Stephen's.

*

Vienna had two defensive rings. The first, a simple earth-
work embankment, bounded its heavily populated suburbs,
where low red-roofed houses crowded in on each other;
the second, a strong defensive wall fortified with moats,

bastions, pillboxes and covered walkways, enclosed the old town, but because the Viennese no longer feared the Turks or Hungarian rebels, hotels and shops had proliferated along the length of its fortifications and trees had been planted to form promenades on the slope.

Lejeune and Beyle passed under the arch of a large gate and made their way at a walk through the city's twisting streets, between tall, elongated houses, a mixture of medieval and baroque, all painted in delicate colours in the Italian manner and with window sills covered in blue flowers and birdcages. The spectacle presented by the other wayfarers was less entrancing: wherever one looked, there was nothing but soldiers.

A conqueror is an ugly thing, Henri thought to himself at the sight of the motley troops. Napoleon had recently handed over Vienna – a city barely the size of a Parisian *quartier* – to his men for four or five days and they were already taking full advantage. It reminded Henri of a pack of hunting dogs. They had risked death a thousand times, it was true, and been brutally forced to leave behind friends' bodies, the maimed, the blind, an arm, a leg, but did the fact that their fear had subsided justify this excess? Dragoons were lowering furniture by ropes into the street, while their accomplices threatened the owners: this could not fail to turn a naturally mild and welcoming people against them. A cuirassier in an iron helmet, swathed in a long white Austrian coat, was attempting to auction off a pile of theatre costumes, clarinets and stolen furs which he had thrown on the ground. Other stalls lined an alleyway where these brigands were selling their plunder: glass and pearl necklaces, dresses, sacramental vessels, chairs, mirrors, chipped statuettes. The throng jostled and seethed like a

Cairo souk, speaking twenty languages and hailing from twenty different countries to merge into a single arrogant army: Poles, Saxons, Bavarians, Florentines (who were nicknamed 'jabberers') – even one of Kirmann's Mamelukes, although the only thing Arabic about him was his baggy trousers, since he had been born at Saint-Ouen. Muskets were stacked in squares and at the junctions of avenues. Infantrymen in high-buttoned gaiters snored on heaps of straw in a church square. Chasseurs in dark blue uniforms flogged black horses through the streets and a group of heavy cavalrymen on foot rolled along barrels of Riesling. Some hussars were sitting outside a café eating boiled beef, their chests puffed out, mightily proud of their sky-blue breeches, their bright red waistcoats, their heavy braided locks to cushion sabre cuts and the extravagant plumes billowing out of their shakos. A rifleman emerged from under a porch wearing a string of sausages as a lanyard; he staggered a little as he held onto a wall to piss.

'Look!' Lejeune said to his friend. 'We could be in Verona.'

He gestured towards a fountain, a narrow building and the pale light which picked out the façades of a little square. Lejeune affected to see nothing else. He was not like other officers. From his tours of garrison duty and his campaigns he had brought back a number of sketches and highly accomplished paintings. Napoleon, when he was First Consul, had bought his *Battle of Marengo*. At Lodi and Somosierra, he went to war as if he was setting up before an artist's model. His figures captured in motion served as props: for example, in the assault on the monastery of Santa Engracia at Saragossa, where a massacre was taking place in the foreground in front of a white stone

22

statue of the Virgin. What held the eye in that composition was the Arabicized building, the stone carving around the cloister, the square tower, the sky. At Aboukir, it was the harsh glare, the heat which made the greys and yellows shimmer. Louis-François, therefore, ignored the soldiers on their drunken spree. He admired the aspect of the Pallavicini palace and was reminded of Palladio by the pediment of the Trautson palace. This enduring love of beautiful things was what had first brought Louis-François and Henri Beyle together, and it had given rise to a friendship, which neither war nor the long absences from each other's company had strained since.

'We're nearly there,' said Lejeune as they turned into the rather more elegant Jordangasse district.

Suddenly, rounding a corner, Lejeune made his horse rear. Ahead of them, dragoons were entering a pink house and leaving with their arms full of linen, china, flagons and smoked hams which they were stacking on an army cart. 'Oh! Those dirty scoundrels!' Lejeune shouted and spurred his horse forward to burst into the swarm of looters. Taken by surprise, they dropped a chest, which split open; one lost his helmet in the scuffle, another was sent flying into a wall. Henri rode nearer as his friend, still on horseback but now in the hall, lashed out with his whip and riding boots.

'The city is ours, sir!' said a tall cuirassier in a greatcoat cut from the sackcloth of a Spanish monk: he wore spurs on his espadrilles and gave the impression of being determined to continue emptying the house of its contents.

'Not this house!' Lejeune yelled.

'The whole city, sir!'

'Leave here or I'll crack your skull open!'

Lejeune cocked his horse-pistol and pointed it at the

forehead of the insubordinate soldier, who broke into a smile. 'Very well, go ahead and fire, Colonel!'

Lejeune struck him a violent blow with the barrel of his gun; the cuirassier, his face badly bruised, spat out three teeth and a mouthful of blood, then drew his sabre, but his companions grabbed him round the waist and pinned his arms to his side.

'Get the hell out! Get the hell out of here!' Lejeune shouted in a hoarse voice.

'If you go into battle, sir, make sure you never turn your back on me!' the cuirassier snarled, his jaw covered in blood.

'Out! Out!' Lejeune said, randomly striking any backs or heads within his reach.

The veterans left the devastated house, abandoning a large part of their spoils, and either mounted their horses or clung onto the cart as it pulled away. The tall cuirassier in the brown greatcoat shook his fist and bellowed that his name was Fayolle and that his aim was true.

Lejeune was trembling with fury. He dismounted and tethered his horse to the ring on the front door. A coatless lieutenant, his hair awry, was slumped on a solitary bench, panting and groaning. It was Lejeune's aide-de-camp, who had been unable to stand up to the rampaging mob. Henri caught up with them at the far end of the vast, austere hall.

'Did they go upstairs?'

'Yes, Colonel.'

'Mlle Krauss?'

'With her sisters and governess, Colonel.'

'Were you alone?'

'Almost, Colonel.'

'Périgord is here?'

'In his rooms on the first floor, Colonel.'

Followed by Henri, Lejeune rushed up the steep main staircase, while his aide-de-camp started picking up the foodstuffs which the dragoons had forgotten.

'Périgord?'

'Come in, old man,' a voice echoed along the empty corridors.

Lejeune, with Henri behind, went into an enormous, unfurnished drawing room where, standing bare-chested and in red breeches before a cheval glass in a mahogany frame, Edmond de Périgord was waxing his moustache, helped by his manservant, a plump, heavy-jowled individual in a wig and a suit of livery trimmed with silver lace.

'Périgord, you let those blackguard soldiers invade this house!'

'It stands to reason that those brutes must amuse themselves before they go into action.'

'Amuse themselves!'

'A brute's amusement, yes. They're hungry, my dear friend, they're thirsty, they're not rich and they have a pretty shrewd idea that they've been condemned to death.'

'Did they go up to Mlle Krauss's floor?'

'There's no need to be alarmed, Louis-François,' said Périgord, leading his colleague through the anterooms on the first floor. Two dragoons were sprawled on the steps of a second staircase which led to the upper floors.

'These imbeciles wanted to do a little looting up there,' Périgord said in a weary voice, 'but I forbade them. They tried to force their way through.'

'Did you kill them?'

'Oh, no, I don't think so. They caught a chair full in the

face and I can assure you, my dear friend, those chairs are devilishly heavy. Having said that, when they fell, they might perhaps have snapped their necks; I haven't had a proper look. In any case, I'll have them removed.'

'Thank you.'

'Don't mention it, my dear friend. My innate gallantry deserves most of the credit.'

Henri, slightly stunned by what he'd just witnessed, followed after his friend, who was now running upstairs and along the corridors until he reached a massive door, which he began pounding on, calling out, 'It's me, it's Colonel Lejeune!'

Having put on a dressing gown sewn with facings and trimmed with brocade, Périgord caught them up, still with only half of his moustache waxed. He started chatting to Henri as if they were at a soirée in the Trianon palace, while Lejeune carried on knocking.

'Pillaging is a part of war, don't you think?'

'I'd prefer not to,' said Henri.

'Do you remember that story of one of Antony's veterans who fought in the Armenian campaign? He had hacked a gold statue of the goddess Anaïtis to pieces to take one of her thighs. When he got home, he sold the goddess's leg and bought himself a house near Bologna, some land and some slaves. How many legionaries, my dear sir, must have returned with gold stolen from the East? That gold was spent developing industry and agriculture across the entire plain of the Po River. Twenty years after Actium, the region was flourishing.'

'Enough, Périgord,' said Lejeune. 'Spare us your history lessons, please!'

'It is in Pliny.'

At last the door opened on an old woman wearing a white crêpe turban. Lejeune, who had been born in Strasbourg, spoke to her in German, she answered in the same language and only then did the colonel feel reassured; he beckoned to Henri to follow him into the room.

'I'll leave you,' said Périgord. 'In such a dishevelled state, I'm hardly fit for company.'

*

Anna Krauss was seventeen, with jet-black hair and green eyes. She shut the book she was pretending to read, sat up as they walked towards her, swung her legs over the edge of the sofa to put on a pair of Roman sandals and then got to her feet in one slow, supple movement. Her long, very fine skirt of cotton cambric from the Indies was figured with jasmine; a lace tunic was draped over her rounded shoulders, and fastened by a clasp of classical design; her hands were bare, her stance both delicate and firm, her slim waist giving way to full hips. Seen like this, against the light which gave clearer definition to her figure under her gossamer-thin clothes, she seemed like an allegory of all that was contradictory in the midst of war. Lejeune looked at her, his eyes shining; he had been so afraid. Both of them started speaking in German, their voices almost hushed. As he hung back by the door, sweat ran down Henri's temples, his cheeks were on fire, his eyes fixed and staring. He felt hot. He felt cold. He didn't dare move. He contemplated Anna Krauss; her oval face, like an Italian woman's, reminded him of a pastel drawing by Rosalba Carriera which he had admired recently at a collector's house in

Hamburg; but no, her velvet skin was real, and the sunshine filtering through the leaded glass windows softened it still further.

After a moment, Lejeune turned to Henri to translate their conversation, because despite two years in Brunswick, when everyone had spoken to him in French – apart from the serving girls he'd sported with and had absolutely no need to understand – Henri had never got used to that country's harsh language.

'I said that on Friday I was going to rejoin the pontoneers on the Danube and then the headquarters staff, to take up my billet on the island of Lobau.'

'Yes,' said Henri.

'I said that in my absence there had to be someone trustworthy to protect the house from the mob our army trails along in its wake.'

'The mob, yes.'

'I said that you'd be moving in because you're going to be staying in Vienna.'

'Ah.'

'Don't you agree, Henri?'

'Agreed.'

'We can't leave her alone in an occupied city!'

'We can't.'

Henri was lost for words and made do with repeating, with emphasis, snatches of his friend's sentences.

'Have you got many things?'

'Things.'

'Henri? Are you listening to me?'

Anna Krauss broke into a broad grin. Was she making fun of this fat, ruddy-cheeked young man? Was there an ounce of tenderness in her mockery? The slightest warmth?

Did she love Lejeune? And Lejeune? The latter took Henri by the shoulders and shook him. 'Are you sick?'

'Sick?'

'If you could see yourself!'

'No, no, I'm fine.'

'Well then, answer me, you dunce! Do you have much luggage?'

'An Italian grammar by Veneroni-Gattel, Bitanbé's *Homer*, Condorcet, Alfieri's *Life*, a few clothes, some other bits and pieces.'

'Perfect! Have your servant bring them round tomorrow morning.'

'My servant has left me.'

'No money?'

'Not much money.'

'I'll take care of it.'

'Daru has to give his permission as well.'

'He will. Do you accept?'

'Of course I do, Louis-François.'

Lejeune briefly translated this exchange for Anna Krauss but she had already grasped the thrust of it and was applauding as if at a concert. Henri, still rooted to the spot, decided to learn German seriously, now that he had a real incentive. What's more, Anna Krauss had actually begun addressing him in her gibberish and he could only make out the melody: the meaning escaped him.

'Louis-François, what is she saying to me?'

'She's offering us tea.'

*

Late that evening, as Lejeune had received orders to return immediately to Berthier at Schönbrunn, Henri accepted

Périgord's suggestion that they take a stroll through Vienna; in point of fact, he had been hoping to draw him out on the details of Anna's life, which, since that afternoon, had become the only subject close to his heart. Lejeune had given his friend one of the bundles of Daru's counterfeit money, so he was in a position to invite Périgord, who was as garrulous as ever but also knew the city and its inhabitants from a previous visit. They set off for the gardens of the Hugelmann café, which overlooked the Danube and its burnt-out bridges. Despite the warm weather, there were no bathers, no café regulars, no Turkish sailors: just as everywhere else there were only soldiers. 'Normally,' said Périgord, 'garishly coloured sailing boats take one out on the Danube here, but they must have either been requisitioned by our men or sunk by the Austrians.' Henri couldn't care less about this piece of information, or about the renowned Hungarian billiards player, who was continuing to practise his craft during the hostilities and had just earned a round of applause. It seemed that he could knock balls around the table for hours without losing a point and the two Frenchmen ended up feeling exhausted. They decided to go to the Prater, which was only a step away in the Leopold suburb.

Périgord wore a pelisse with gilded braid, black trousers and top boots and, to spare them any ridicule, he'd lent Henri a decent horse. In Spain recently, several expensive horses of his had been stolen and so, while they picked at crayfish, he'd had their mounts looked after by a very young soldier who had been passing by. The boy was waiting patiently for them.

'Bravissimo!' Périgord said to him. 'Your name?'

'Voltigeur Paradis, sir, Second Infantry of the Line, 3rd

Division of General Molitor, under the command of Marshal Masséna!'

Périgord tucked a few florins in the voltigeur's jacket and said to Henri, who was looking pensive, or distracted, as if overcome by anxiety, 'My man will bring your belongings round tomorrow, Beyle, don't worry.'

'Do you know Anna Krauss?'

'I've lodged in her house for three days, no, two – well anyway, curious as I am and diaphanous as she is . . .'

'Her family?'

'The father is a musician. A close relative of Herr Haydn.'

'Where is he?'

'He has followed Francis of Austria's court to its place of refuge somewhere in Bohemia, so they say, but can one be certain?'

'Her mother?'

'I happen to know that she is dead. Air could no longer reach her lungs.'

'So Mlle Krauss stayed behind in Vienna on her own?'

'With her younger sisters and her older governess.'

'Her father abandoned her in the middle of a war!'

'My dear sir, the Viennese take nothing seriously. Consider: finding Monday a sad day which used to spoil Sunday, they simply turned Monday into a public holiday. Not bad, eh, for insouciance?'

'Do you think Lejeune is in love?'

'With the Viennese?'

'No, no! With that young girl.'

'I don't know, but the symptoms are fairly conclusive: agitation, anxiety, near-swooning. As a matter of fact, she gives you palpitations as well.'

'Sir, I did not give you leave . . .'

'Tut tut! You can't do anything about it, and nor can I, but the battle between you two promises to be a sight more delightful than the one between the rest of us and the Archduke Charles's troops! You see, what I don't like about war, what I simply can't abide, is the dirt, the wretched uniforms, the dust, the vulgarity, the unsightly wounds. To come back in one piece, ah, now that's the thing! Then one can cut a dashing figure at balls and dance with faux duchesses and real bankers.'

They reached the sandy avenues of the Prater. The park's tall trees had been felled for derisory barricades. Dotted around the lawns stood grottoes, miniature houses, lodges, a Chinese pavilion, a Swiss chalet, savages' mud huts: a gallimaufry of pleasure haunts to which, in times of peace, crowds flocked from every corner of the planet. The ladies and gentlemen of Vienna would rub shoulders with Egyptians, Cossacks and Greeks, and the Emperor Francis often came to take his daily walk unescorted, raising his hat to his subjects like any respectable bourgeois. On summer evenings insects plagued one in swarms, and Périgord joked, 'A German explained to me recently that if it wasn't for these insects, love would wreak terrible havoc here!'

They lingered in front of a caravan which was staging a curious show, in which the parts were performed by puppets and dwarves. Most of the audience of French and allied soldiers didn't understand a word, but were amusing themselves instead by distinguishing which of the actors were flesh and bone, and which wood.

'What are they playing?' asked Henri.

'Shakespeare, old man. Do you see the tiny fellow with the fake beard and the cardboard crown? He's delivering the famous monologue, "What, do I fear myself?"' Péri-gord acted out the scene as he recited. '"There's none else by. Richard loves Richard: that is, I am I. Is there a murderer here? No; – yes; I am: Then fly. What, from myself? Great reason why, – Lest I revenge. What, – myself upon myself! Alack, I love myself. Wherefore? For any good that I myself have done unto myself? Oh no! Alas, I rather hate myself for hateful deeds committed by myself!"'

'And I,' sighed Henri, 'I hate myself for not knowing German!'

'Don't worry, my dear Beyle, I'm garbling it, but the play's title is written up on that board and I know *Richard III* by heart.'

On the platform, the puppets and dwarves were flinging themselves at each other around a painted wooden throne. Périgord added, 'Act V, scene 3.'

*

At Schönbrunn, in the Lacquer Saloon where flowers and gilded birds chased one another around the walls, Napoleon was rummaging in his tortoiseshell snuffbox and filling his nostrils with snuff. Wearing a white flannel dressing gown, and with a Madras bandana wound round his head like a shawl from the West Indies, he was examining maps. Different coloured pins showed the current position of his troops, of the stores of provisions, forage, and shoes, and the artillery park.

'Monsieur Constant!'

The head valet, a tall, heavy-lidded figure who moved noiselessly as if gliding above the ground, appeared at his side. The Emperor pointed to his glass, which the servant filled with Chambertin mixed with water.

'My chicken, Monsieur Constant.'

'At once, sire.'

'*Pronto!*'

'Sire . . .'

'Has that devil Roustan eaten my chicken again, like the other night?'

'No, sire, no, the chicken is safely locked away in its wicker basket and I have the key to the padlock.'

'Well?'

'Sire, the Prince of Neuchâtel, His Excellency the Chief of Staff . . .'

'Keep it simple, Monsieur Constant! Say Berthier.'

'He is waiting, sire.'

'*Io lo so*, I had him summoned. Bring him in, the dullard, and my chicken as well!'

Immaculate in full-dress uniform, Major-General Berthier entered the study followed by Lejeune and put his cocked hat down on a pedestal table. The Emperor turned his back on them and they were forced to listen to his monologue without moving.

'The English fleet lies at anchor off Naples. Tyrol is in revolt. Prince Eugene is in difficulty in the Kingdom of Italy and the Pope is becoming unruly. Our army's finest men are wearing themselves out in Spain. Can I count on the Tsar's neutrality for long? The English are bankrolling rebellions at every turn. In France the mood is souring and the people's impertinence is no longer to be contained by censorship. Talleyrand and Fouché, alas both so valuable, are conspiring to have me replaced by that puppet Murat, but I keep them in check, like everyone else, through fear and self-interest! Public funds are dwindling, desertions are on the increase, my gendarmes are shackling conscripts to bring them into barracks and camp. There's a shortage of non-commissioned officers, they have to be plucked from outside school gates . . .'

The Emperor tore a drumstick off the chicken which Constant had left on a black table. He bit into it, grease spilling onto his chin, and growled, 'What do you think of this dismal picture?'

'That it is unfortunately all too accurate, Your Majesty,' said Berthier.

'Goddamn, I know that only too well! I've had to send for that scavenger Masséna and insist that Lannes leave the peace and quiet of his château, which is all he cares about! *Venga qui!*'

With the chicken bone, Napoleon pointed to the island of Lobau on his large map. 'In three days we will take up position on this wretched island. The bridge?'

'It will be thrown over the Danube,' answered Lejeune, 'since that is what you have decided.'

'*Bene!* On Friday, Molitor's riflemen disembark and mop up the few Austrian cretins still bivouaced there. Organize enough boats. Meanwhile, with the material which you will have transported to Bredorf—'

'Ebersdorf, sire,' Berthier corrected.

'Keep your damned thoughts to yourself! Did I ask your advice? What was I saying?'

'The material, sire.'

'*Si!* Straight away we throw the pontoon bridge over the broad arm of the river to join Lobau to this bank. Lasalle's cavalry instantly reinforce Molitor's men, who then cross over to the left bank and occupy the two villages.'

'Essling and Aspern.'

'Whatever you like, Berthier! By Saturday evening, the

main bridge and the second one, which will cross from the island to the left bank, must be fixed and secure.'

'It will be done, sire.'

'Sunday, at dawn, our troops occupy your damned villages, whatever their names are, entrench and wait. The Archduke sees us. He wakes up. He thinks me a fool for stationing my troops with their backs to the river. He attacks. Masséna meets him with cannon. You, Berthier, with Lannes, Lasalle and Espagne, lead the charge to break up the Austrian centre and cut their army in two. Then Davout crosses the main bridge with his reserves, reinforces your attack and we crush those *coglioni*!'

'May it turn out that way, Your Majesty.'

'That's how it will turn out. I see it and I wish it. You don't approve, Lejeune?'

'I listen, sire, and in listening to you, I learn.'

The Emperor slapped him hard on the cheek to show that he was pleased with the reply, without really being taken in by it. He detested familiarity and advice: all he wanted from his officers, like his courtesans, was mute obedience. Lannes and Augureau were the only two who dared speak their minds to him. Otherwise, he had fashioned a court of spurious princes and trumped-up dukes, each as compromised, crass and dissembling as the other. He asked nothing of them save low, scraping bows which he rewarded with châteaux, titles and a fortune in gold.

Constant was shuffling from one foot to the other by the door, which Napoleon eventually noticed. Grumbling, he said, 'What is this new dance, Monsieur Constant?'

'Mlle Krauss has arrived, sire.'

'Have her undress and wait for me.'

At the mention of that name, Lejeune thought he was

going to faint. What? Anna was at Schönbrunn? She was going to spend the night in the Emperor's bed? No. It was unthinkable. Nothing in her character suggested such a thing. Lejeune watched his sovereign finish the chicken, then wipe his fingers and mouth on the curtain. What could Lejeune do? Nothing. When Napoleon dismissed Berthier and him with a wave of his hand, like a pair of lackeys, he hastily asked permission to return to Vienna.

'Off you go, my friend,' Berthier answered paternally. 'Have a whale of a time, but don't waste all your energy, we'll be needing it.'

Lejeune saluted and rushed out.

Will we still be alive next week? Berthier thought as he watched Lejeune leap into the saddle and ride away.

Lejeune galloped to the pink house in the Jordangasse district. He ran up to the floor where Anna Krauss should have been asleep, went into her room without knocking, walked silently, holding his breath, up to the sarcophagus-shaped bed, there she was, dreaming, lit up by the last quarter of the moon, calm, almost smiling. He listened to her even, untroubled breathing. She moaned softly and stretched without waking. Lejeune pushed a chair over to the bed and and watched her sleeping. Later, he found out that the young lady visiting the Emperor may have had the same surname, with one less 's' that is, but that her Christian name was Eva. She was the adopted daughter of a commissary of war. The Emperor had noticed her one morning at a parade in the palace courtyard; amongst so many women in bright colours, she alone had been dressed in black, like a terrifying portent.

Henri also couldn't get to sleep in his room in an inn on

the outskirts of Vienna, which he shared with another deputy commissary. His room mate was snoring thunderously. So, by candlelight, Henri prepared his leather trunk for the next day's move. Leafing through each of his books before packing them away, he fell by chance on a passage in Alberti's *Shipwreck*. 'We didn't know in which direction we were drifting in the vastness of the sea, but the very fact that we could breathe with our heads above water struck us as marvellous enough.' These lines written during the Renaissance matched his state entirely. A little while before, as he and Périgord were wandering with torches through the catacombs under the Augustiner-Kirche, they had come across row upon row of corpses, sitting or standing, crowded together, dry, miraculously intact and without the slightest sign of decomposition. They both thought of the King of Naples who used to spit on his enemies' embalmed bodies, which he'd hang in rows like puppets, in the days when a Visconti trained mastiffs to tear men to pieces and the Individual emerging in Italy was armed with claws and fangs. Eventually, Henri lay down on his mattress and he dozed off just before dawn, fully clothed, with the haunting, tender image of Anna Krauss in his mind's eye.

Two

WHAT SOLDIERS
DREAM ABOUT

IT WAS GLORIOUS WEATHER and the acacia trees smelled sweet. On that particular Saturday, the eve of Whitsun, Private Paradis was lying on the island of Lobau's bank. He had taken off his voltigeur's jacket and laid down next to it his yellow and green-plumed shako, his knapsack and all the other kit he had to strap himself into. His greatcoat was rolled up as a pillow. He was a tall, red-haired peasant with down on his upper lip, and broad hands more suited to the plough than to arms: he'd only ever used a musket to scare off wolves. He dreamed incessantly of deserting and reaching his parents' farm before harvest time, where he'd be of more use, but how was he to take advantage of the imminent battles to get there? Nevertheless, the oats would still have to be brought in in a month, and then the wheat in August. His father would never manage on his own and his eldest brother hadn't come back from the wars. He chewed a twig, thinking that he hadn't even had time to spend the florins he'd earned the other night in Vienna looking after Edmond de Périgord's horses. Suddenly the birds stopped singing. He propped himself up on his elbows in the grass. Masséna's IVth Army Corps was crossing the Danube on the long bridge which the Engineers had finished at midday, only moments before. All one could hear was the sound of thirty thousand feet hitting the planks in step. Precariously balanced on light craft, tied together so as not to fall into the swirling water, sappers were using boathooks and oars to turn aside the tree trunks swept down by the current so that they wouldn't sever the mooring ropes. The Danube was turning savage. Two days earlier, after nightfall, Voltigeur Paradis's division had embarked on rafts and long boats and, risking the river's violent swell, had made a sudden landing on the island to dislodge the hundred or so Austrians on picket duty. There had been a short exchange of fire, bayonet thrusts in the thickets, a few Austrians taken prisoner in the dark and many more who had fled . . .

Paradis was expert at laying snares and wielding a catapult and on Lobau, a former game reserve, there was plenty to keep him occupied. That morning he'd hit a bird, he didn't know what sort, a golden-headed oriole perhaps, which he'd spotted on a willow branch. It was roasting on his bayonet and he stood up to turn it on the fire of dry brushwood. On the other side of the island, he'd also seen pike and roach in an oxbow of the Danube, and he'd promised to teach one of his comrades to fish, a man with more education but no experience of the countryside. Paradis shrugged his shoulders, because he knew that the future, even the near future, didn't belong to him any more. Sergeant-Major Roussillon's shout confirmed this painful thought.

'Hey! Lazybones! We're short-handed over here!'

On the main bridge, now, wagons were transporting the pontoons and boats needed to throw a second bridge from Lobau across fifty metres of fast current to the left bank.

By their uniforms which glinted in the sunshine, Paradis recognized, from a distance, Marshals Lannes and Masséna riding at the head of the convoy, surrounded by their plumed officers.

'Look alive!' yelled Sergeant-Major Roussillon, glowing with pride at the brand-new *Légion d'honneur* which he'd pinned in a prominent position on his chest and stroked from time to time with a sigh of pleasure.

Paradis took the half-roasted bird off his bayonet, burning his fingers as he did so, trampled on the fire, which started to smoke, picked up his gear and set off after Roussillon, who had mustered thirty riflemen at the edge of a broad-leaved wood. In shirt-sleeves or bare chested, each of them was holding a woodcutter's axe. Orders had come through that the small bridge needed timber, since there weren't enough trestles, girders or posts to support its roadway of planks.

'Put your backs into it, lads!' the sergeant-major harangued them. 'In two hours it has to be ready!'

The men spat on their palms and began striking the base of the elms; the bark sheared away and splinters flew into the air.

'Attention!' bellowed Roussillon, as straight as a ramrod.

'Stand at ease!' said, in unison, the two officers who were riding towards them through the high grass. Colonel Lejeune, who had been closely following the construction works for two days, was accompanied by Sainte-Croix, Masséna's orderly. The latter asked the sergeant-major, 'Are these Molitor's men?'

'They are, sir!'

'What are they doing with axes?'

'The second bridge, Colonel, and there's no time to waste.'

'But that's the sappers' work.'

'They're dog-tired, that lot, from what I'm told.'

'I don't give a damn! They can rest later. I want these men on the left bank where they're to establish a bridge-head. Marshal Masséna's orders!'

'Did you hear that, you bunch of layabouts?' shouted the sergeant-major. 'Get your kit on!'

Paradis sighed as he put down his axe. He had made a good start on his tree, he felt satisfied with it, but what the hell. Tribulations like this were a soldier's daily bread: put the musket down, pick it up again, buckle your belt, march, keep on marching, sleep a couple of hours wherever you found yourself, take cover, lie in wait, back on your feet again like a jumping jack, march mindlessly on and never any question of stumbling or one's ankles being sore or getting one's breath back or eating anything except those foul greasy beans which two men had to share from a single mess tin. Paradis checked that he had everything in his cartridge pouch: the thirty-five cartridges, the musket flints. He pulled up his gaiters which pinched his calves, took his musket from the stack and fell in behind his comrades as they started for the coppices facing the Danube's left bank.

'Halloa!' Sainte-Croix said to Lejeune. 'The river is rising and the current's running fast.'

'Yes. It worries me.'

'Let's not waste time. I have to take these fellows over to the other side by boat. Were you assigned to choose a suitable place for the bridge?'

'If it comes out over there, do you see, those spinneys will hide it from any Austrian scouts.'

As he said this, Lejeune heard someone talking in the riflemen's ranks. Paradis was explaining to his neighbour that there had once been a ferry ten metres upstream. Lejeune called to the lad, 'What's that you were saying?'

'There was a ferry here before, sir, by that clump of reeds.'

'How do you know?'

'Well, it's easy, sir. Look on the bank, you can see where the farmers' tracks went down to the river.'

'I can't see a thing.'

'Nor can I,' said Sainte-Croix, despite his field glass.

'You can!' insisted the soldier. 'The grass is shorter and bent back. It's been trodden down so much that it's not grown back the same. There were tracks here, I swear.'

Lejeune gave the soldier a grateful look.

'You're a mine of infomation, young man.'

'Oh, no, sir, I'm only a peasant.'

'Sainte-Croix,' Lejeune said, turning towards Masséna's orderly, 'I leave you to cross with your riflemen, but I'm going to keep this one.' He pointed to Paradis. 'He's got a very sharp eye, which I've no doubt will stand me in good stead on my reconnaissances.'

'Very well. I only need two hundred men to cover the pontoneers.'

Paradis could barely make head or tail of what was happening to him.

'Your name?' asked Lejeune.

'Voltigeur Paradis, sir, Second Infantry of the Line, 3rd Division, Commander General Molitor.'

'You have a Christian name too, I presume.'

'Vincent.'

'Well then, Vincent Paradis, follow me.'

Lejeune and his discovery moved off towards the centre of the island as Sainte-Croix gave the order to launch the boats which had been unloaded from the wagons: this was a difficult undertaking in such a strong current, and, standing in water almost up to their waists, skirmishers had to hold the boats steady so that the company could embark without their powder or muskets getting wet.

*

A hundred metres away, in a clearing guarded by sentries, the vast tent of the General Staff was being erected, swaths of canvas forming what, in effect, would be a suite of apartments where Berthier would receive the Emperor's orders and have them conveyed to the commanding officers. The furniture still lay on the grass but Berthier hadn't waited for everything to be in place to organize operations. He was sitting outside, in an armchair, and his aides-de-camp were spreading out maps and weighting them with stones to prevent them blowing away. The Austrians taken prisoner the previous night were lined up in front of him for questioning and Lejeune arrived just in time to translate. Lost in the midst of such a crowd of officers, Paradis didn't know what to do with himself; he wrung his hands, feeling extremely awkward, and blushed with agitation. He had felt important when Lejeune had told the sentry barring his path, 'This one's with me. He's a scout.'

'He hasn't got the uniform for it, Colonel.'

'He will do.'

What on earth did a scout's uniform look like, Vincent Paradis wondered.

Their faces dark with three days' growth of beard, covered in dirt and with their light uniforms in rags, sixteen Austrian privates stood gaping stupidly in the middle of the clearing, shooed together like bantams and stunned still to be alive. They meekly answered the questions put by Lejeune, who was entirely at ease with his role and passed on such information as they gave to Berthier.

'They belong to the 6th Army Corps of Baron Hiller.'

'Are there any other outposts?' asked the Chief of Staff.

'They have no idea. They say that the main body of troops is encamped up there on the Bisamberg.'

'We know that. How many men?'

'They say at least two hundred thousand.'

'Exaggeration. Halve it.'

'They say there's five hundred cannon.'

'Let's put three hundred.'

'This is more interesting: they maintain that the Archduke Charles's army has recently been reinforced by some detachments from Bohemia and two regiments of Hungarian hussars.'

'How do they know?'

'The Hungarians have reconnoitred right up to the Danube. They recognized their uniforms, they even talked to them.'

'Good,' said Berthier. 'Have them sent to Vienna, they can work in the hospitals.'

A moment later, before Lejeune could even enquire about a new uniform for Vincent Paradis — supposing such a thing was possible — news reached them that the small bridge was fixed. Lasalle's cavalry and Espagne's cuirassiers were to cross immediately and occupy the villages on the left bank, followed by the rest of Molitor's division. Lejeune rode off to deliver the orders.

Now he was waiting at the mouth of the small, hastily built bridge, which was being shaken by the swirling waters. The planks of the roadway had been laid double and most of the pontoons were tied to the bank by thick ropes, but the river was continuing to rise and such improvisation made Lejeune anxious. Still, what matter, it looked as if it would hold. Lasalle's chasseurs rode across after their general – his curved pipe jutting out, as ever, from under his bristling moustache – and, reaching the other side, forced their horses to climb the slope and disappeared into the trees. Next Espagne, tall, square-jawed, the pallor of his face accentuated by his black, bushy sideburns, watched his cuirassiers trotting across the sway-ing bridge. He looked concerned but they crossed without mishap. One of the troopers stared pointedly at Lejeune. This tall fellow, with his maned helmet and his brown coat, was Fayolle, whom Lejeune had struck in the face the other night when he was looting Anna Krauss's house. Caught up in the forward movement, Fayolle had to be satisfied with knitting his brows and then he, in turn, crossed the small bridge and vanished with his squadron behind the dense thickets on the other bank. Finally, as the Emperor had planned and Berthier had ordered, Molitor's division followed at full strength, with the sole exception of a relieved Paradis, who watched his companions of the previous day crossing at arm's length from artillery pieces. The voltigeur was glued to Lejeune's heels, worried that he'd be forgotten, and he ventured, 'What shall I do, Colonel?'

'You?' said Lejeune, but he hadn't time to elaborate: shots could be heard on the left bank.

*

'Ah! Now it's underway . . .' Cuirassier Fayolle said to his horse, patting its neck. But no, it wasn't really. Some uhlans had let themselves be shot at by the infantry on the edge of a wood, and they could be seen galloping away through the green crops. General Espagne sent Fayolle and two of his companions ahead to reconnoitre. The villagers of Aspern and Essling had fled, the French following their exodus of overloaded carts, livestock and children through spy-glasses, but some snipers might have stayed behind to harry them and shoot them in the back. Fayolle and the two others rode their horses at a walk through the meadows, skirting the copses and the ponds, more often than not surrounded by tall trees, which broke up the countryside.

They reached Aspern first, which ran alongside the river, its two broad streets converging on a small square in front of a rectangular belfry. Narrow lanes – which put the troopers most on their guard – wound between the village's low stone houses, each identical with a courtyard in front and a hedged garden behind. A wall ran round the church, high enough to cover the French against skirmishers but not cannon, and they guessed that a substantial house adjoining the cemetery, with a garden enclosed by an earth wall, was the parsonage. They took careful note of each of these details. A few stray birds flew off at their horses' approach. But no human sound. The cuirassiers turned in their saddles for a moment, scanning the windows, and then met up with a party of Lasalle's chasseurs on patrol, who they left to continue the inspection of Aspern. They wheeled their horses towards the neighbouring belfry of Essling, which they could see about fifteen hundred metres to the east. Avoiding the swampy ground where the Danube had overflowed, they pushed on to it across the open fields.

Fayolle was the first to enter Essling.

The deserted village was like the first one, but on a smaller scale, with only one main street and more space between the identical houses. They had to keep a sharp lookout and stay on their guard for the slightest unusual sound. There was probably nothing to fear, but these ghost villages created a sense of unease. Fayolle tried to imagine them full of life, with men and women standing under the oaks of the avenue and bent over their vegetables in the gardens. Normally there'd be a market here, stables there, a loft over there. Wait, he said to himself, suppose I pay a visit to the lofts? They can't have taken everything with them. At that moment, sunlight glinted on his helmet and in his eyes. He looked up at the second storey of a white house. Was that a ray of sunshine reflected by the panes of glass or had someone in hiding opened a window? Nothing stirred. He handed his horse to one of his companions and, with the other's help, tried to force the wooden door. It was bolted. He kicked the lock hard, without success, then reached for the pistol in his saddle holster to shoot out the crude lock.

'Not very subtle,' said the other cuirassier, who was called Pacotte.

'If there's anybody here, they're bound to have seen us. If it's only a cat or an owl, why should we give a damn?'

'That's right: we'll just cook up a nice stew.'

On their guard, with a loaded pistol in one hand and a sabre in the other, they entered the house. Fayolle shouldered open the shutters with his shoulder so that they could see what they were doing. The room was sparsely furnished with a thick table, two straw chairs, a wooden chest that stood open and empty and a fireplace full of ashes. The ashes were cold. A steep staircase led upstairs.

'Shall we go?' Fayolle asked Cuirassier Pacotte.

'If it makes you happy.'

'Did you hear that?'

'No.'

Fayolle stood stock-still. He had heard a creak: a door or a floorboard.

'It's the wind,' said Pacotte, nevertheless lowering his voice. 'I don't see who could be dumb enough to stay in this rat trap.'

'Maybe a rat; maybe that's just what it is,' said Fayolle. 'We'll soon find out.'

He put his foot on the first step and then hesitated, his ears straining; Pacotte pushed him and they went on. Upstairs, all they could make out in the dark room was the blurred shape of a bed. Fayolle groped his way along the wall until he reached a window and smashed it with his elbow without letting go of his sabre. He opened the shutters and turned round. His companion was at the head of the stairs. They were alone.

Pacotte pulled open a low door and Fayolle ducked down. As he went into the next room someone jumped on him. He struggled, hearing the blade of a knife screech on the metal of his breastplate under his brown coat. He flung out his arms, sending his attacker flying against a wall and then, in the half-light, ran him through the stomach with a violent sabre thrust. He could barely see, but he felt warm blood coating his sword hand as the man's body started convulsing in spasms. With a hard tug, he pulled out his sabre and his enemy slumped to the ground. Cuirassier Pacotte rushed over and opened the window. A fat, bald man in leather breeches lay dying on the ground, moaning as blood gushed out of his mouth, his eyes as white as hardboiled eggs.

'Not bad, those boots, eh, Fayolle?'

'The jacket's not half bad either. A bit short, but damn it all, the fat pig has made it filthy!'

'I tell you what, I fancy those braces. Blow me if they're not velvet...'

He crouched down to take them off, but, before he could, they both started. Someone behind them had stifled a cry. A young peasant girl in a short pleated skirt was squeezed into a corner, behind a bedpost. She was covering her mouth with both hands, her huge dark eyes open wide. Cuirassier Pacotte levelled his pistol at her but Fayolle pushed down his arm. 'Stop, you idiot! It's not worth killing her: well, at least not yet.'

He went up to her, blood dripping from his sword. The Austrian curled up into a ball. Fayolle put the point of his sabre under her chin and ordered her to stand up. She didn't move: only trembled.

'She can't understand a word you say, Fayolle. Have to give her a hand.'

Pacotte caught her arm and pulled her to her feet: she

leant against the wall, shaking. The two cuirassiers looked at her. Pacotte whistled in admiration: she was full-breasted, just the way he liked. Fayolle raised his sabre and wiped the back of it against her blue bodice. With the sharp edge he sliced off the bodice's silver buttons and tore off her lace blouse; lunging at her, he snatched off her woollen cap. The girl's golden-brown hair fell down over her shoulders. It was smooth and glossy, with a sheen like Indian silk.

'Shall we take her to the officers?'

'You must be mad!'

'Maybe there's more of these bloody yokels spying on us with their cleavers and scythes.'

'We'll think about it,' Fayolle said, tearing away the skirt and what was left of the blouse. 'Had any Austrian girls, have you?'

'Not yet. Only Germans.'

'German girls, they don't know how to say no.'

'Not to me, they don't.'

'What about Austrian girls?'

'From the look of this one, she knows how to say no and something a lot stronger than that.'

'You think so?' Turning to the girl, he asked, 'Don't you find us handsome?'

'Have we given you a fright?'

'Mind you,' Fayolle said, chuckling, 'if I was her, your mug would put the wind up me!'

They heard the third cuirassier calling to them from outside: Fayolle went to the window. 'Don't yell like that! There are snipers . . .'

He stopped in mid-sentence. The cuirassier was not alone. Jingling, dust, the rattle of hooves: the cavalry had

occupied Essling and General Espagne in person was waiting at the foot of the house.

'Have you spotted any of them?' he asked.

'Well, that's just it, General,' said Fayolle. 'There was
one tub of lard who wanted to butcher me alive.'

Cuirassier Pacotte dragged the peasant's body to the
window, lifted it onto the ledge and tipped it over. The
corpse crashed limply to the ground like a a sack of wet
dough, and Espagne's horse shied away.

'Any others?'

'He's the only one who saw a few stars, General.'

Through his teeth, Fayolle said to his companion,
'You're a bit of a sap, aren't you? We could have kept his
boots, they looked sturdy, at least a lot sturdier than my
espadrilles.'

'You up there!' the General shouted again. 'Come down!
Every one of these shacks has to be checked and a sweep
done of the whole village!'

'Yes, General!'

'What about the girl?' Pacotte asked Fayolle.

'We'll keep her on the boil.'

Before rejoining their squadron, Fayolle and Pacotte
tore the blue petticoat and lace blouse into strips and
bound the peasant girl; they stuffed her cap in her mouth,
tied it in place with the dead man's braces and threw
her on a horsehair mattress. Before slipping off, Fayolle
kissed her on the forehead. 'Be good, sweetheart, and
don't you worry. How could we forget a lovely looker
like you? Hey! Feel that, our treasure has got a boiling
hot forehead . . .'

'Must have a fever.'

Shouting with laughter, they went down to their comrades.

*

Vincent Paradis poked at some charred logs.

'Just need to blow on there and they'll catch, Colonel.'

'They saw us, then they bolted.'

'I don't think so. There are only two of us. There were more of them. Look at the brushwood trampled by their horses.'

Accompanied by his new scout, Lejeune had reconnoitred far beyond the villages, suspecting Austrian spies in even the smallest copse.

'It must have been the same uhlans as before,' he said.

'Or some other lot who haven't gone far. There's plenty of places to hide around here.'

A rustling of leaves put them on their guard: Lejeune cocked his pistol.

'Don't you be afraid, Colonel,' said Paradis. 'It's only an animal climbing that beech. It'll be more terrified than we are.'

'Are you scared?'

'Not yet.'

'But you're not entirely at ease either, by the look of you.'

'I don't like galloping through crops and ruining a harvest.'

Lejeune had borrowed a mount from the horse artillery for his protégé, who was still wearing his voltigeur's uniform. Looking at him, Lejeune said, 'Both sides are going to slaughter each other with their cannon on this green plain tomorrow. There'll be plenty of red then, and it won't be poppies. When this war is over . . .'

'There'll be another one, Colonel. With this Emperor, war will never end.'

'No, you're right.'

They wheeled their horses, and headed back towards Essling at an easy pace but still watchful. Lejeune would gladly have stayed behind, with his sketchbook, to draw this gentle, deserted countryside. Troops were still pouring into the village. On the square in front of the church, Lejeune recognized Sainte-Croix and some of Masséna's staff officers, which meant that the marshal couldn't be far off. In fact he was visiting the village granary, a three-storeyed brick and stone building at the end of an avenue of oaks, separated from a large farm by a walled garden, which had dormer windows on the roof and round loopholes covered with bars under the gables, where sharpshooters could take up position.

'I have counted forty-eight windows,' Masséna said to Lejeune. 'The walls are more than a metre thick, the doors and shutters are lined with sheet metal: it's a solid piece of work. If the worst comes to the worst, we can entrench here and hold it. Here, Lejeune, I've had it measured. Take these figures to the Chief of Staff – they're accurate.'

Masséna thrust the piece of paper into the colonel's hand, who glanced over it: the building was 36 metres long and 10 metres wide, the ground-floor windows were placed 1.65 metres above the ground . . .

'Are you staying in Essling, Your Grace?'

'I haven't a damned notion,' said Masséna, 'but on this bank, yes. How far did you push up to?'

'That clump of beeches, over there.'

'And? Any luck?'

'Tracks, but no people.'

'Yes, that's just what Lasalle says. Espagne as well. His cuirassiers only killed one skulker, but why had that imbecile stayed behind? I smell the Austrians all around us, and I've got a nose for that particular scent!'

Masséna came closer to murmur in Lejeune's ear, 'Have you got my information?'

'What information, Your Grace?'

'You numskull! Gad, the Genoese millions of course!'

'Daru claims that they don't exist.'

'Daru! Of course he would! That liar pockets anything with a shine to it! Like a magpie! Never ask Daru a thing! You may go.'

Grumbling, Masséna went back into the village granary.

*

In the main courtyard of Schönbrunn, Daru had perched on the hub of the first cart in a supply convoy and was opening sacks at random. Each one caused him to exclaim furiously, 'Barley!'

'There are no more oats, my lord,' a deputy commissary said in an embarrassed voice.

'Barley! Out of the question! The cavalry needs oats!'

'The new crop isn't ripe yet, we could only find barley . . .'

'Where has M. Beyle got to? This was his job, damn it all!'

'I am his replacement, my lord.'

'And that sloth?'

'In bed, most probably, my lord.'

'With whom, if you please?'

'With his habitual fever, my lord: here, I have a note vouching for him, I was meant to give it to you . . .'

Daru tore the piece of paper out of his hand and read a bona fide notice of sick leave, signed by Carino, a German doctor, and countersigned by the Surgeon-Major of the Guard. Unable to find fault with it, Daru almost choked with rage; he took a handful of barley and threw it in the deputy's face. 'Fine, our cavalry will feed on barley! Go!'

And he signalled to the convoy to start off for the island of Lobau.

*

Henri did indeed have terrible migraines, for which he was taking belladonna, but the true cause of his suffering was the pox, as unfortunately there was no other choice but to call those ailments that plague a gallant's adventures, those painful, although not serious, conditions about which a man might smile amongst his fellow men, but still feel embarrassed by in a woman's company. This handicap, to which Henri had eventually become accustomed, did not, however, prevent him fighting other battles on his own behalf. He wasn't actually in bed, despite his exhaustion and unpleasant, feverish sweats. Instead he was waiting at the far end of the Prater in a ruined hunting lodge, not far from a group of bizarre-looking mock-Gothic construc- tions. A few months earlier in Paris he had lost his heart to Valentina, an actress of easy morals who, off-stage, was known simply as Louise. She, like so many of her kind, had followed the troops to Vienna, and Henri had given her this rendezvous in order to break off their liaison, since he dreamt only of Anna Krauss and, stoked by his fever, this new love burned white-hot in his breast. How to get rid of Valentina? She had become a burden. Henri wanted absolute freedom. How to announce the split? Brutally? Henri couldn't set about anything in that fashion. With a feigned weariness? Coldly? Henri began to smile to himself. He had been so jealous over Valentina! He wondered how he'd ever risked fighting a duel with her official lover, a leathery captain in the horse artillery: that was another occasion when his migraines had saved him from being wounded or making a ridiculous spectacle of himself. Valentina was late. Perhaps she'd forgotten? He had noticed her that winter at the Feydeau theatre in Paris: she was singing in *The Inn at Bagnières*, a fresh, unpretentious comic opera by MM. Jalabert and Catel:

> When I wear my little hat,
> My dress of amaranthine,
> My shawl and my poppy red shoes,
> What a picture's to be seen ...

Valentina arrived in a barouche, dressed very like the character in her song, that's to say just as flimsily, but her crêpe dress was a shade of hydrangea, she wore satin ankle boots, a heavily embroidered bodice, and two long feathers waved above her black velvet toque. Her brown hair fell in corkscrew curls about her temples. As pale as the fashion demanded but rather plump, Valentina favoured certain mannerisms: she wrinkled her nose, swivelled her hips and made a point, whenever she smiled, of showing her teeth, which she knew to be perfect.

'*Amore mio!*' she said, her Italian heavily laced with a suburban Parisian accent.

'Valentina ...'

'This is it! The theatre at the Carinthian gate is going to reopen: the theatre on the Wien too!'

'Valentina . . .'

'I'm going to appear, Henri! It's a dream! Me, on stage, here, in the capital of theatre! Can you imagine, my sweetheart?'

Oh yes, her sweetheart could imagine, but he couldn't get a word in edgeways and, seeing the pretty actress so elated, he was hardly brave enough to crush her spirits.

'There are four rows of boxes! The sets change without the curtain having to fall! And Vesuvius is even going to erupt on stage!'

'Is it an opera about Pompeii?'

'No, nothing like that, it's *Don Juan.*'

'By Mozart?'

'By Molière, of course!'

'But, Valentina, you're a singer.'

'It's sung from start to finish.'

'*Don Juan?* By Molière?'

'That's right, you silly old roly-poly!'

Henri became sullen. He didn't feel silly and he couldn't stand references to his weight. He decided to extricate himself by taking evasive action, reflecting that flight is sometimes the most sensible tactic, at least in matters of the heart. It helped that his teeth were chattering and that he was shivering despite such a mild May. He wiped his forehead with his handkerchief, exaggerating his discomfort only slightly.

'I am ill, Valentina.'

'Then I will look after you!'

'No, no, you have to rehearse Molière's songs.'

'We'll manage. Why, you can help me learn them!'

'I don't want to be a millstone round your neck.'

'Don't worry, my sweetheart, I'm strong enough to carry it all off: my career and you. No, no, what I mean is: you and my career as well!'

'I'm convinced of that, Valentina . . .'

'So, do you agree?'

'No.'

'Must you leave Vienna?'

'Most probably.'

'Well, then, I'll follow you!'

'Be reasonable . . .'

What a blunderer I am, thought Henri as he uttered these words. How could one appeal to Valentina's reason? She possessed everything save that. He was tying himself in knots. The more pitiful he made himself, the more attentive and loving she became. Vienna's church bells started ringing.

'Five o'clock already!' said Valentina.

'Six,' lied Henri, 'I counted.'

'Oh, no, I'm terribly late!'

'Come on, off you go quickly and try on your costumes and learn your part.'

'I'll take you back in a barouche!'

'No, no, I'll take you.'

Henri dropped the actress off at the theatre where she hoped to make her debut. Before leaving, she kissed him frenziedly; he closed his eyes and could only respond by imagining that he was kissing the lips of another, whom he loved too deeply and at too great a distance. Valentina ran towards the theatre door and, under the columns, quickly turned to sketch a last wave of her gloved hand. Henri sighed. What a coward I am, he thought, and then gave the coachman the address of the pink house in the Jordangasse where he had lodged for the last three nights. He instantly forgot the war, his illness and his friends and fell into a reverie about Mlle Krauss, who displayed all the human virtues, each in its purest form. Every second he discovered something new to add to the sum of her qualities. He had considered Cimarosa to be the finest of all composers only the week before and yet, here he was, humming Mozart. Every evening, in their large, bare drawing room, Anna and her sisters would play Mozart on the violin for no one's pleasure but his alone.

*

There was only one stone house on the island of Lobau, a former hunting lodge where the Habsburg princes took shelter from sudden storms. M. Constant was laying logs in the fireplace on the first floor. Valets were cleaning, sweeping and setting out the furniture transported on wagons from the neighbouring castle of Ebersdorf where the Emperor had spent the previous night. Cooks were unpacking pans and spits, the obligatory Parmesan which His Majesty ate with everything, his favourite macaroni and his bottles of Chambertin. Two lackeys were carrying his iron bedstead upstairs. The chamberlains, meanwhile, were overseeing the preparations and chivvying along His Majesty's domestic staff.

'Hurry up there!'

'The china! The chandeliers!'

'Carpet, here, at the top of the stairs!'

'I very much regret it, Marshal, but this is the Emperor's house!'

Marshal Lannes was taller, less refined and considerably

stronger than the chamberlain barring his path; catching
the man by the silver lapels of his uniform, therefore, he
simply pushed him hard in the chest. M. Constant rushed
downstairs when he heard the servant's yelp of protest and
the Marshal's gruff voice, growling in exasperation. But he
too had no choice but to give way to the intruder, who had
no patience with protocol. Lannes set himself up on the
ground floor in a low-ceilinged room filled with straw, and
furnished his new quarters with a candlestick, a chair and
a desk on which he threw his sabre and tricorn covered in
feathers. Renowned for furious bouts of rage which,
although he mastered them, still turned his face a deep
red, Lannes's square features otherwise bore a tranquil
expression. His light, wavy hair was cut short and, at forty
years old, his stomach was still flat and his back still
straight, thanks to a stiff neck – the legacy of a wound he'd
received at Saint Jean d'Acre. Whenever the old ache made
him bring a hand up to his nape, his mind would go back
to that battle. It was their twelfth assault on the citadel. His
friend, General Rambaud, had come within a hair's breadth
of taking Djezzar Pasha's seraglio, but the reinforcements
he hoped for had not arrived and he had barricaded himself
and his men in a mosque. Lannes could still see the ditches
piled with Turkish corpses. General Rambaud had been
killed. Wounded in the head, he had himself been believed
dead. The next day he had climbed back into the saddle
and led his men over the hills of Galilee . . .

The marshal was worn out by fifteen years of fighting
and danger. He had just led the horrific siege of Saragossa.
Rich and married to the most beautiful and discreet of the
duchesses at court, the daughter of a senator, he would
have liked to retire to his native Gascony and live with his

family and watch his two sons grow up. He was tired of always leaving and not knowing whether he'd come home as a corpse packed in a crate. Why did the Emperor refuse him this tranquillity? Like him, most of the marshals only aspired to the peace of the countryside now. These adventurers were turning bourgeois with time. At Savigny, Davout built wicker runs for his partridges and got down on all fours to feed them bread; Ney and Marmont adored gardening; MacDonald and Oudinot only felt comfortable when they were surrounded by their villagers; and on his land at Grignon, Bessières was out hunting whenever he wasn't playing with his children. As for Masséna – ensconced in his property at Rueil, looking onto Malmaison, the Emperor's retreat – he was fond of saying, 'I can piss on him from here!' And yet they had all come to Austria on an order, at the head of a motley army of young soldiers who had no good reason to kill. The Empire was already in decline; it had only existed for five years. They sensed this. Yet still they followed.

Lannes's moods shifted quickly from anger to affection. Once he had written to his wife that the Emperor was his worst enemy. 'He is only fond of one on a whim, when he needs one.' But then Napoleon had lavished favours on him and they had fallen into each other's arms. Their destinies remained inseparable. Only a short while before, the Emperor had clung to his arm on the treacherous escarpment of a Spanish sierra. Inching forward in their high leather boots, lashed by a snowstorm, they had struggled to keep their footing. Together they had climbed onto the barrel of a cannon and, as though on a sleigh, had been hoisted by grenadiers to the top of the Guadarrama pass. Fond memories jostled with nightmares. Lannes sometimes regretted not having become a dyer. He had enlisted early and drawn attention to himself by his reckless and headlong courage in the army of the Alps, commanded by Augereau. Slumped in the straw, he was thinking of a hundred conflicting episodes of his life when Berthier entered the room.

'Whenever there's a commotion, it's bound to be you.'

'You're right, Alexandre. Go on, clap me in irons: at least I'll get a decent night's sleep.'

'His Majesty is entrusting you with the cavalry.'

'And Bessières?'

'He is to be your subordinate.'

Lannes and Bessières detested each other as bitterly and as roundly as Berthier and Davout. The marshal smiled and his mood lifted. 'Let the Archduke attack! We'll meet him with our sabres!'

At that moment, Périgord and Lejeune arrived out of breath. 'The small bridge has broken!' they announced to the major-general.

'We're cut off from the left bank. Three-quarters of our troops are trapped on the island.'

*

The moon in its last quarter lit up Essling's main street with a feeble light, but nonetheless the Emperor had authorized bivouac fires to be lit under the trees on the lane leading to the village granary, in the square and at the edge of the fields; the enemy must know that the Grande Armée had crossed the Danube since, his plan went, this would provoke them to attack, even though the Archduke Charles was known for his timidity in taking the offensive. Fires were blazing in every direction. Women canteen workers moved between them, filling tumblers to the brim with brandy and getting slapped on their ample buttocks for their pains. Some of the soldiers sang crude drinking songs, while others bolted down their rations and told jokes to give themselves courage for the battle that was now certain to begin the following day. They had unfastened their cuirasses and taken off their maned helmets, and the polished metal of their equipment lying on the ground reflected the red glow of the fires. Like their horses, the men were preparing to sleep under the stars, protected by a handful of mostly slightly drunk sentries, who scanned the plain without seeing anything. Some of them had found a bag of flour, a bottle of wine or a duck: nothing really to speak of, since the villagers had taken almost everything with them, all their poultry, casks and grain. The cuirassiers occupied the village on their own. Masséna had returned to Aspern before nightfall to be close to the small bridge which the river had breached and which the sappers were attempting to repair by torchlight, their fingers frozen and their uniforms soaked by the turbulent, icy waters.

General Espagne's staff officers had taken refuge in Essling's church for the night. The painted wooden balustrade dividing the nave had been chopped into firewood for braziers which gave off a thick smoke and cast hellish silhouettes on the church walls. Wrapped in an overcoat, Espagne stood away from the others and leant his elbows on the altar. He could find no reassurance in the shadows which the flames sent dancing over the stone floor. Premonitions had been troubling him for the past few weeks. He felt no love or fear for this campaign, only the sense that a judgement had been passed on his life and then deferred:

in silence, he thought about death. His cuirassiers were aware of their general's superstitious fears, even though he never allowed a sign of them to alter his grave expression. Each of them respected his silence. Each repeated his strange story.

Troopers Fayolle and Pacotte had shared from a single mess tin a thick, ill-defined soup which now lay like lead on their stomachs. Their conversation had turned to the general, about whom Pacotte knew nothing since he hadn't been with the regiment long. Fayolle knew the whole story.

'It was at the castle in Bayreuth. We get there late, he's tired, he goes to bed. I wasn't far off, on the main staircase with the others, and suddenly in the middle of the night, we hear shouting.'

'Someone was trying to kill the general?'

'Not so fast! Well, the shouting was coming from his room, right enough, so the orderly officers run to it and I follow them with the sentries. The door has been locked from the inside. We break it down, using a couch as a battering ram, we go in . . .'

'And then?'

'Patience, man! What do we see?'

'What?'

'The bed upended in the middle of the room and the general underneath it.'

'And he's shouting.'

'No, he's unconscious. Quick as a flash, our doctor bleeds him and checks him over, he opens his eyes, he's pale, terrified, he stares at us, the doctor has to give him powders to calm his nerves. Then he says, listen carefully, Pacotte, he says, "I've seen a ghost and it wanted to slit my throat!"'

'No!'

'Don't laugh, you fool. It was when he was wrestling with the ghost that the bed got tipped over.'

'You believe that?'

'He's asked to describe this phantom, which he does to the last detail, and do you know what it was, eh? No, you don't know. Well, I'm going to tell you. It was the White Lady of the Habsburgs!'

'Who's she?'

'She appears in the palaces of Vienna when the time has come for a prince of the House of Austria to die. She had already come to Bayreuth three years before, and Prince Louis of Austria had fought with her, just like the general.'

'And was it the death of him?'

'Oh, yes, my friend, it was. Near Saalfeld, a hussar's sabre through the throat. The general is as white as death, he says in a very low voice, "Her visit foretells that my end is near," and he goes off to sleep somewhere else.'

'You believe in fairy tales like that, do you?'

'We'll see tomorrow.'

'So you do, Fayolle, you believe in them!'

'And suppose the general is killed?'

'Suppose we are?'

'Oh, us, that'd just be bad luck . . .'

Cuirassier Pacotte felt very sceptical about the general's misadventure. At home, in his market town of Menilmontant, no one set too much store by that sort of fancy. An apprentice joiner before being recruited, Pacotte was used to tangible things: turning a table leg, nailing down boards, blowing your pay on cheap wine. Seeing that Fayolle was troubled by the story, he slapped him on the back. 'Got to take your mind off it, man. What say we go and pay our respects to our little Austrian friend? She's expecting us. Tied up the way we left her, I can't see her turning into a ghost!'

'Do you remember where it was?'

'We'll find it. The village has only got one street.'

They took a lantern down from a cart and set off through Essling where all the houses looked the same. Twice they chose the wrong one. 'Plague on this,' grumbled Fayolle, 'we'll never find it again.' Further on, by the light of the lantern, Pacotte recognized the body of their attacker, who no one had buried. They smiled at each other and pushed open the door. Pacotte tripped on the step and the candle in the lantern went out.

'Very smart, you fathead!' said Fayolle, wrapping his hand in his cape to lift off the burning-hot glass while Pacotte struck his tinderbox. When they reached the first floor, they walked to the room at the back of the house, and saw that the girl hadn't moved.

'How do you say "Hello, my beauty" in German?' asked Pacotte.

'Darned if I know,' said Fayolle.

'It's strange she's having such a good sleep . . .'

They put the lantern down on a three-legged stool and Fayolle cut her free with his sabre. Cuirassier Pacotte took out the gag, pocketed the velvet braces with which it had been tied in place, bent down and kissed her full on the mouth. He jumped back. 'Hell!'

'Can't you wake her up?' asked Fayolle, grinning.

'She's dead!'

Pacotte spat on the ground, then wiped his mouth on his sleeve.

'But our little doll has still got warm feet,' Fayolle said, prodding the girl.

'Don't touch her, it's bad luck!'

'You don't believe in my ghosts, but what, now your teeth start chattering? Out of the way, you sparrow.'

'I'm not staying here.'

'Well, get out, then. Leave me the lantern.'

'I'm not staying here, Fayolle, you can't do this, any of this . . .'

'You're talking to a real soldier,' Fayolle laughed mockingly, undoing his belt.

Pacotte raced down the stairs in the pitch black. Outside, he leaned against the wall of the house. He breathed deeply several times. He felt sick. His legs prickled. He didn't dare imagine his accomplice taking that poor peasant girl, suffocated to death by the gag that he, Pacotte, must have tied too tight. He played the part of the swaggerer, true enough, but he had never wanted to kill anybody. In battle, of course, there was no other way of getting out alive, but this?

Slow minutes passed.

Over by the church, soldiers were singing.

Fayolle came out. Neither said a word about the Austrian, Pacotte only asking, 'Give me the light, will you, I'm going to be sick.'

'You don't need to see for that, but I do.'

'See what?'

'My new shoes.'

He pointed to the body lying in the courtyard.

'Now's the time to relieve this fellow of his boots. I think my need's greater than his, wouldn't you say?'

Fayolle crouched down and put the lantern on the

ground. He undid his spurs to try them on the corpse's shoes and cursed: they didn't fit at all. Disappointed, he stood up and called out, 'Pacotte!'

Holding the lantern at arm's length in front of him, he set off down the street, grumbling, 'Can't you answer me, you swine?'

He made out a figure near a tree and walked towards it.

'What, do you need a tree to chuck up your guts?'

Striding through the grass and nettles of the verge, he bumped into something: a tree trunk, probably. He kicked it. It wasn't wood. It was soft, like a body. He bent down, the light of the lantern picking out a uniform. As the soldier was lying face down, he turned him over. Smeared with vomit and blood, his friend Pacotte had a knife stuck in his throat.

'Stand to arms!'

Nearby, in the shadows, a group of Austrians in mouse-grey jackets and black hats with a cutting of leaves pinned to the crest – the uniform of the Landwehr, their people's militia – ducked down and disappeared into the wheat-fields.

*

Masséna had ordered braziers to be lit and lamps strung along the stanchions of the small bridge. Handing his gold-embroidered coat and cocked hat to his orderly, he flung himself into pressing on the repairs. Boots sunk in the muddy riverbank, he caught a pontoneer by the collar who had almost drowned in the swirling waters. Masséna had the stamina of a wild animal. He scaled girders, carried planks, did as much work as ten of the men whom he led by example. He had never been ill. No, he had, once, in Italy, when he had established such a successful traffic in import licences that he made a profit of three million francs. The Emperor found out and asked Masséna to pay a third into the Treasury: the marshal pleaded that they were his savings, that his family cost him a fortune; he said he was poor, in debt. The Emperor finally became so exasperated that he confiscated the entire fortune, which was deposited in a bank in Livorno. That was when Masséna fell ill.

But in action, the marshal forgot about his banditry, his avarice and the Genoese gold which he imagined to be slumbering in some safe in Vienna: he'd worry about that later. Without seeming to strain, he lifted up an enormous beam for the sappers to rope to one of the boats ballasted with cannonballs which danced in the violent waves. Some planks broke away from the unfinished roadway and span off in the current. Masséna yelled like a devil. Over on the island of Lobau, other pontoneers were trying to join their half of the bridge to his, the two detachments having to make contact somewhere near the middle of this raging branch of the Danube. Now almost within reach, the detachments had started throwing out cables weighted with stones, catching them in mid-air and stretching them taut like the skeleton of a bridge's parapet. The rolling waters were still rising beneath them and they inched forward, beam by beam, plank by plank, pulling, knotting and nailing in the blurred, reddish glow of the bonfires, drenched by the sheets of water which broke on their handiwork, exhausted, numbed and roped together like rosaries of men. Like a lion tamer, Masséna exhorted and insulted them by turns, cutting a majestic figure with his stock pulled up to his chin and his sleeves rolled up to his elbows. Standing at the edge of the reconstructed roadway he picked up a tangle of chains in his right hand and threw them to a sergeant who was clinging to a pontoon. 'Round that log!' The sergeant's fingers were frozen, he couldn't hook them round the post, and as his boat pitched and the cold waves hit him full in the face he almost lost his balance. Masséna climbed down the ropes towards the helpless soldier, pushed him out of the way and fixed the chains in place. A gust of wind blew the smoke back into the men's faces, they coughed and blindly kept on working. 'To the right! More to the right!' Masséna shouted, as if, with his one eye, he saw better at night than the pontoneers with all their experience. On the other side of the river, the rest of the army were waiting on the island of Lobau to cross, their knapsacks on their backs, their muskets at their feet. The front ranks watched the marshal, and if they did not love him, they nevertheless admired him that night. Others were praying that this lousy bridge would never hold, that the Danube would shatter it to pieces and that they'd be able to go home.

*

Two hundred metres away, in a clearing at the centre of the island, the officers of the General Staff and their entourages were reclining on the turf. Many of them carried rings, or miniatures, or a lock of their mistress's hair in small, finely worked boxes and they extolled those ladies' merits in an attempt to distract themselves from the present. Others sang nostalgic airs in chorus,

Patrick Rambaud

You are leaving me, my dear, to go where glory waits
My tender heart will follow, at every step you take.

Lejeune was silent, sitting under an elm tree. His orderly, on all fours, was fanning a fire of branches while Vincent Paradis skinned two hares he had killed with his catapult. Inspired by the bucolic night and the serene, verdant countryside, Périgord was concluding a disquisition on Jean-Jacques Rousseau. 'Sleeping on the grass, under the stars, is all very fine, but one shouldn't make a point of it. There are ants, for one thing. And then the birds wake you up at dawn with their racket. One is far better off between sheets, with the window firmly shut, and, if at all possible, in company: I am somewhat sensitive to the cold.'

He turned to Paradis. 'Keep the skins for me, my boy. They will be perfection itself when my boots need a polish ... Rabbits! Every time I see those little creatures it makes me think of that charade of a shoot at Grosbois. What a fool he is, our major-general!'

'Clumsy perhaps,' Lejeune corrected him in a somewhat vexed tone, 'but not a fool. Don't exaggerate, Edmond. Anyway, we weren't even at that shoot.'

'What are you talking about?' asked a colonel of Hussars, who was keenly looking forward to the stew.

'About the day when, to flatter the Emperor ...'

'To oblige him,' corrected Lejeune.

'It amounts to the same thing, Louis-François!'

'No, it doesn't.'

'The marshal, in order to flatter His Majesty,' repeated the hussar, encouraging Périgord in his scandalmongering.

'Marshal Berthier,' the latter continued, 'had invited the Emperor to a rabbit shoot on his land at Grosbois. Well,

74

Grosbois may have small game, but it hasn't a single rabbit. So what does the marshal do? He orders a thousand. The day arrives and the rabbits are set loose but instead of scampering away from the guns, these animals run straight towards the guests, make a great fuss of them, nuzzle against their boots – none of them in the slightest bit wild – and almost trip up His Majesty. The marshal had forgotten to make it clear that they had to be wild, so the suppliers had delivered a thousand tame rabbits. When they saw such a crowd of people, they quite naturally thought it was feeding time!'

This made Périgord and the hussar cry with laughter. Lejeune, however, had stood up before the end of the story, which he had heard too many times and no longer found amusing. Everybody was making the major-general out to be an ass and it upset Lejeune, who owed his rank and his duties to Berthier. A young infantry officer in Holland and then, through merit, an officer in the engineers, Lejeune had been picked out by Berthier and taken on as an aide-de-camp. His first mission, Lejeune remembered, had been to deliver sacks of gold to some priests in the Valais who were to help drag the artillery over the Alps. He hadn't left the marshal's side since. He, more than anyone, was aware of the marshal's courage and his record: the battles he'd fought alongside the American rebels at New York and Yorktown, his meeting with Frederick II at Potsdam, his devotion to the young General Bonaparte, whose destiny he foresaw during the war of Italy, and his equal devotion to the Napoleon this general had become, for whom, by turns, he played the part of secret agent, confidant, nursemaid and whipping boy. Davout and Masséna had been spreading unjust rumours about him for weeks. It was true that when

Berthier was in sole command of operations at the start of this Austrian campaign, he had relied on dispatches sent by the Emperor from Paris. These directives frequently arrived late, but in the field the position changed from moment to moment, and consequently a number of dangerous manoeuvres had been attempted which nearly brought disaster on the army. The Emperor allowed all the blame to fall on Berthier, who never sought to exonerate himself, just as he hadn't on that day at Rueil when the Emperor fired at random into a flock of partridges and only succeeded in blinding Masséna. Turning to the loyal Berthier, he had said, 'You have wounded Masséna!'

'Not at all, sire, it was you.'

'Me? Everyone saw you shoot across!'

'But, sire . . .'

'Don't deny it!'

The Emperor was always right, and never more so than when he was lying: to contradict him was out of the question. Masséna's hatred for Berthier, however, harked back to an earlier incident. When Masséna was commanding the Army of Italy he had set about looting the Quirinal, the Vatican and the convents and palaces for his personal benefit. The unpaid army had mutinied against the profiteer, and in the chaos the Romans of Trastevere, who had been maltreated and kept on rations of black bread, had also risen up in arms. On the square in front of Agrippa's Pantheon, the rebel officers had offered the command of the French army to Berthier, and, to calm the mood, he had had no choice but to accept and ask the Directory to recall Masséna. Compelled to flee the fury of his own army, Masséna had never forgiven him.

Lejeune shrugged his shoulders. These rivalries struck

him as pitiful. How he would have loved to be in Vienna, to take off this gaudy uniform and go strolling in the hills with his sketchbook and pencil, to take Anna with him, to travel with her, live with her, gaze endlessly at her. Yet, as a reasonable man, Colonel Lejeune knew that good had come from bad: if it hadn't been for this war he would never have met the young girl. A great uproar startled him from his reverie. On the main pontoon bridge, riding behind the Grand Equerry Caulaincourt who was steadying his horse by the bridle rein, the Emperor was crossing over to the island of Lobau. All the troops were cheering.

*

In Vienna, on the second floor of a house painted pink, Henri Beyle was admiring by candlelight his friend Lejeune's drawings of Anna Krauss. The young girl had been happy to pose, uninhibited by any sense of shame. Henri was struck by the likeness. He stared intently at the sketches until they gained another dimension, her figure seeming to take on flesh, to come alive and move. In one, Anna wore a high tunic which lifted a lock of her black hair from the nape of her neck; another showed Anna pensive, in profile, her eyes fixed on some mysterious sight out of the window; Anna asleep on a pile of cushions; Anna standing naked, like a goddess sculpted by Phidias, unreal in her perfection and yet, at the same time, provocative in her wild abandon; Anna in a different pose, drawn from the back; or again, perched on the edge of a sofa, her knees drawn up to her chin, gazing frankly into the artist's eyes. Henri was dazzled and discomfited, as if he had surprised the Viennese girl in her bath, and yet he couldn't tear himself away from the sketches. What if he stole one? Would Louis-François notice? There were so many of them. Was he going to use them for paintings? Then terrible thoughts began to run through Henri's mind, which he abjured with all his reason, but did he still possess sufficient reason to withstand them? In short, he wished in a confused way, without spelling out his desires, that Louis-François would die in battle, that he would be left to console Anna and take Louis-François' place – because one thing was clear: the model could feel nothing less than love for the painter.

The window was half-open, the night still. Henri heard a piano being played with a limpid grace and he leaned out of the window to see where the music was coming from.

'Do you like that music, Monsieur?'

Henri turned round as if he had been caught doing something improper. A young man whom he didn't know had entered his room. In the candlelight, Henri couldn't see him clearly.

He asked, 'How did you get in?'

'Your door was open and I saw the light.'

Henri moved closer to the intruder and observed him. His eyes were pale grey and he could almost have been mistaken for a girl. He spoke French with a thicker accent than was usual in Vienna.

'Who are you?'

'A lodger, like you, but my room is under the eaves.'

'Are you passing through?'

'Yes, passing through.'

'Where do you come from?'

'Erfurt. I work for a trading company.'

'Ah, I see,' said Henri, 'you're German. I work for the commissariat: army supplies.'

'I have nothing to sell,' said the young man. 'I am not in Vienna on business.'

'No doubt you're a friend of the Krauss family?'

'If you like.'

As he was asking these questions, Henri had turned over Lejeune's drawings to hide them, but the young German hadn't glanced in their direction. He stared fixedly at Henri. 'My name is Friedrich Staps. My father is a Lutheran pastor. I have come to Vienna to meet your Emperor. Will that be possible?'

'If he returns to Schönbrunn, request an audience. What do you want of him?'

'To meet him.'

'Ah, so you're an admirer?'

'Not in the way you think.'

The conversation was taking an unpleasant turn; Henri wanted to bring it to an end. 'Well, Monsieur Staps, I'm sure we'll see each other tomorrow. As I am ill, I hardly leave the house.'

'The man playing the piano opposite is also ill.'

'Do you know him?'

'It's M. Haydn.'

'Haydn?' said Henri, returning to the window to hear the celebrated musician better.

'He took to his bed when he saw French uniforms on the streets of his city,' Friedrich Staps continued. 'Now he only gets up to play the Austrian anthem he composed.'

With these words, the young man snuffed out the candle with his fingers. Henri was left in darkness. He heard the door shut and swore, '*My God!* He's mad, that German! Where did I put the tinderbox?'

*

At three o'clock in the morning, repairs finally allowed the troops to cross the small bridge and establish themselves on the left bank of the Danube in the villages of Aspern and Essling. Watches were posted. The men slept little or badly. Marshal Lannes didn't take his eyes off his dress uniform hanging over the back of a chair, its gold lace and braid glinting in the light of a candle. He would put it on at dawn and, most likely, lead his cavalry out to be butchered, but at least their slaughter would have an air about it. Riding at the head of his troopers, he would wear all his decorations, even the great ribbon of St Andrew which the Tsar had awarded him. His dress would single him out to the enemy, he knew that, he wished as much: more even, that he would cut an elegant figure as they sabred him – that was its purpose. Oh yes, he had had enough. What he'd seen in Spain still filled him with disgust: he had not slept easily since. There had been no conventional battles with troops in ordered ranks there, only a faceless war which had broken out on the same day at Oviedo and Valencia, without a word of command, armies of twenty ploughmen led by their alcalde suddenly rising up before them. In no time these armies had grown to several million strong. The Andalucian oxherds had prevailed at Bailén, wielding the lances they used for branding bulls, and then guerrilla warfare had broken out in the mountains, a warfare fuelled by hatred. At Saragossa, little boys slid under the horses of Polish lancers to disembowel them and monks made cartridges in their monastries, scraping dirt off the streets to extract the saltpetre. Lannes's soldiers were attacked with broken bottles and paving stones, and if they were unlucky enough to be captured their noses were sliced off and they were buried up to their necks for a game of skittles. On the pontoons at Cadiz, how many of them had been eaten by the vermin? How many had had their throats slit or been sawn between two planks? How many had been thrown into fires, mutilated, their tongues torn out, their eyesockets left hollow, their noses and ears hacked off?

'What are you thinking, Your Grace?'

Lannes, the Duke of Montebello, refused to unburden himself to Rosalie, an adventuress who, like so many others, marched in the army's rearguard in search of happiness: a few sous, some trinkets, some stories to tell. Lannes was not unfaithful, he adored his wife, but she was so far away and he felt too alone, so he had yielded to this tall, blonde girl with tousled hair who had just tossed her clothes into the straw. He didn't answer. He was haunted by other nightmares. He saw again the children impaled on bayonets in their cribs and the grenadier who had confided in him, 'It's not easy at the start, Marshal, but you get used to it.' Lannes couldn't get used to it any more.

'I'm not your mistress, am I? It's him, up there . . .'

Rosalie was not mistaken. The Emperor was pacing about on the floor above and the sound of his footsteps wore on the marshal's nerves. If a cannonball cuts me in two tomorrow, he thought, at least I'll stand a chance of sleeping without dreaming!

'Come here, he's going,' Rosalie said.

The Emperor was walking down the staircase with his escort of Mamelukes, who surrounded him like guard dogs wherever he went. Lannes heard the sentries present arms. He got up to consult his gold engraved watch. It was three thirty. What hour would the sun rise and what scenes would it reveal?

Rosalie insisted, 'Come!'

This time he obeyed.

*

Napoleon had gone to meet Masséna, who was keeping watch in the belfry of Aspern.

'They're getting ready, sire,' said the Marshal.

The Emperor made no reply. He took the spyglass from Masséna's hands and looked out, steadying himself against a dragoon's shoulder. The horizon was coloured with the flickering red dots of the enemy bivouacs. He imagined the battle in the green crops, he heard the cannon fire, the shouts, the tumult which struck terror into Europe. A great reputation, he thought, is a great noise. The more one makes, the further it carries. Laws, institutions, monuments, nations, men: all these disappear, but the noise continues to echo down the length of the centuries. On the Marchfeld plain before him, Napoleon knew that Marcus Aurelius had crushed the Marcomans of King Vadovar, just as he would crush the Austrians of the Archduke Charles. The echo of that other battle gave him pleasure. In Roman times, there was no wheat here, only marshes, reeds, herons and banks of heather. The legions had charged out of the Bohemian forests, hacking their way through with axes and slaughtering bears and bison for their daily rations. Theirs was no longer the famed peasant army of Latium, heavily armed and rigorously disciplined, but centuries drawn from all over the Empire, who marched behind horn players, half-naked under the pelts of wild animals. Moroccan cavalry, Gallic crossbowmen, Bretons, Iberians ready to choose from their prisoners those who'd dig the Asturian silver mines, Greeks, Arabs, Syrians as vicious as hyenas, Getans with straw-coloured hair, crawling with lice, Thracians in skirts of hemp. And Marcus Aurelius on horseback in this flood tide, unarmed and without a cuirass, but unmistakable, even to the most distant observer, in his purple mantle . . .

Three

THE FIRST DAY

AT DAWN, A HEAT HAZE VEILED THE PLAIN. Not a breath of wind disturbed the wheat. In front of the villages where his army was preparing, Napoleon observed the unnaturally still countryside, hunched over the mane of his white Arab and surrounded by his marshals, their staff officers, orderlies and equerries. They presented a fine target, this cluster of commanders – Berthier, Masséna, Lannes and Bessières, who had arrived from Vienna – and generals of division glitteringly arrayed as if on parade – Espagne with his tight jaw, Lasalle chewing his cold pipe, the points of his moustache twisted up into his eyes, Boudet, Claparède, Mouton, Saint-Hilaire, his head sunk deep in his collar, Oudinot, with his short hair, bushy eyebrows and dogged expression, Molitor, unkempt hair curling onto his cheeks, his nose as thin as a knife blade, and lastly the commanding figure of Marulaz, his stomach straining against a scarlet sash. The fierce tension precluded any movement or conversation. As their stiff-legged horses gently shook their manes, they sat motionless, a mass of plumes and colours festooned with braid and gold thread down to the tops of their boots, which had been polished until they shone. Together, these heroes composed an anachronistic tableau which Lejeune regretted not being able to capture – even

in a pencil sketch, dashed off in a second – so keenly did
he feel, and so excited was he by, the discrepancy between
the soldiers and their surroundings, the impatience of the
one and the serenity of the other. Nothing was happening.
Lejeune thought of the power that settings have, their
capacity to alter the meaning and actions of the people they
frame. He remembered one of his passing lovers, a rosy-
cheeked German girl, bathing in a mountain stream in
Bavaria: innocently high spirited in the natural surroundings, she had simply been pretty. But at night, when she'd
undressed again in a drawing room heavy with wall hang-
ings, draperies, ornaments and dark furniture, when she
was equally naked but more solemn, she had become
disquieting; her abandon, her agility, her clothes strewn on
the carpet all contrasting with the severe decor. It's funny,
mused Lejeune, here I am thinking of love while we wait
for war ... He smiled. The Emperor's voice brought him
back to the present.

'They must still be asleep! Damned Austrians! *Mascal-
zoni!*'

No one commented, no one agreed: the time for servility
had passed. Before the day was out, a number of these
princes, barons, counts and generals would, in all probabil-
ity, be dead. The haze was clearing, only strips of it now
floating above the fields. The sky was a purer blue, the
wheat a more vivid green. On the horizon, on the slopes of
Gerasdorf, they could see where the Austrians had stacked
their arms.

'What are they waiting for?' the Emperor shouted.

'Soup,' said Berthier, his eye to his telescope.

'It's only a rearguard, sire,' Lannes grumbled, 'let's go
and bowl them over!'

'My troopers encountered nothing on their patrols,' Bessières agreed.

'No,' Masséna insisted, 'the Austrian army is out there: they're very close.'

'Sixty thousand of them, at least,' said Berthier, 'if my intelligence is correct.'

'Your intelligence!' Lannes growled. 'Those prisoners of yours have been talking twaddle! They were sacrificed on that damned island, what on earth are they going to know of the Archduke Charles's intentions?'

'Skirmishers slit one of my men's throat last night,' Espagne stated in an expressionless voice.

'That's all it amounts to,' Lannes continued, 'skirmishers and marauders – meanwhile the main body of their regiments has stayed behind, snug in Bohemia!'

'They're probably waiting,' added Bessières, 'to be reinforced by the army of Italy . . .'

'*Basta!*'

The Emperor had shouted with exasperation. He was tired of hearing their chatter. He had no need of their advice. He signalled to Berthier with a quick wave of his hand then moved away from the group, accompanied by the Grand Equerry Caulaincourt, the young Count Anatole de Montesquiou, his aide-de-camp with the fleshy face, and, as always, the Mamelukes he had brought back from Egypt, who swaggered beside him self-importantly in their plumed turbans and scarlet Turkish trousers, their richly ornamented daggers tucked in their belts. Berthier began speaking in a loud voice, without even looking at the marshals.

'His Majesty has devised a deployment which you will implement immediately. There must be no mistakes. We find ourselves with our backs to the river, whence fresh troops, supplies and munitions will be arriving. Our objective is to present the enemy with an unbroken front stretching from one village to the other. Masséna will hold Aspern, with Molitor, Legrand and Carra-Saint-Cyr. Lannes will occupy Essling with Boudet and Saint-Hilaire's divisions. The bare ground between the villages must be barred: Espagne's cuirassiers and Lasalle's light cavalry will deploy there. That is all!'

There was nothing to discuss. The group broke up and each went to take up his appointed post. Deep in thought, Berthier took the road to his encampment, flanked by Lejeune and Périgord. 'What are your thoughts, Lejeune?' the major-general asked.

'I have none, your Highness, none.'

'Truthfully.'

'This light makes me want to paint.'

'And you, Périgord?'

'Me? I obey.'

'We're all reduced to obedience, my children,' sighed Berthier.

In single file, they crossed the small bridge, which bobbed up and down in the current. On the island, Périgord brought his horse level with Lejeune's and whispered confidentially, 'Our major-general is very sombre.'

'It must be the uncertainty. The Emperor seems to have chosen to go on the defensive: we entrench, we wait. Are the Austrians going to attack? The Emperor believes so: he must have his reasons.'

'Good Lord,' said Périgord, raising his eyes to heaven, 'just as long as he knows where he's leading us! Even so, my dear friend, we would all be far better off in Paris or Vienna and our major-general on his estate with his two wives! Look at him, I could swear he's thinking of the Visconti . . .'

Lejeune didn't reply. It was common knowledge that Berthier maintained a *ménage à trois* and that the arrangement tormented him. For thirteen years he had been madly in love with a grey-eyed woman from Milan, alas, married to the Marquis Visconti, a good-natured diplomat of advanced years and complete discretion who was only mildly disconcerted by the constant infidelity of his immoderately beautiful and passionate wife. When Berthier had resolved to follow Bonaparte to Egypt and part from his mistress, it had caused him terrible heartbreak. In the middle of the desert, in his tent, he erected a sort of altar to Giuseppa and endlessly wrote her despairing and salacious letters. And so it continued. Eventually Napoleon found this interminable passion ridiculous. Created Prince of Neuchâtel, Berthier had been compelled to choose a genuine princess with whom he could found the semblance of a dynasty. Submissive, wretched and choking back tears, Berthier decided on Elizabeth of Bavaria, a princess with a pointed little face and no chin, of whom Giuseppa Visconti couldn't conceivably be jealous. And what happened, two weeks after the enforced ceremony? The marquis died in his bed and Berthier could no longer marry his widow. He had been wracked by fevers, and on the verge of a nervous collapse: he had had to be consoled, supported, rewarded, even though the two women tolerated one another, spent time in each other's company and played whist together. On that particular Sunday, 21 May 1809, while the French waited for the Austrian cannon to open fire, that is why Berthier was sighing.

*

Marshal Bessières sighed to himself for similar, although secret, reasons. Cold, unusually polite, taciturn, without obvious feelings and beyond suspicion of having committed even the most minor amorous indiscretion, he had managed to shield his double life from the gossip-mongers. He also wore two lockets under his blue and gold coat. One showed his wife Marie-Jeanne, a pious, very gentle lady, who was well regarded at Court: the other his lover, a dancer at the Opéra on whom he spent millions – Virginie Oreille, known as Letellier.

Bessières's *ancien régime* appearance, with his long powdered hair swept back from his temples in crow's wings, never gave any intimation of the less than soldierly thoughts that often preoccupied him. When he entered Essling for the first time at General Espagne's side, he immediately glanced up at the clocktower. What a Whitsun! The Holy Spirit wouldn't be coming down on their heads today, but other tongues of fire: the Archduke's shells and roundshot. On the square, the saddled horses were feeding from heaps of barley. Troopers helped one another fasten their breastplates or cleaned their weapons with curtains torn from the windows of the village.

'Espagne, go and inform your officers of His Majesty's wishes,' said Bessières as he dismounted.

Then he walked thoughtfully towards the church and entered. The choir had been turned into a camp and the remains of two prayer stools were burning in front of the bare altar, which had been stripped of its ornaments. Bessières stood in front of the crucifix, which soldiers had attempted to prise loose, bent his head, searched inside his jacket and looked at the pictures of his beloveds, a locket in each palm. Marie-Jeanne would be attending mass in the chapel of their chateau at Grignon, while Virginie, at this hour, would be asleep in the large apartment he'd bought for her near the Palais-Royal. And he, what was he doing in this half-destroyed Austrian church? He was a Marshal of the Empire, forty-three years old. Circumstances had favoured him this far. So much ground covered in such a short time! As a very young member of Louis XVI's guard he had tried to protect the royal family during the August 10th riots. He had never approved of the Revolution's crudeness, or its subjugation of the clergy. A suspect himself at one moment, he had been forced to hide in the countryside at the Duke de la Rochefoucauld's before joining the Army of the Pyrenees and then that of Italy as part of Bonaparte's entourage, whose coup d'état he had assisted, and for whom he had created a praetorian bodyguard which was to become the Imperial Guard ... In an hour, he would be on horseback. His soldiers loved him. His enemies as well. Those monks at Saragossa, for instance, whom he had protected from his own regiments. Had he been born to command? Bessières couldn't make sense of anything any more.

Outside, Espagne had already gone into action. He was giving orders, hurrying preparations forward, inspecting horses and weapons. He noticed that some cuirassiers were digging a grave under the elms at the end of the main street and sent a captain to get this burial over with as quickly as possible. Captain Saint-Didier set off on foot, without any great urgency.

Three cuirassiers were finishing digging a hole with spades they'd stolen from a shed. Trooper Pacotte lay white and stiff in the grass.

'Let's get a move on, lads,' said Captain Saint-Didier.

'Got to be done, Captain,' was Fayolle's only answer as he drove his spade into the earth piling up round the ditch.

'We're moving out of this cursed village!'

'And we're burying our brother, Captain,' Fayolle again replied, 'so the foxes won't gnaw on his bones.'

'We've got our principles,' added another cuirassier, a strapping blacksmith called Verzieux.

'What about the fellow you disembowelled yesterday evening in that house: not burying him?'

'Him!' said Fayolle. 'He's an Austrian.'

'If the foxes make a meal of him, then at least they'll be his own foxes,' sniggered the third soldier, a small, brown-haired man.

'That's enough, Brunel!' the captain upbraided him

'Would you, by any chance, be a religious man, Captain?' asked Fayolle mockingly, stroking the black braces which he'd found in Pacotte's pocket: he wore them round his neck like a cravat, a souvenir or a trophy.

'In three-quarters of an hour, I want to see all three of you back with your troop!' ordered Captain Saint-Didier, and he turned on his heels. He walked away, disgusted at having to command such brutes.

As soon as he was out of earshot, Brunel asked the others, 'Saint-Didier, that's an aristo's name, isn't it, or am I getting that wrong?'

'Could be the one who'll save us from the worst of it,' said Fayolle. 'I saw him at work at Ratisbon. He knows his trade.'

'That's right!' agreed Verzieux, starting to dig. 'I'm sick of those little upstarts fresh from school who are out there drilling us, before a fortnight's past, just because they can speak Latin!'

Behind them, on the banks of the Danube, some gulls started screeching with what sounded like laughter. Fayolle grimaced, and threw his brown coat over his shoulder. 'If even the birds think we're a bloody joke, this isn't getting off to a good start . . .'

*

The cavalry regiments quartered in Vienna moved out en masse at the start of the morning and the ground shook as they rode past. Friedrich Staps flattened himself against a wall to give way to some dragoons, who'd spurred their horses to a gallop and would have trampled him without a second glance, then he plunged into the old streets surrounding St Stephen's Cathedral. He pushed open the glazed door of an ironmonger's which had just opened for business and already had a customer, a corpulent, sombrely dressed gentleman, with long, sparse grey hair which bunched up on his collar. The man was speaking French and the wide-eyed shopkeeper was trying to explain in Viennese – that German that sounded as if it was being sung – that he couldn't understand. The Frenchman took some chalk out of his pocket and drew something on the counter, undoubtedly badly because the tradesman remained perplexed. Staps stepped forward and offered his help. 'I have some knowledge of your language, sir, and if I can be of any service . . .'

'Ah! Young man, you have come to my rescue!'

'What have you drawn?'

'A saw.'

'You wish to buy a saw?'

'Yes, a fairly long and solid one with fine teeth that won't bend too easily.'

Informed of this by Staps, the shopkeeper darted off amongst the boxes and returned with several models which the Frenchman picked up. Staps studied him with curiosity.

'Sir, I cannot picture you at all as a carpenter or joiner.'

'And you would be right! Forgive me, I'm in rather a hurry this morning, I haven't even introduced myself: Dr Percy, Chief Surgeon of the Grande Armée.'

'Do you need a saw to treat your patients?'

'Treat them! I'd much prefer to do that, but in a battle, one doesn't treat: one repairs, one hunts death down, one cuts off arms and legs before gangrene sets in. Gangrene, do you know that term?'

'I don't think so, no.'

'In this heat,' said Percy, shaking his large head, 'a wounded limb quickly starts to rot, young man, and it's best to amputate before the whole body breaks down from within.'

Dr Percy chose a suitable saw which the tradesman wrapped up: he paid, peeling off a note from a bundle he'd taken out of his bag, pocketed his change, thanked the man and put on a black three-cornered hat with a cockade. Through the shop window, Staps watched him walking towards the Kärtnerstrasse where he climbed into a barouche.

'And for you, sir?' asked the shopkeeper.

Staps turned and said, 'I need a large sharp-pointed knife.'

'For carving meat?'

'Exactly,' he replied, with a faint smile.

When he left the ironmonger's, Friedrich Staps put the

96

kitchen knife wrapped in grey paper in the inside pocket of his wrinkled frock coat and set off at a good rate through the tumultuous city: squadrons were still streaming towards Vienna's gates to take the road to Ebersdorf, the Danube, and the main pontoon bridge. Reaching the pink house in the Jordangasse, Staps found a team of bare-chested men, with policemen's caps on their heads, unloading one of the commissariat's covered wagons. Without asking any questions, he followed two of them who were sweating heavily as they carried a huge basket up to the first-floor kitchens. When he walked in, he saw chickens, decanters, round loaves of bread and vegetables piled up on the long dark table. The Krauss sisters and their governess were plucking, chopping, peeling and washing, while Henri Beyle was returning from the pump with two pails of water, despite looking very unwell. Staps took them from him, saying, 'You should rest, you are ill.'

'That's very kind of you, Monsieur Staps.'

Then, indicating the foodstuffs with a wave of his arm, Henri explained, 'My colleagues at the commissariat are, as you can see, looking out for my health.'

'And that of the young ladies.'

Henri looked at Staps, with his angelic air and ambivalent smile: this excessively polite boy bothered him. Everything he said could have a double meaning. Should one mistrust him? Why? Henri forgot his suspicions as he heard Anna Krauss joking with her sisters, and realized that he couldn't understand who or what they were joking about. Staps quickly joined in the conversation, speaking German as well, which made him odious to Henri, who was forced to observe their laughter from his end of the table without being able to take part in it. He paled, gritted his teeth and as he tried to stand up, felt faint and started shivering. Suddenly anxious, Anna rushed to hold him up. When she gave him her arm and he felt her warmth against him, Henri blushed as red as a beetroot.

'He's getting his colour back!' exclaimed Friedrich Staps in French.

Henri would have liked to have bitten him, the little imbecile.

*

With his jacket open and trousers rolled up over mud-caked clogs, Vincent Paradis no longer resembled a volti-guer, nor, quite yet, a scout: one's first guess would have been a civilian in fancy dress. Lejeune's aide-de-camp had had to shake the colonel to wake him up. He yawned and stretched in front of the yellow Danube, which was now unlike any river he had seen before – as broad as a sound and yet, with its whims and sudden violent furies, as unstable as a mountain torrent. The sun was beginning to beat down and Paradis picked up his shako, put it on and adjusted the gilt leather strap under his chin. Who on earth had come up with hats as tall as this? Protected by an officer of the headquarters staff, Paradis felt that he was out of harm's way on the island of Lobau and he was amused by the hustle and bustle he could make out in the distance, on the other bank, towards the densely packed houses and farms of Ebersdorf. Then he heard music. At the head of the troops filing onto the jolting main bridge, the clarinets of the Imperial Guard had struck up a march of Cherubini's which had been composed for them. Behind came the eagles with outspread wings mounted on diamond-shaped tricoloured standards, then the immaculate grenadiers. No one in the army could stand them, that crowd. They were entitled to every privilege and they showed it. The Emperor's pampering made them arrogant. They never entered the front line except when a battle had ended, to parade amongst the corpses of men and horses; they ate out of individual mess tins, and travelled in carts lined with straw, or cabs, so as not to spoil their uniforms. At their encampment at Schönbrunn , the commissariat had provided him with coppers for warming sweet wine. They wore kerseymere breeches, like the Emperor, tucked into white cloth gaiters, and their commander Dorsenne – an inordinate dandy who kept his black curls set with tongs and had the haughty manner of a salon habitué – regularly inspected the buttons and false pleats of their uniforms and ran a gloved finger over their bayonets to check that they were clean.

The grenadiers of the Guard advanced in three ranks over the interminable bridge, its planks resting on boats of unequal shapes and sizes which rocked in the current. As they marched forward with a slow, measured tread, they threw off their cocked hats, which the river whirled out of sight, and each man untied a case from the knapsack of the grenadier in front of him, opened it and put on one of their famous bearskins.

'What a sight!' said Lejeune's aide-de-camp, who was standing behind Paradis.

'Yes, Lieutenant.'

'That sends the blood racing through your veins!'

'Yes, Lieutenant,' Voltigeur Paradis repeated, not wanting to contradict his benefactors who were keeping him away from the front, but this affected ceremonial got on his nerves.

No such consideration was ever shown to the foot soldiers: always up to their knees in mud, always hunched under the weight of their weapons, legs aching, backs broken; they slept on the ground, even when it rained, and fought amongst themselves for a warm place not too far from the bivouac fire.

Lejeune walked towards them, with his hands behind his back, looking morose. It didn't bode well. He took Paradis by the shoulder with an exaggerated display of affection and steered him towards the bank of the island. Suddenly Lejeune jumped backwards: he'd just stepped on a snake slithering between the tufts of grass.

'Don't be afraid,' said Paradis, smiling, 'it's a grass snake, they only eat frogs and newts.'

'You know a great deal.'

'So do you, Colonel, just not the same as me.'

'You have been very useful to me.'

'I say what I know, that's all.'

'Listen . . .'

'You look worried.'

'I am.'

'Oh, that's what it is! I've understood what's up!'

'What have you understood?'

'You don't need me any more.'

'I do . . .'

'Well then, what?'

'The Austrians are going to attack, since the Emperor believes that they will. From now on you'll be of more use in your division.'

'That's exactly what I understood, Colonel.'

'I'm not the one who decides.'

'I know. No one decides.'

'Take your things . . .'

The voltigeur returned to the officers' encampment, put on his kit, checked his weapons and his cartridges and without looking back set off towards the small bridge which crossed to the left bank. Lejeune would have liked to have shouted after him that there was nothing he could do, but it wasn't absolutely true, and so he held his tongue, feeling pained, as if he had betrayed a decent lad's trust. And yet they were all risking their skins: here, just as much as in the trenches of Aspern where Paradis was going to join up with Molitor's division.

*

'Ah! They're moving! At last! Let's have done with this!'

Simultaneously anxious and relieved, with that excitement which precedes an engagement before the blood starts to flow, Berthier handed his spyglass to Lejeune to be sure that his eyes weren't deceiving him. They were at the top of Essling's belfry, from where they could take in the entire plain. Lejeune could only confirm what Berthier had seen: the Austrian army was marching down into the plain, its line describing a semicircle.

'Inform His Majesty at once!'

Lejeune raced down the wooden spiral staircase, nearly knocking himself senseless against a beam and catching his feet in his spurs, across the church, out through the great open doors and into the square, where he found the Emperor sitting in an armchair, leaning his elbows on a table on which he had spread a detailed map of the region: it showed every relief, almost down to the maze of bridle paths hidden in the wheat.

'Sire!' exclaimed Lejeune. 'The Austrians are advancing!'

'What hour is it?'

'Midday.'

'Where are they?'

'On the hills.'

'Bravo! They won't be here until one o'clock.'

The Emperor stood up, rubbed his hands together and good-humouredly called for his minestrone, as a mobile kitchen had anticipated. Cooks' boys stoked the braziers to reheat the broth and threw in the already cooked macaroni, the Emperor constantly badgering them because it wasn't ready. Berthier came up in turn, to repeat the news.

'Everything is in place?' asked the Emperor.

'Yes, sire.'

Then he drank the soup in large spoonfuls, swearing because it was boiling hot, spilling it on his chin, shouting for the Parmesan they'd forgotten and half-shutting his eyes the better to savour, not the taste, so much as his thoughts. Standing around his armchair, the officers watched him eating, so composed all of a sudden, and their master's sang-froid restored their confidence, even though their throats were knotted in anticipation of the battle. Their orders had been clear: it was now up to them to carry them out to the letter, since everything seemed to have been planned, even their victory. The Emperor knew the Archduke's talents as a strategist, his gift for organiz-ation, his tentativeness as well, which he could turn to his advantage. Berthier was pouring out a glass of Chambertin – in response to a flick of Napoleon's hand – when Périgord rode into the square, exhausted, jumped off his steaming horse and announced, 'Sire, the main bridge has this minute broken loose.'

The Emperor swept his soup and glass off the table with his sleeve and stood up in a fury. 'Who in the devil's name has burdened me with such jackasses? Shot for desertion in the face of the enemy: that's what the pontoneers deserve!'

'Explain yourself!' Berthier asked his aide-de-camp.

'Well,' said Périgord, catching his breath, 'there was a sudden spate, the river rose very fast . . .'

'Wasn't that taken into account?' roared the Emperor.

'It was, Your Majesty, but what wasn't was that the Austrians stationed a long way upstream at a bend in the river would launch boats full of stones at the bridge: they smashed the posts and broke the mooring ropes . . .'

'*Incapaci!* Incompetents!'

The Emperor paced up and down, shouting. He caught Lejeune by his fur dolman. 'You were in the engineers, go and rebuild this bridge for me!'

The officers summed up the situation: no passable bridge, no communication with the right bank, the supplies, the munitions, the troops arriving from Vienna or Davout's army. Lejeune saluted, mounted the first horse to hand – Périgord's, who didn't dare protest in the emergency – and disappeared, digging his spurs into his mount's ribs. Enraged, the Emperor glared round at his entourage and said in an icy voice, 'Why are you standing there rooted to the spot like buckets of shit? This contretemps changes nothing! Return to your posts, *massa di cretini*! Good for nothings!'

Then to Berthier alone – suddenly milder tempered, as if his anger had been feigned – he said, 'If the Archduke finds out about this mishap, he will want to take advantage. He will speed up the advance and attack us in force, presuming that we're now trapped on the left bank.'

'We will meet him, sire.'

'Idiots! The Danube is with us!'

'Let's hope it can hear you, sire,' the major-general muttered.

'Périgord!' called the Emperor. 'Inform the Duke of Rivoli that the Austrians may suddenly appear along the bend of the Danube which ends at Aspern.'

Périgord also borrowed the first horse he could find, which happened to be fresher than his own, and set off to deliver the order to Marshal Masséna. The Emperor watched him riding away through the brushwood, smiled and murmured to Berthier, 'If they're launching boats against the bridge, Alexandre, then they must already have taken up position by the Danube.'

'A vanguard at least . . .'

'No! Come here.'

Napoleon pushed his major-general towards the table, turned over the map and sketched a rough diagram on the back in pencil:

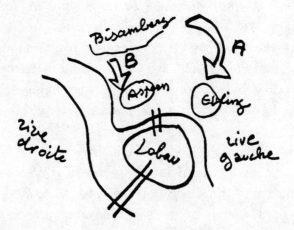

Berthier watched and listened.

'Charles is sending troops down into the plain, they're arrow A...'

'Who are the only ones we can see.'

'Exactly! Meanwhile, from the Bisamberg – there, on the top left of my map – where we know the Austrians have been encamped for several days, he sends another body of men, probably more sizeable and with cannon, to march along the Danube – they are arrow B. They plan to come out behind Aspern, attack us by surprise while we're expecting them somewhere else, swarm in behind our lines and encircle us.'

The Emperor continued sketching until his map became an illegible scribble, but Berthier had understood.

*

As he galloped round a copse, Lejeune recognized the plumes of Molitor's voltigeurs; he didn't want to delay, first because there was no time to waste and secondly because he had no desire, by a wretched stroke of luck, to come face to face with Private Paradis, who had had such hopes of remaining with the headquarters staff, far away from the firing line. How could he explain to him that Berthier had been very firm. 'No favouritism, Lejeune: everyone must go to their post. Send your rabbit catcher back to his regiment. I don't want anyone setting a bad example!' Lejeune hadn't known what to say. At this stage of events, what the devil use could a scout be? Gunners and marksmen were what was needed. Obedience, however, did not preclude remorse. But anyway, it would all be swept away by the fighting.

The colonel walked his horse across the small bridge as

the swirling water beat against its sides: the Danube had swollen greatly, the planks were unsteady and his horse trod in puddles of water. On the island, he was able to pick up speed and quickly saw the catastrophe on the other side. The large pontoon bridge was gaping open towards the middle of its span, and fierce waves rolled into the breach, continuing to tear its beams loose. Stretched too tight, the mooring ropes were snapping, one after another, and a section of the bridge was on the verge of floating away, despite the efforts of the bridging troops and the pontoneers. With poles, boathooks, axes and pickaxe handles, they were trying to repel the boats loaded with rubble which the Austrians were launching into the current. One of these craft had run aground on the bank of the island of Lobau and Lejeune inspected it. It was a small, triangular, steep-sided boat, filled with large stones: because of their shape, they span around as it floated downstream and, whatever the angle of impact, collided at high speed with the row of boats chained together which kept the long bridge afloat. What folly, Lejeune thought, throwing a pontoon bridge in haste over a river in spate! Now the enemy were taking advantage, and with good reason: nothing could have been simpler. He cursed the rushed, slipshod workmanship, not that he would have dared do so in anybody's presence. The sensible thing would have been to wait for the Danube to subside and regain its natural course – two weeks, a month at the very most – and then establish a solid bridge on piles driven into the riverbed. This speculation was useless. What he had to do was direct the repairs and find a way to deflect onto the island the crafts and tree trunks which the Austrians were sending downstream to destroy the fragile bridge.

With a certain weariness, Lejeune took off those accou-
trements to his uniform which might get in his way – his
sabre, shako and sabretache – and dropped them on the
grass. He caught sight of an officer of engineers trying to
fend off one of the terrible triangular boats. He and ten
other men were holding a thick beam swung out into the
river as a buffer, and bracing themselves for the impact.
The fast-moving craft hurtled into the improvised battering
ram, the men lost their grip, four of them flew into the
turbulent waters, but they managed to hang on to the posts
and moored pontoons, shouting and swallowing mouthfuls
of the muddy water; the projectile veered off course and
overturned against the island.

'Captain!'

The officer of engineers, his uniform drenched, his
moustache dripping with water, took the hand Lejeune
offered him and hauled himself up onto the bridge. He
didn't ask any questions and stood ready for the orders of
the headquarters staff's envoy in the red trousers. This was
a relief to Lejeune.

'Captain, how many of the boats supporting the bridge
have been swept away?'

'About ten, Colonel, and there's no chance of coming up
with any others.'

'I know that. Let's make rafts.'

'Gad! That'll take hours!'

'Do you have another solution?'

'No.'

'Round up your men.'

'All of them?'

'All of them. They have to fell the trees, strip them,
collect them together, nail them with planks, lash them –

whatever you think best. But we have to have rafts as soon as possible, and as many of them as boats have been sunk.'

'Agreed.'

'Look, not all the planks of the roadway have been lost: I can see some from here that have been washed onto the island. Have someone go and fetch them.'

'There aren't that many . . .'

'It's a start! We must re-establish the link with the right bank at all costs and we must do so quickly!'

'Quickly, quickly, Colonel.'

'Captain,' said Lejeune, remaining calm, 'the Austrians are going to attack at any moment. I hope that at Ebersdorf, over there, they know that and are taking appropriate action.'

*

Molitor's soldiers were crowded into a long sunken lane which ran from the rear of Aspern to one of the Danube's many oxbows. They had loaded their muskets and were waiting, as if in a trench, under cover of the lane's natural parapet, which was overgrown with brushwood. They thought that they were in reserve, since the Austrians were marching across the plain towards the villages and so would encounter the cavalry or Masséna's cannon first. Anxious, but at least certain that they wouldn't have to endure the first onslaught, some were listening to Sergeant-Major Roussillon's stories to distract themselves, despite knowing all of them by heart. He had fought everywhere and the fact that he had survived filled him with pride: so, for the umpteenth time, he was telling the story of his wounds and horrors he'd seen that would make one's hair stand on end. How, for example, in Cairo, a single executioner had decapitated two thousand Turkish rebels in five hours without spraining his wrist. Vincent Paradis had moved away from the group. He dreaded the thought that this could be the last day of his life and, to clear his mind of everything except the immediate present, he was teasing a large tortoise with a reed; curled up in its shell, on its back in the mud, it struggled as he tickled it.

'That little fellow will never manage to right himself,' commented another voltigeur. 'His legs are too short, like ours. Now if I had longer legs and they didn't shake so much, I swear I'd run for it before you could snap your fingers!'

'Where to, Rondelet?'

'To bury myself in a hole, of course, until all this is over. Right now, I envy moles, I can tell you that.'

'Quiet . . .'

Paradis strained his ears.

'Do you hear that, Rondelet?'

'I can hear the sergeant-major's tall stories, but that doesn't mean I'm listening.'

'The birds . . .'

'What about the birds?'

'They've stopped singing.'

Voltigeur Rondelet couldn't care in the slightest. He chewed a biscuit that was so dry it nearly cracked his teeth and, with his mouth full, started singing,

> 'Long live Napoleon
> He keeps us in
> Roast chicken
> Bread and wine by the gall-e-on
> Long live Napoleon.'

Paradis pulled himself up to the edge of the sunken lane, which screened his company. He saw a yellow flag fluttering above a hill, then black iron helmets, pointed bayonets glinting in the sun and, soon, a column of white uniforms, then a second, then a third: no drums, not a sound. Paradis slid down the bank on his backside and managed to utter the words, 'They're coming!'

'This is it, they're coming our way,' repeated Voltigeur Rondelet to his neighbour, who passed it on and, whispered from one young soldier to the next, the news sped to Aspern.

They formed up into about ten ranks and stood ready to climb up into the meadows and hills to face the danger. Without changing their tone, their voices firm, the officers ordered the first three ranks to assume the firing position. Roughly five hundred voltigeurs scaled the bank of earth and loose stones in silence. Going down on one knee in the grass, behind the bushes lining their entrenchment, they levelled their muskets and took aim at the hills. Behind them, their comrades prepared to take their places as soon as they'd fired, so as to give them time to reload and ensure a continuous field of fire.

'No impatience now!' grumbled Sergeant-Major Roussillon. 'Wait until they get close . . .'

The voltigeurs lowered their muskets.

'When they reach that little stunted tree: do you see the one? At five hundred metres. Then you can let them have it!'

To their right, halfway towards the village, they could see the shakos of another company under a barn and behind the low walls of a large, stone farm. Molitor had positioned his troops so as to take advantage of every irregularity in the ground, even the banks of dried mud which the peasants used as flood barriers. Paradis suddenly felt very

calm. He became absorbed in watching the columns –
white, orderly, slow-moving, almost immaterial – which
were marching straight at him one moment and then
vanishing behind a rise the next, as if they had been
swallowed up. The rugged ground near the banks of the
Danube distorted the perspective and those damned Austrians knew it.

It was one o'clock, and hot, when isolated gunshots rang
out near the farm. Tense, their muskets pointing at the
ground, the soldiers stared fixedly at the shimmering horizon and the nearest hill, from behind which, at any second,
the Archduke's skirmishers could emerge. Where were
they, for God's sake?

They suddenly appeared in the tall grass, formed up
in perfect order in diagonal lines, with their long, grey
gaiters and their spotless matching uniforms, levelling
their bayonets in a single movement as if they were on
parade. Paradis glanced down at his breeches, which had
been torn by brambles that morning; Rondelet was wearing
a civilian's jacket and a cross-belt whitened with chalk.
Their officer had lost his hat and his face was flecked with
two days' growth of stubble. In front of them, the Austrians
were still advancing, and more of them kept on coming;
how many of them could there be?

'There's ten times more of them than us,' muttered
Rondelet.

'Don't get bloody carried away,' Paradis replied, so as
not to lose his nerve.

The enemy were on the verge of passing the stunted tree:
everyone took aim, their fingers trembling on the trigger.

'Fire!' commanded the officer, who had drawn his sabre
and held the empty scabbard in his left hand.

Paradis fired and the recoil was so violent he thought he'd wrenched his shoulder. He ducked down to let his comrades in the second rank take his place. Aiming straight ahead, at chest height, he had fired blindly and had no idea if he'd hit anything.

'Fire!'

He heard the next volley, but couldn't see anything from the sunken lane where he had taken cover to reload. He took a cartridge, tore it open with his teeth, poured the powder in the hot barrel, tamped it down with the ramrod and slid in the ball: each time the whole operation took three minutes and it felt like a respite. Above his head, the voltigeurs were still firing. And the Austrians? Paradis hadn't seen any wounded yet. When it was his turn to climb back up, the smoke had cleared and the Austrians had again disappeared behind the hills.

*

Rather than vanishing, as Vincent Paradis convinced himself they were doing, the Austrians were forming up according to a carefully designed plan. What the infantryman was not in a position to know as he fired at random in the field, Marshal Masséna was discovering for himself from Aspern's belfry. Brushing past the bronze bell, he moved from one window to the next, and, looking through the tall, narrow, ogival slits, he was beginning to make sense of the enemy's manoeuvre. Three vast, disciplined masses of men were enveloping the village, their lines stretching from the swampy ground by the bend of the Danube to the middle of the Marchfeld plain, and perhaps even on past Essling at the other end of the front line. Here and there regiments were opening up to let through dozens of horse-drawn cannon and caissons, the gunners astride the cannon barrels as if on horseback. Pale and silent, Masséna struck the walls with the whip hanging from his right wrist; he cursed himself for not having loopholed the buildings or had trenches dug to delay the remorseless Austrian advance. He realized that the Archduke was planning to encircle the villages, destroy the bridges, hem in the thirty thousand soldiers who had already crossed onto the left bank, deprive them of reinforcements – and then annihilate them with an army three times their size. From now on, Masséna sensed, everything depended on what he decided. Descending the staircase of the clocktower with Sainte-Croix, his aide-de-camp, following, he shouted, 'They're going to besiege us and pound us to dust!'

'Most likely,' said Sainte-Croix.

'Without a shadow of a doubt! You've got two eyes, haven't you? What would you do in a situation like this?'

'I'd protect the bridges, first and foremost, Your Grace.'

'That's not enough! What else?'

'Well . . .'

'Did you see any bears in Bavaria?'

'Bears? Only in the distance.'

'When a bear's wounded, does he lick himself and go to sleep?'

'I don't know, Your Grace . . .'

'He attacks! And we will do the same! Our rascals are going to punch holes through their pretty battalions with their fine uniforms! Take them by surprise! Throw them into disarray! We're going to cut them to pieces, my little Sainte-Croix!'

In the sacristy, Masséna picked up a magnificent stole embroidered with gold thread and threw it over his shoulders, saying, 'These sort of things are worth a fortune, Sainte-Croix; it would be stupid just to trample on this priest's scarf! Do you believe in churches, eh, with a name as suspect as yours?'

'I believe in you, Your Grace.'

'Good answer,' said Masséna, and he burst out laughing.

He was going to take the initiative and attack and it made him supremely happy. Under the elms in the square, he said to the officers gathered to await his orders, 'We have a two-kilometre-long front line to hold until our troops arrive from the right bank. We are facing an army three times our size, with at least two hundred cannon which they are putting in position now. It is up to us to launch the first assault!'

'The main bridge hasn't been repaired yet . . .'

'Precisely! There's no time to waste.'

Masséna leapt on a horse which one of his equerries held out to him by the bridle, put on his white gloves, gave his mount a flick of his whip and rode over to the gunners whom he had deployed on the periphery of Aspern, under cover of trees or at the corners of buildings. Everything was ready. The crews were standing behind some twenty loaded guns. At Masséna's signal, they lit the fuses with their linstocks. In clear view on the plain, the VI Austrian Army Corps commanded by Baron Hiller – a skilful, if old, officer – were standing at ease in close order, their ranks densely packed.

'Aim just above the wheat!' the marshal ordered.

He snatched a linstock from a gunner and, without dismounting, his eyes blazing fiercely, he gave his instructions. 'When I light the charge of the first cannon, wait for one breath and then fire number four cannon, followed by numbers seven, ten, thirteen, and then numbers two, five, nine, and so on. I want a line of fire! Those dogs are within our grasp!'

He lowered the linstock, lit the charge and the cannon fired with a roar, followed by the fourth cannon and then the rest at matching intervals, while those that had already been fired were hastily reloaded in a cloud of smoke.

The battle hadn't a name yet. Everyone had been imagining it, fearing it or contemplating it for a week, but only now had it begun in earnest.

*

At three o'clock in the afternoon, the inhabitants of Vienna heard the rumble of the cannonade. The most inquisitive rushed, en masse, to the city's vantage points to witness the spectacle. They perched on roofs, steeples and the ramparts' medieval crenellations, quarrelling over the best seats as if they were at the theatre. Accompanied by his German doctor, Carino – who had given in to him by saying it wouldn't do any harm to take some air – and despite shooting pains, Henri Beyle had installed himself on top of a bastion from where he could see the Danube's meandering progress and the vast green plain. He had been dragged here by the Krauss sisters and, by a stroke of good fortune, the infuriating M. Staps had not tagged along. Far away on the Marchfeld, the battalions on the march looked as harmless as miniature replicas, and the smoke from the cannon hung in the air like balls of cotton. Henri felt as if he was in a stage box, and it made him uncomfortable. There was little delight to be had from the flames rising up from Aspern's bombarded houses. Anna was muffled in a large Egyptian shawl, as if it was cold, and she trembled slightly, her lips pinched. She undoubtedly foresaw the worst for Louis-François in that distant mêlée, but Henri, without any jealousy, simply admired the image of helpless grief she presented.

A spectacle-maker from the old town was renting out spyglasses and, with frequent glances at his watch, zealously checking that no one overran their allotted time. Using Dr Carino as an interpreter, Henri asked for one, but the fellow had been cleaned out and he replied that that fat gentleman, there, on the left, his time would soon be up; it only cost two florins, a pittance for such a high-quality performance, they'd not see the like of it again in a hurry. When Henri's turn eventually came, he pointed the spyglass towards Aspern, where a barn was in flames. A pillar of black smoke rose into the air, the house next to it was catching fire, the roof was about to collapse, but who was underneath? He turned towards the bridge where men the size of ants were scurrying back and forth. A rumour was going around, which Henri did not believe, that the Emperor had breached the large pontoon bridge to prevent a retreat and compel his soldiers to keep fighting until they were victorious. Anna stretched out her hand with a sad smile; Henri gave her his spyglass and she peered through it anxiously, but at that distance, even with such an instrument, one could only make out general movements – nothing specific, and certainly not individual faces or even familiar silhouettes. The hirer protested. His spyglasses were not for the use of more than one person at a time, they should pay an extra two florins. When Dr Carino translated this complaint for Henri, the latter leaned forward, until he was face-to-face with the tradesman, and bellowed, 'Non,' making the man flinch. At that moment a female voice called out, 'Henri!'

He swore through his teeth. It was Valentina. She had come to show herself on the ramparts, with the troupe of actors who were rehearsing for their performance, in the Viennese manner, of Molière's *Don Juan*. They were all very elegant, the girls in cotton cambric coats, the boys in tight-fitting tailcoats and plush knee-breeches tucked into yellow top-boots. They had brought their theatre glasses and were commenting on the battle, which did not give them a great deal of satisfaction. It was too far away for their taste. They referred to *Count Waltron*, a play with elaborate stage machinery, crowds of extras in costume and cavalry charges that thundered within a hair's breadth of the audience.

'Tell your friends that they can get nearer to the cannonballs, if they wish,' Henri said to Valentina.

'As charming as ever!' she said, taking offence.

'Down below, they'll see real dead, real blood, and who knows, if they're lucky enough, a charred beam might fall on their heads.'

'That's not funny, Henri!'

'No, it's not funny, you're right, because there's no reason for it to be.'

He turned back to the edge of the bastion where Anna had been standing anxiously, but, as Dr Carino explained, she had left with her sisters. 'And you would do well to follow their example, my poor friend. If you could see yourself ... You've got a bad fever, I'd advise you to go back to your bed and drink some broth.' Henri left without saying goodbye to Valentina, whose friends were still holding forth on the merits of the fires burning in Aspern. They found them less realistic than the storm in *The Magic Flute* which they had seen at the great, and celebrated, Schikaneder open-air theatre.

*

Masséna's cannonade had played havoc with the Austrians' ranks, but after a moment of dangerous confusion and a brief withdrawal, their artillery had gone into action. A wooden granary had gone up in flames and then, under the barrage of two hundred guns, roofs had collapsed and fires broken out all over the village which there was neither the time nor the means to put out. The first casualties had burnt like torches, desperately rolling over and over in the sand. The voltigeurs were some way off, covering the village's left flank, but they felt the heat of the inferno; sparks flew which they slapped out with their coat sleeves and a light wind blew the thick black smoke at them which stuck in their throats. Private Rondelet spat on the ground and joked half-heartedly, 'It's hardly started and we're already cooked.'

Paradis grimaced as he fingered the hammer of his musket. Molitor's division hadn't changed position and after several exchanges of fire in which no one had been hurt, having nothing else to do the men had broken ranks. Their captain sheathed his sword and took out a pair of pistols from under the tails of his tunic. Sergeant-Major Roussillon calmly rallied the company. 'Come on, boys, we're going to clear the ground! Fan out! We're going on the attack!'

'What are we attacking?' Paradis had the temerity to ask.

'The Austrian infantry is concentrating on Aspern. We have to attack them from the rear,' explained the captain.

Wrapped in thought, the officer loaded his pistols and strode forward through the grass. Three thousand men spread out over the fields and the hollows, and climbed away from the Danube, on their guard and in some semblance of order. But the crackling of the fires hard by, the roar of the cannon and the splintering roof frames made it impossible to hear the squadron of Austrian hussars who burst out at a brisk trot on their flank. The hussars bore down on them, yelling, their sabres outstretched at arm's length, the curved edge pointing at the sky to make it easier to drive downwards and skewer the infantrymen to the ground.

The earth vibrated under the stampede and a trumpet sounded, merging with the cries of the hussars. Caught by surprise, Paradis and his comrades half-turned and instinctively levelled their muskets. With both arms held straight out in front of him, the captain emptied his pistols, threw them to the ground and gripped his sabre. Then the voltigeurs fired at neck height, without taking aim and without waiting for orders. In the rolling horde coming to crush them, Paradis saw a horse rear; the rider was thrown under the hooves of the next horse and knocked it off balance. Another Austrian took a bullet in the forehead but his mount, carried forward by the impetus, kept on galloping with the trooper still in the saddle, facing backwards. Paradis drove the butt of his gun into a mound of loose earth and gripped it with both hands, dropping his shoulders and head and tensing his body as if he was hunching over a lance; he felt his comrades shoulder to shoulder with him, so that together they formed a harrow.

He closed his eyes. The shock came immediately. The leading horses were torn to pieces on the bayonets but they opened a way and Paradis, curled up in a ball on the grass and knocked half-senseless, his arms bruised, felt a hot, thick liquid sticking to his fingers. He must have been wounded. He pushed himself up and looked at the mêlée of voltigeurs and hussars around him. He shook his neighbour, then turned him onto his back; his eyes had rolled up into their sockets. Behind him a disembowelled horse was kicking in pain and banging its hooves together; its stomach was open and intestines spilled onto the ground. On a battlefield, Paradis said to himself, there isn't a damn thing that makes any sense. Am I dead? What about this blood? No, it's not mine. Is it the horse's? Or my neighbour's whose name I can't even remember?

'Psst!'

Paradis saw Rondelet lying flat on his stomach, winking at him.

'Are you hurt?' he asked him.

'No, but I can't go through that again. I'm playing dead: it's safest.'

'Watch out!'

An Austrian, who had been thrown from his horse, was coming towards them, limping. He'd heard Rondelet talking and, realizing that he was shamming, had raised his sabre. Alerted by his friend, Rondelet rolled onto his side without waiting for an explanation and Paradis threw a handful of earth in the hussar's eyes; blinded, the latter stumbled and started trying to slash them, windmilling his arms dangerously, until Sergeant-Major Roussillon, who had picked up a bayonet, drove it into his back with a hard thrust.

'Wounded or not, on your feet!' the Sergeant-Major commanded. 'They're going to come back.'

'Have they left, then?' sighed Rondelet. The Sergeant-Major seized him by the fleshy part of the arm and pulled him to his feet. 'You didn't even get a hoof in the face. What about you?'

'It's blood, that's for sure,' Paradis answered, 'but I don't know whose.'

'Regroup behind the sunken lane, at the double!'

Those who by some miracle had survived, stood up, dazed and unsteady on their feet.

'And pick up the cartridge pouches,' Sergeant-Major Roussillon harangued them, 'musn't waste the cartridges.'

At the other end of the field the hussars in their green uniforms were re-forming for a fresh attack. The two voltigeurs obeyed immediately, without looking too closely at the real corpses.

*

After the fourth murderous cavalry charge, General Molitor decided on a retreat towards the village where he thought they'd find more protection. Sword in hand, he was steadying his terrified horse to organize a withdrawal just as a further assault, the fifth, dashed itself against the sunken lane. Thinking they were hurdling a gentle rise, the hussars crashed into the lane as if into a ravine: they broke their necks, and ended up either bayoneted or with their brains blown out at point-blank range. The voltigeurs gave ground but they took with them a mass of kit they'd collected from the dead; one had a carbine under his arm and another slung over his shoulder, another had picked up a black leather cross-belt into which he had slid the bare blade of a sabre; Paradis, his chest crisscrossed with cartridge pouches, had put on an Austrian's red shako. They pulled back towards the outlying houses of Aspern, stepping over the great brown chargers, which lay whinnying where they had fallen, dying slowly, but there was no question of putting them out of agony – the cartridges were too precious and had to be saved for men, ideally aimed at the head and the stomach.

By a quirk of perception, the fire was less spectacular close to. Most of the houses on the high street, along which the herd of soldiers were advancing, were practically intact, because Baron Hiller's cannon eventually had fallen silent and the flames blazing violently a while before were now dying down for lack of fuel. All around, men were trying to put out the fires by throwing earth on them. Ruined, blackened beams smoked and cracked, sometimes falling to the ground in great sections and raising clouds of ash. Suffocated by the belching smoke, voltigeurs were tearing strips off their shirts and clamping them over their faces. The heat of the embers was becoming unbearable.

On the immense terrace in front of Aspern's church, gunpowder was adding to the thick black smog of the fires, since the artillerymen, without being able to see a thing through the dense smoke, were still firing. With blackened faces and dry lips, they picked up the enemy's cannonballs to fire them back at their lines. The square bell tower of the church had been blown up by a shell and, as it fell, the bronze bell had smashed the stairwell. Wounded soldiers, who had been kept under cover in a shed spared by the bombardment, crowded onto the platform of a wagon. They were going to be evacuated to the bridgehead on the island of Lobau, where Dr Percy was setting up his first ambulance. Legs or arms bandaged in strips of uniform, they groaned, limping or crawling along like devils, and the least hurt carried the most seriously wounded in their greatcoats.

Masséna was standing in the church square. With the priest's stole wrapped round his neck like a scarf, he was holding a loaded musket and bellowing orders in a hoarse voice, 'Two cannon in enfilade in the second street!'

As the artillerymen limbered up the guns, Molitor approached the marshal, leading his horse by the bridle.

'Many dead, General?'

'A hundred, two hundred, Your Grace – perhaps more.'

'Wounded?'

'At least as many, I think.'

'Around me,' said Masséna, 'the rest of your division will have suffered similar losses. And there's another thing...'

The marshal pushed Molitor towards Aspern's second main street in order to show him, through a haze of fog, the yellow flags emblazoned with black eagles that were three hundred metres away.

'You're coming in at one end of the village, Molitor, and the Austrians at the other. I can hold them with cannon, but we're going to run out of powder soon. Gather together your freshest men and let them have it!'

'Even the freshest are not that fresh, Your Grace.'

'Molitor, you've beaten the Tyrolese, the Russians, even the Archduke himself at Caldiero! All I'm asking is that you do the same again.'

'My voltigeurs are very young, they're afraid, they are

not accustomed to war as we are, nor do they feel the same contempt.'

'Because they haven't seen enough dead! Or because they think too much!'

'This is not really the place to lecture them.'

'True, General. Give them wine! Get those whipper-snappers drunk and show them the regimental colours!'

Colonel Lejeune came charging into the square and made his horse rear in front of Masséna. 'Your Grace, His Majesty requests you to stand firm until nightfall.'

'I need gunpowder.'

'Impossible. The large bridge will not be passable until this evening.'

'Well, then, we'll fight with batons!'

Masséna carelessly turned his back on the colonel and picked up the thread of his interrupted conversation with Molitor.

'Wine, General. The nave is full of it. I had it unloaded from those commissariat wagons which are evacuating our wounded.'

Lejeune was already galloping back to Essling and the Emperor, over terrain crisscrossed with hedges and fences, by the time the compulsory drinking bout got underway. The enemy shells had so far overlooked the roof of the church and about a hundred stout barrels were stacked up inside, which Molitor ordered to be rolled out under the elms. With the heat of that particular May, which was doubled by that of the burning ruins, and the clouds of smoke drying out their throats, the appearance of the casks caused a stampede. Approximately two thousand exhausted voltigeurs barged forward to have their metal mess tins filled to the brim, drained them in one, as if they were quenching their thirst, and then went back for more. Whilst not transforming boys who wanted to escape death more than they wanted to kill into staunch warriors, the wine did make them less aware of their situation and better able to confront it. Drunk, or at least with a spring in their step, they encouraged each other by mocking the Austrians, whom Masséna kept on cannonading to keep at a distance. Every explosion provoked crude or vengeful rejoinders and when their morale had revived, Molitor lined the voltigeurs up in something resembling ranks and brandished the tricoloured flag on which the name of the regiment was embroidered in yellow. They set off after him, boldy marching towards Baron Hiller's infantry, which had appeared at the other end of the High Street. After coming under an opening round of fire and seeing some of his comrades fall to the ground, whom he blamed for their bad luck, Private Paradis, as drunk as the rest of them, fired straight ahead. Then, on a command, his bayonet levelled at stomach height, he started running to break through the crowd of white uniforms, which looked slightly blurred.

*

The Emperor, on horseback beside Lannes, was waiting in front of Essling on the edge of the plain, surrounded by grenadiers in the blue uniforms and fur caps of the 24th Light Infantry Regiment.

'Well?' he asked Lejeune.

'The Duke of Rivoli has sworn that he will hold his ground.'

'Then he will hold it.'

The Emperor bent his head, a disgruntled look on his

face. He was paying little attention to the Austrian cannon, which were now pouring the same barrage of fire into Essling as Aspern, but a roundshot came and struck the haunch of his horse; with a whinny it shook its mane and fell to the ground, taking its rider with it. Lannes and Lejeune leapt out of the saddle; officers helped the Emperor to his feet, while Roustan, the Mameluke, picked up his hat.

'It's nothing,' the Emperor said, brushing his riding coat with his hands, but they all remembered the recent incident at Ratisbon, when a Tyrolese skirmisher's bullet had hit him in the heel. He had had to sit on a drum and have his wound dressed before he was able to remount.

A general in a hat covered with plumes threw his sword onto the grass and shouted, 'Down arms if the Emperor does not retire!'

'If you do not leave here,' another yelled, 'I will have my men remove you!'

'*A cavallo!*' said Napoleon, putting his hat back on.

As his Mamelukes finished off the wounded horse with their daggers, Caulaincourt led another forward which Lannes helped the Emperor to mount. Berthier, who hadn't moved, asked Lejeune to accompany His Majesty to the island and devise a lookout post from which he could survey operations without being exposed. Surrounded by an escort and in absolute silence, the Emperor rode at a jog-trot back through Essling and a large, thick wood which lay between the village and the Danube. The troop followed the river as far as the little bridge, which they went over at a walk, an equerry holding the Emperor's horse by the bridle for the short crossing. Once on Lobau, the latter flew into a rage. He insulted Caulaincourt in

Milanese dialect, as it dawned on him that not only had his officers given him orders and threatened him, but that he had also complied. Would they have dared take him to the rear by force? He put the question to Lejeune who replied that yes, they would have. Then his fury died down and he began grumbling, 'You can't see a thing from here!'

'It can be arranged, sire,' said Lejeune.

"What do you suggest?' said the Emperor in an ugly voice.

'That thick fir tree . . .'

'Do you take me for one of the chimpanzees in Schön-brunn's menagerie?'

'We can fix a rope ladder to it and, from up there, nothing will escape you.'

'Well then, *presto*!'

An encampment, after a fashion, was improvised at the foot of the fir tree. The Emperor fell into an armchair. He didn't watch the young soldiers agilely climbing up through the branches to put a rope ladder in place, he barely heard the constant cannon fire or smelt the smell of burning which came from the plain. He stared impassively at the tip of his boots, thinking: They all hate me! Berthier, Lannes, Masséna, the others, all the rest of them, they hate me! I'm not entitled to make a mistake. I'm not entitled to lose. If I lose, that rabble will betray me. They'd even kill me! I'm the one they have to thank for their fortunes and it's as though they resent me for it! They feign loyalty, but the only reason they march is to amass gold, titles, chateaux and women! They hate me and I love nobody. Not even my brothers. No, perhaps Joseph. From habit, and because he's the oldest. And Duroc as well. Why? Because he can't cry, because he is stern and resolute. Where is he? Why isn't he here? What if he hated me too? And me? Do I detest myself? Not even that. I have no opinion about myself. I know that a force drives me and nothing can restrain it. I must proceed, in spite of myself and against the rest of them.

The Emperor took a pinch of tobacco and sneezed over Lejeune who announced, 'Sire, the ladder is in position. With your campaign telescope, you will be able to cover the entire battlefield.'

The Emperor glanced up at the fir tree and the flimsy ladder hanging from it, swaying slightly. It was so hard holding himself steady in the saddle, how was he going to climb up that high? He sighed. 'Go up, Lejeune, and give me a detailed account.'

Lejeune was already on the lower branches when the Emperor added, 'Don't pay any attention to individuals, just concentrate on the masses, like you do in your damned pictures!'

When he reached the top of the tree, the colonel wound the rope ladder round one hand, rested a foot on a stout branch and extended the telescope to scan the countryside. Masses, that was all he saw. Since serving with Berthier, he had learnt to recognize the Archduke's regiments by their insignia. He could name them all, and their commanding officers, and estimate the number of soldiers. With the Emperor's spyglass, he could even make out the uhlans' yellow pennons and the dragoons' helmets bound in black chenille. In the welter of troops, he saw the Hohenzollern infantry and Bellegarde's cavalry on the right flank, massing on Essling without breaking through. On the other wing, he saw Baron Hiller's formidable offensive closing on Aspern, which was still in flames. Between these two intact positions he also saw, slightly withdrawn and facing the fields, Marshal Bessières's green standard slashed with silver, Espagne's motionless cuirassiers formed up in seventeen squadrons ready to attack, and Lasalle's chasseurs. Facing them, in the smoke, rows of cannon were spitting fire but there were fewer battalions and fewer cavalry. The Austrian troops were moving towards the two villages to bring the bulk of their effort to bear on them; at each moment their centre was becoming more depleted. Lejeune climbed back down the tree to give the Emperor this information. He reached the ground just as two horsemen rode up, one from Essling and the other from Aspern.

The first, Périgord, was smiling. The second, Sainte-Croix, his hair scorched by flames, looked tired and grave. The Emperor quickly sized them up. 'Let's start with the good news. Périgord?'

'Sire, Marshal Lannes is holding Essling. With Boudet's division, he hasn't lost a scrap of ground.'

'Brave Boudet! Ever since the siege of Toulon, he has been brave, that one!'

'You know, sire, that the Archduke was leading the attack in person ...'

'Was leading?'

'He has been seized by one of his convulsive fevers.'

'Who is his replacement?'

'Rosenberg, sire.'

'*La fortuna è cambiata!* Where Charles has not succeeded, the unfortunate Rosenberg will fail!'

'The Major-General thinks so too, sire.'

'Rosenberg is courageous but rather too much so, and he lacks resolve too: his nature is to be cautious ... Sainte-Croix?'

'The Duke of Rivoli has urgent need of munitions, sire.'

'He has experienced this manner of situation before.'

'What reply should I give him, sire?'

'That night falls at seven o'clock and that he is to find a way to hold Aspern – or its ruins – until then. By seven, the bridge will be repaired and the battalions kicking their heels on the left bank will have crossed the Danube. Then there will be sixty thousand of us ...'

'Not including the dead,' Sainte-Croix murmured.

'You were saying?'

'Nothing, sire, I was clearing my throat.'

'Tomorrow morning Davout's army will arrive from Saint-Polten. We will have ninety thousand men and the Austrians will be exhausted ...'

The two messengers had scarcely remounted before the Emperor turned to Lejeune without a word: Lejeune instantly replied to this silent enquiry. 'Sire, the Austrians are heading for the villages en masse.'

'So, they're lightening their position in the centre.'

'Yes.'

'Then they've got a soft underbelly! Berthier is bound to have remarked on it; go and find him at the tile factory in Essling, tell him that now is the moment to launch our cavalry against the Archduke's artillery. The major-general can sort out the details with Bessières. Caulaincourt! Take Lejeune's place at the top of the fir tree.'

The colonel left to deliver the order: the Emperor slumped sullenly into his armchair, muttering, 'I don't object to being accused of recklessness, but dilatoriness: if anyone so much as dared!'

*

Exposed to the hot sun since morning, Fayolle was beginning to swelter under his breastplate and iron helmet. His horse stamped the ground to keep its blood circulating, or rubbed its neck against that of its neighbour. In the sixth rank of his squadron, the battle appeared to the trooper as nothing but a muffled rumble, and on either side he saw the flames billowing up from houses that had been bombarded. Suddenly, up ahead, between the backs of his comrades, he glimpsed movement. The standard of Bessières's chasseurs floated up over the troops, then Fayolle recognized the long powdered hair of the marshal, who was raising his sabre. The trumpets sounded, the officers' voices passed on the order to march and, across a front a kilometre wide, thousands of cavalrymen moved off towards the cannon hidden by a fog which reeked of gunpowder.

Fayolle advanced. His heavy armour, jolted up and down by the trot, bruised his shoulders. He had rolled up his Spanish coat like a bolster and tied it across his chest. His sabre blade, held pointing downwards, hung slackly against the grey cloth of his breeches. He concentrated, imagining the imminent attack; the sight of his friend Pacotte with his throat slit came back to him and he felt ready to hack those filthy Austrians to pieces. When, at last, the trumpets blew the order to charge, he dug his spurs into the flanks of his black horse and found himself galloping ferociously, neck and neck with his comrades, his sword outstretched, stung by the wind and the dust, his mouth twisted in an endless scream, howling to forget the danger, to insult death, to terrify it, to give himself courage, to make himself dizzy, to feel that he was nothing but one component of an invincible body of men. A previous charge by the chasseurs had dashed itself on the batteries, the bulk of them cut down by the burning roundshot, and they had to jump their horses over the shattered corpses in their path and make sure that they didn't stumble or lose their footing in the bloody pulp of intestines and bone. In the distance, they could make out the bright green plumes of Bade's dragoons, led by the corpulent Marulaz, and the heavy fur caps of Bessières's non-commissioned officers who were re-forming their cavalrymen towards the rear, as the cuirassiers drove forward before the gunners had time to reload. The first ranks suffered the shock, and those behind, of which Fayolle, Verzieux and Brunel were a part, flew over the kegs and wheels of the limbers. Fayolle plunged his sword into one fellow's heart, trampled another who was carrying a cannonball, nailed a third to his gun and then kept on slashing at random with the cutting edge of his sabre until he came up against a square of white-uniformed infantrymen firing in his direction. As he pulled his horse about a bullet rapped on his helmet and he was poised to hurl himself against the bristling wall of bayonets when a trumpet sounded the retreat to make room for the next wave of attacks led by General Espagne in person. Disfigured by rage, alone at the head of his men, his eyes staring madly and completely exposed, it seemed as if Espagne wanted to prove right the ghosts which had been haunting his dreams ever since his misadventure at Bayreuth.

Carried too far forward behind the line of artillery, Fayolle watched his general ride up like a fury; he tried to turn and rejoin his troop, but his horse was hit between the eyes and reared on its hind legs. Thrown to the ground, Fayolle fell on his back and the chinstrap of his helmet cut into his jaw. Lying half-stunned in the trampled wheat, he stretched out his hand to retrieve his sword, and as he propped himself up on one elbow he felt a sabre cut, partly cushioned by the plume of his helmet, that screeched across his metal backplate. The Austrian officer in a russet jacket, the cuirassier on all fours at his feet, and everything else was swept away by General Espagne's charge; Fayolle felt a hand grab hold of his arm and the next moment he was riding pillion behind his comrade Verzieux. They surged to the rear with Espagne's squadron, leaving the field open for a fresh charge. Once out of range of the musketry and cannon fire, Fayolle let himself slide off onto the grass. He wanted to thank Verzieux, but the latter had slumped forward and was clinging to the pommel of his saddle, unable to move. Fayolle called to him. Verzieux had been hit by canister shot in the breastplate, on his left side, at stomach height. Fine jets of blood spurted out of the bullet holes, and ran down his leg. Fayolle and Brunel helped him off his horse, laid him on the ground and pulled off his coat, which was soaked in warm blood and stuck to the leather-straps of his breastplate. Verzieux groaned and then screamed when Fayolle jammed a handful of grass into his wound to stop the bleeding. With red, sticky hands, Fayolle stood and watched the wounded man being taken away to the ambulances by the little bridge. Would he get there? Was that all? Cuirassiers were carrying him on a stretcher made out of branches and greatcoats. Fayolle unfastened his helmet and threw it on the ground.

'One thing's for sure,' said Brunel, 'he's not coming back.'

*

Protected by the still warm, soft belly of a dead horse, Vincent Paradis was sniping at Baron Hiller's Austrians. Having been driven out of Aspern by a furious bayonet charge led by Molitor, they were returning in strength. Some of them were falling to the ground but fresh troops instantly took their place and closed the ranks. It was as if the Austrians were rising from the dead, as if it made no difference whether one aimed true or not. The exhilaration produced by the wine had worn off and Paradis was left with a rasping tongue, a throbbing pain in the nape of his neck and heavy eyelids. They weren't men any more at the end of the main street, he thought, but rabbits disguised in uniforms, or spectres masked by the smoke, demons from a nightmare or a fairground show. After each round, he held out his musket, hands snatched it from him, and another was put in its place. In a doorway, soldiers were loading and reloading without pausing.

'Don't fall asleep,' Rondelet said.

'I'm trying not to,' Paradis answered, pulling the trigger, his right shoulder bruised by the countless recoils.

'If you fall asleep, they'll butcher you. A dead man who snores: not that convincing.'

To prove his point, he lifted up the limp arm of one of their companions, whose brains had been splattered across his face when his forehead was blown apart by a hail of bullets.

'Look, he's not making any noise,' Rondelet went on.

'Yes, all right!'

Pounded by the salvoes from the Austrian muskets, the horse's body juddered. In front of them in the street, a group of voltigeurs had taken cover behind an overturned plough. Suddenly they got to their feet to fall back at a run.

They dragged a wounded soldier behind them like a sack, holding him by the neck. He was groaning, his face contorted like a child's in a grimace of pain and he left a glistening red trail which was instantly soaked up by the dry ground. As they ran past the dead horse shielding Paradis, Rondelet and several badly mutilated corpses, the fugitives shouted, 'They've got cannon. Got to get out of here or we'll be blown sky high!'

Pieces of ordnance had started enfilading the row of little houses: they'd best make themselves scarce. Rondelet and Paradis agreed to head for the church square, where the bulk of the battalion was assembled.

'Got to go round the back, fast!'

They crawled through the dirt and gravel back to the doorway, and once inside got to their feet. Their comrades were still biting open cartridges.

'The powder's running out,' complained a tall moustachioed rifleman with his hair tied back in a queue at the nape of his neck.

'We're clearing out through the gardens! Cannon!'

'The sergeant agrees, does he?' asked the moustachioed man.

'Are you blind?' Paradis shouted at him, pointing at the corpses in the street.

'Oh, no!' said the other obstinately. 'The sergeant moved his leg.'

'He didn't move a bloody thing!'

'We can't leave him here!'

'Come back, you idiot!'

The private was already running outside, crouching low, but before he could reach the body he'd seen moving, he was cut down by musketry; he span round, a trickle of blood at the corner of his mouth, and crumpled against the stiff legs of the horse they had been using as a barricade.

'Very clever!' muttered Rondelet.

'We're wasting time! Let's go!' shouted Paradis.

The survivors of this position, now too far advanced, gathered up the muskets and slung them under their arms like bundles of firewood. Rondelet picked up a spit which had been left in the fireplace, and they ran out into the small garden. Scratching themselves, they forced their way through the low hedges, to bypass the lethal main street. They tried to take their bearings from the shell of Aspern's belfry, but instantly ran in the wrong direction and lost their way. They turned back on themselves, colliding with the debris of a low wall. They plunged into bushes, scaled heaps of rubble, twisted their ankles, limped, crashed into obstacles they couldn't see, tore themselves on brambles, but their terror of being buried under the splintered buildings or burnt to death filled them with a frenzied energy. They heard cannon fire raking the main street; a shell fell on the house they'd just run from and the roof beams burst into flames. They came upon other runaways in scorched uniforms and their numbers had swollen by the time they reached the cemetery walls; still with enough strength to climb them, they jumped down onto the tombs and, leaping from cross to cross, they reached the church. Masséna and his officers were on their feet and, as roundshot blasted the tall elms, branches fell all around them.

*

Fayolle had taken his friend Verzieux's horse, which was more highly strung than his own and needed to be kept on a tight rein, but the day was beginning to lengthen, and after nearly a dozen brutal charges the horseman and his mount were each as exhausted as the other. Riding back to their lines, setting off again, sabreing the enemy: their ranks were thinning out and still the Austrians did not withdraw. Fayolle's back hurt, his arm hurt, his whole body hurt and sweat ran into his eyes which he wiped with a sleeve encrusted with Verzieux's dried, brownish blood. As his horse baulked, he dug his spurs in hard enough to draw blood. With a sabre in one hand, a lit Austrian linstock in the other, and the bridle between his teeth, he was preparing to fall back with his troop for a minute's rest between charges, when a group of Lasalle's chasseurs brushed past him, bawling, 'This way! This way!'

In the tumult and confusion of the battle, who was in command? Fayolle and his fellow cavalryman Brunel glimpsed their captain, Saint-Didier, emerging from the smoke; he'd lost his helmet and was signalling to them and other cuirassiers from the scattered troop to follow the chasseurs. Forming up in a group, they rode their horses as hard as they could and swept down on the rear of the uhlans who were overwhelming Bessières's cavalry. Caught by surprise, the Austrians turned their lances with the fluttering pennons towards their attackers but they hadn't time to manoeuvre their horses or mount a charge, and they took the thrust side on. Fayolle forced the flaming match of his linstock into an uhlan's open mouth, driving its shaft into the man's throat with all his might, and the uhlan toppled over onto the ground, writhing, his body convulsed by violent spasms, his eyes turned back into their sockets, his throat burnt black. A few paces away, Marshal Bessières himself was on foot, hatless and with one of his sleeves torn, parrying blows with two swords crossed above his head. The uhlans' lances were too long for hand to hand fighting, and finding themselves tangled up in them and without time to draw their sabres or horse pistols, they rapidly disengaged, giving up their dead and several horses. Bessières mounted one of those short-maned horses with red saddles trimmed with gold, then set off for the rear, accompanied by his saviours and the shattered remnants of his squadron.

An officer in full-dress uniform was waiting in front of his bivouac. It was Marbot, Marshal Lannes's favorite aide-de-camp, who announced, in a slightly embarrassed voice, 'Marshal Lannes directs me to tell Your Excellency that he orders you to charge home . . .'

Bessières felt insulted. He turned ashen and retorted, scornfully, 'I never do otherwise.'

The marshals' old animosity flared up again at the slightest provocation. Both Gascon, they had each jealously tried to thwart the other for nine years, ever since Lannes had set his hopes on marrying Caroline, the First Consul's frivolous sister. He accused Bessières of having supported Murat's claim against his own: hadn't he been the witness at their marriage?

*

Berthier had established his staff headquarters in the solid buildings of Essling's tile factory, which resembled a redoubt, with lookouts posted on the roofs, skirmishers at every window and even cannon on the ground floor. In a fury, Lannes entered the room where Berthier's maps were spread out on trestles, which he altered as he received news from the front or orders from the Emperor.

'The cavalry is incapable,' said Lannes, 'of extricating us from this situation!'

'It will do so eventually.'

'And Masséna? Everything's in flames where he is! When Hiller's finished with him, how many enemy troops will we have on our back?'

'Aspern hasn't fallen yet.'

'How much longer before it will? Why not send in the Guard as reinforcements?'

'The Guard will remain in the front of the small bridge to safeguard the passage onto the island!'

The Emperor strode into the room, having delivered this last sentence in an angry voice. He pushed Berthier roughly aside to consult his maps. Anxious at the course events were taking, he had not been able to stand being kept out of the way under the fir trees on Lobau for long. Napoleon realized that if the Archduke had attacked earlier in the morning he would have carried the day, but their luck could still turn; victory at Austerlitz had been decided in fifteen minutes. The sun would set in an hour and a half: now was the time to retaliate. 'Part of the Liechtenstein corps has reinforced Rosenberg's troops, sire,' Berthier was explaining, 'but Essling will hold until nightfall. Our entrenchments are solid.'

'Alas,' Lannes added, 'our cavalry mounts charge after charge, which have no effect on the Austrians and give us little relief.'

'They must rout the Austrians on the plain,' shouted the Emperor. 'Lannes, round up the entire cavalry, you hear me, and hurl it against them *en bloc*! Attack! Bring back the Hohenzollern cannon! Turn them against the enemy!

I want you to sweep everything before you in a hail of fire and iron!'

Lannes bowed his head and left the room with his officers. The main pontoon bridge was still not repaired. Oudinot and Saint-Hilaire's men couldn't rush to the rescue. And what if the cavalry were lost in this massive assault? Given fresh heart and with no one to bar their path, the Austrians would move on the villages in number and from every point on the battlefield.

'What have you to say, Pouzet?' Lannes asked, taking his old friend by the arm, a brigadier-general who had been at his side from campaign to campaign and had formerly tutored him in strategy.

'His Majesty always reasons in the same fashion. He continues to base his actions on speed and surprise, as he did in Italy, but the battlefields on these large northern European plains are ill suited to such an approach. What's more, movement and offence depend on light, highly mobile, highly motivated troops who can live off the land like bands of *condottieri*. But our armies have become too heavy, too slow, too tired, too young, too demoralized . . .'

'Hold your tongue, Pouzet, hold your tongue!'

'His Majesty has read Puységur, Maillebois, Folard, and then Guibert and Carnot who wanted to restore war to its original savagery. What Carnot and Saint-Just advocated was fitting for their era. Of course an army with a soul is bound to win out against mercenaries! But where are today's mercenaries? And what side are the patriots on? You don't know? I'll tell you: the patriots are rising up in arms against us in Tyrol, in Andalucia, in Austria, in Bohemia, and they will soon do the same in Germany and Russia . . .'

'You're right, Pouzet, but please hold your tongue.'

'I'm quite prepared to do so, but at least be honest with me. Do you still believe in it all?'

Lannes put his boot in the stirrup and pulled himself up onto the horse which had been led forward for him; Pouzet followed suit, but, as he did so, he sighed heavily enough for his friend to hear.

*

Anna Krauss's face was drawn as horrendous thoughts ran through her mind. She imagined soldiers trapped in a burning farm or stretched out on the ground, their stomachs slit open. Her ears rang with the pounding of the guns and the crackling of the flames. She seemed to hear diabolical screams. No reliable news of the battle had reached Vienna yet and the city was gleaning its information from malicious gossip, with the only certainty everyone could agree on being the fact that both sides had been senselessly slaughtering one another down on the plain for hours. Anna's gaze played aimlessly over the pinkish light of the setting sun as it fell through the leaded glass windows. She had distractedly untied the laces of her Roman sandals and curled up in a corner of the sofa, not saying a word, hugging her knees to her chest. A lock of hair fell onto her forehead, which she didn't brush back. Sitting near her on a padded stool, Henri forced himself to speak to her in a soft voice, as much to reassure himself as to reassure her, and although she couldn't exactly understand French, his soothing tone comforted the young girl a little — but not too much, since Henri's voice lacked that note of sincerity which cannot be imitated. He had taken Dr Carino's repellent potions, which had given him some respite from his fever and, feigning conviction, he spun out his phrases and studied Anna lying prostrate in her shawl. After a while, he fell silent. Anna had closed her eyes. Viennese women's devotion, Henri thought to himself, is like a mystic's faith: their lovers go away and they simply shut out the world and turn in on themselves. The only thing Italian about Anna was her pretty face: her moods and gestures were entirely unselfconscious, she never played the coquette and her enthusiasm was moderated by tenderness. Henri would have liked to have made notes of these observations, but what would it look like if Anna woke up?

She slept a sombre, troubled sleep, her lips moving as she murmured. To ward off Lejeune's death, Henri continued in a very low voice, 'Nothing will happen to Louis-François, I promise you ...' At the other end of the room, Anna's two slender little sisters came skipping towards him, chattering noisily, and Henri turned round, signalling to them that Anna was resting; *'Quiet, please!'* The girls tiptoed nearer with exaggerated caution, as if it was a game. They had lighter hair than Anna, more pointed little faces and they were more soberly dressed. Henri silently stood up to shoo them away from the sofa and they started talking to him, pulling faces and gesticulating and bursting out laughing whenever they caught the other's eye. None of it made any sense to Henri. Finally, they started tugging at his frock coat and he had to follow them. They took him to the staircase which led to the eaves, trying, like cats, not to make the wooden steps creak, and Henri let himself be pulled along. What did they want to show him? One of them slowly opened a door and he found himself in a minute room, in complete disarray, which was used as an attic. The little girls rushed onto a chest and, squabbling over the best view, peered through a fairly wide crack between two slats in the wall. When they asked him to come and have a look, Henri, in turn, peered into the next room. There was M. Staps, unaware that he was being watched. Lit by a ray of sunlight in which motes of dust floated, the young man was kneeling before a gilt statuette and holding a butcher's knife by the handle, its blade pointing downwards, like a knight on the eve of his investiture. Wearing a canvas shirt and with his eyes shut, he was intoning a sort of prayer.

Henri thought he must be delirious. He's mad, he thought, I'm certain he's mad, but with what sort of madness? Who does this poor boy take himself for? What does that statuette represent? Why that knife? What scheme is he hatching in his overheated brain? What sorcery does he want to inflict on us? Is he dangerous? We are all dangerous; the Emperor most of all. We are all mad, as well. I'm as mad as anyone, but Anna is the cause of my madness, and Louis-François is the cause of hers. And he is mad as only a soldier can be . . .

*

At that moment, Colonel Lejeune was having to fight alongside Masséna's men. Since riding back into Aspern, to confirm Masséna's orders to hold out until dusk and to inform him that the Emperor intended to launch the entire cavalry against the Austrian batteries, the village had come under siege and he hadn't been able to leave. Only the cemetery and the church remained in the voltigeurs' control; the Austrians had opened numerous breaches in the village's ruined defences and taken a firm hold everywhere

else. Masséna had had every large object that could afford
protection – harrows, ploughs, furniture – lined up in the
gaps between the guns, which were useless now the gunpowder had run out. On top of them, grenadiers were
piling dead bodies to barricade the church square up to
the cemetery wall, which men without ammunition were
defending with whatever they could lay their hands on –
bronze crosses, a beam, knives. Paradis had brought out his
catapult and Rondelet was holding his spit like a rapier.

Masséna was proving his true worth in the chaos.

When he realized that Hiller's artillerymen were rolling
a cannon into a lane to shatter the church façade, he had a
handcart filled with straw and leaves. He picked up a fallen
branch and walked into the sacristy, which had been blown
open by a shell, to light it off the burning embers. Coming
back out, he threw the branch into the cart which caught
fire instantly, and spotted Lejeune, who had no idea where
to turn in the mayhem. 'Come with me!' he ordered. The
two men each took an arm of the blazing cart, and, running
hard, pushed it towards the lane. As soon as their incendiary device had picked up speed, they threw themselves on
the ground, the bullets skimming over them, and the cart
rolled forward, collided head-on with the mouth of the
cannon and broke into pieces. The open powder kegs
exploded and everything was blown sky-high, the blast
tearing the gunners to shreds. A group of grenadiers
mounted a bayonet charge to rescue Masséna and Lejeune,
who had half-stood up, but it was impossible to get into the
lane, which the burning houses had turned into a furnace.
So they turned back and ran towards the shattered elms
around the church. Some Austrians tried to block their
path, but another group of grenadiers wielding beams like

clubs broke a few skulls. Masséna picked up a ploughshare and, with one swing, beheaded a couple of strapping soldiers who were pinned against a flight of steps. A white-jacketed officer slashed at Lejeune, who parried the cut, and then drove his knee into Lejeune's stomach, bending the Frenchman over double – fortunately for him, since the bullet aimed at the nape of his neck buried itself instead in the Austrian's forehead and blood gushed from the wound.

Sitting on a stone bench attached to a house without a single wall left standing, Masséna looked at his watch. It had stopped. He shook it and wound the key, but there was nothing he could do: it was broken. He swore. 'Plague it! My souvenir of Italy! It belonged to a monsignore in the Vatican! Pure gold and silver-gilt! Well, I suppose it was bound to pack up one day or another ... Don't stay there on your hands and knees, Lejeune, come and sit down for a moment and compose yourself. You ought to be dead but you aren't, so take a couple of good, deep breaths ...'

The colonel dusted himself off and the marshal continued, 'If we come through this, I'll commission you to paint my portrait, but it's got to be in action, eh? Holding the ploughshare like just now, for instance, and flattening a horde of Austrians! We'd entitle it, *Masséna in Battle*. Can you imagine the effect that would have? No one would dare hang a picture like that. Reality has no admirers, Lejeune.'

A roundshot shattered part of the roof of the house in front of which the two men were sitting; Masséna leapt to his feet. 'There it is, right on cue, that damned reality! Upon my word, those dogs are trying to bury us under rubble!'

A horseman galloped into the village from the direction

of the plain, slowed his horse near the church, questioned a non-commissioned officer, and, catching sight of Masséna, who had broken into a stream of oaths, made straight for him. It was Périgord, as impeccable as ever.

'Where the devil has this fellow come from?' asked Masséna.

'Your Grace!' Périgord handed a note to the marshal. 'A dispatch from the Emperor.'

'Let's see what harm His Majesty wishes me . . .'

He read the dispatch, and then glanced up at the sun sinking in the west. The two aides-de-camp chatted to each other.

'Are you wounded, Edmond?' asked Lejeune.

'Good Lord, no!'

'But you're limping.'

'That's because my man didn't have time to break in my boots; the leather hasn't really softened up and every step is agony. As for you, my dear friend, your breeches could do with a good brush!'

Masséna interrupted them. 'Monsieur de Périgord, I presume that you did not cross the Austrian lines.'

'The small plain this side of the village was clear, Your Grace. I only encountered one of our battalions of volunteers from Vienna.'

'So, we could fall back there for the night, before we allow Molitor's entire division to be massacred . . .'

'There are hedges, windbreaks of thickets, and a good number of ditches for cover . . .'

'Fine, Périgord, fine. At least you've got sharp eyes.'

Masséna called for a horse.

An equerry brought one immediately. Masséna wanted to mount, but the right stirrup was too short. Swinging his leg over the withers to sit sidesaddle, he called the man back. As the equerry hurriedly lengthened the leather, a roundshot sliced off his head and shattered the stirrup. The horse bolted and Masséna fell into Lejeune's arms.

'Your Grace! Are you hurt?'

'Get me another decent horse!' Masséna bellowed.

*

Lannes, transfigured by the fighting, Espagne, Lassalle and Bessières were charging at the head of their thousands of cavalrymen to break through the Austrian centre, hack it to pieces, cut it off from the wings, relieve the two villages in flames and make off with the enemy cannon. Fayolle didn't have this overall view. In the frenzied mêlée he behaved like an automaton, fearing nothing but desiring nothing either, wishing neither to draw rein nor to give chase, without a will of his own, a puppet swept along by the sound of bugles and war cries, yelling, sabreing, parrying, lungeing, shattering ribcages and running men through the neck. The cuirassiers had slaughtered a company of artillery and were hitching the captured cannon to the gunhorses. Espagne was directing the operation, his horse covered in foam and tossing its head up and down. Fayolle observed him out of the corner of his eye as he tied a harness to the trail of a howitzer: the general was grey with dust, straight-backed on his sheepskin saddle, but the distant look in his eyes belied the brief, precise orders he was dictating from habit. The trooper knew what was tormenting the officer: he couldn't silence his fear of portents. What was this? Could the hero of Hohenlinden – the same man who, years ago, in a snowstorm, had cleared the road to Vienna for the French – really be afraid of ghosts? Fayolle, as we have said, had witnessed the outcome of that strange scuffle at the chateau of Bayreuth, when General Espagne had been worsted by a ghost, but what had been the real cause of that? Hallucinations? Exhaustion? A malignant fever? Fayolle had not seen the spectre with his own eyes. The White Lady of the Habsburgs! He knew of the evil spirits that parents used to threaten children in his village with; they prowled around crosses at the roadside and terrified wayfarers. He had never believed in them.

'Think you're on holiday in the country, Fayolle?' Captain Saint-Didier said, shaking his dripping red sword. He was hurrying the manoeuvre forward, so that the fourteen enemy cannon could be towed back to their lines without delay.

General Espagne lifted his gloved hand and the troop hurried off. Fayolle and Brunel whipped the draught horses into a gallop, but on their right, grenadiers' bearskins suddenly appeared through the thick layers of smoke, followed by white uniforms and grey gaiters worn high to the knee.

'Watch out!' shouted Saint-Didier.

Most of the cuirassiers were wheeling their horses to bear down on the infantrymen, when a hail of roundshot caught General Espagne full in the chest and pierced his cuirass. The wounded man slipped and fell from his saddle, his foot caught in a stirrup; his horse bolted and dragged him along like a sack, his body bouncing over the wheatfields ploughed up by the explosions. Fayolle spurred his horse in pursuit, crouching down low over its mane, and cut the stirrup leather with the edge of his sabre. The others came after him and gathered up the general's mangled body. His breastplate and backplate were taken off, he was wrapped in an Austrian officer's long white cape, which immediately bloomed with bright red stars, and then his body was laid on a gun carriage, head and arms hanging down, like a ghost.

*

There were more dead lying on the tombs in Aspern's cemetery than in the graves. Overwhelmed, the voltigeurs were resisting as best they could by hurling stones at Baron Hiller's skirmishers. Paradis even had the satisfaction of hitting several with his catapult, but like the rest of his decimated battalion he was falling back, hoping to scatter across the fields and duck out of sight behind the bushes and tall grass. Austrians blustered triumphantly on the cemetery walls, and waved their standards emblazoned with a double-headed black eagle or a Madonna in a sky-blue dress, who seemed out of place in that hellish spot. The drums beat arrogantly. The French let themselves be shot at, as if they were prey running headlong before a hunt. A cannon aimed through an opening in the splintered wall and Paradis and Rondelet fled without being able to return fire. They crouched down to catch their breath behind the body of a stocky non-commissioned officer, who had fallen on a cross and was pinned there like a scarecrow. Rondelet straightened up a little behind the corpse to see how far the enemy had got. 'Strike me, it's the sergeant-major!'

He took the dead man under the arms to show Paradis. Sergeant-Major Roussillon's eyes were wide and staring, his blue lips peeled in a smile. Rondelet pricked his finger as he unfastened the Légion d'honneur from the tattered uniform. 'A souvenir,' he started to say.

These were his last words which he wasn't able to finish because a roundshot skimmed the ground and tore off his shoulder. Crouching next to his friend, Vincent Paradis was stupefied by the blast and flung against a gravestone overgrown with nettles and moss. His ears rang. He could only hear muffled sounds. He raised a hand to his face and gasped. All he could feel was a fleshy pulp. It was in his hair and his mouth. He spat out gobs of it: they were soft, lukewarm and tasted of nothing. Was he disfigured? A mirror! Didn't anyone have a mirror? A puddle, even? No? Nothing? Was he nearly dead? Where was he? Still on earth? Asleep? Would he wake up? Where? He felt hands grab hold of him and pick him up like a parcel; the next thing he knew, he was propped against a wooden fence which ran through a field. Voltigeurs were lying on their backs, mumbling incomprehensibly, covered in blood, their wounds dressed with handkerchiefs and rags; one had his arm in a sling, another was hunched over a branch as if on a crutch, his foot bandaged in a piece of fatigue jacket. Young men in long aprons were inspecting the wounded and deciding on the seriousness of their condition: those closest to death would not be transported to the rear. They held up the shattered soldiers to help them squeeze onto the platform of a haycart pulled by two draught horses wearing blinkers. Paradis let himself be examined. He didn't answer the apprentice medical orderlies who were astonished that, with his face in shreds, he hadn't yet lost consciousness.

The makeshift ambulance took a long time to reach the small bridge over to the island of Lobau. They constantly had to zigzag across the broken fields, and tear down fences to avoid detours. The assistant surgeons followed on foot, studying their cargo and occasionally pointing to a wounded man. 'That one's not worth the trouble any more . . .'

The dying man would be dragged off the platform and laid on the grass, as the ambulance moved on at the draught horses' slow pace. Paradis remained on his feet, in a daze, clinging to the uprights of the haycart as if they were prison bars. In the distance, he recognized the bivouac of the Guard and then they reached the small bridge. It was seven o'clock, night was falling and the reddish glow of the fires lit up a horde of at least four hundred wounded who had been stretched out on bales of straw or on the ground. Paradis was put near a hussar with one leg crushed to a pulp, who dragged himself along like a snake and tore at the dirt with his fingernails, raging against the Emperor and the Archduke. There was no respite for Dr Percy and his assistants: drenched in sweat, they amputated arms and legs in a hut, using carpenter's saws. All that could be heard were screams and curses.

Four

THE FIRST NIGHT

By CANDLELIGHT, HENRI SEARCHED THROUGH his tin trunk stamped with an eagle and took out a grey notebook, which he put on the table. Across the well-worn cover ran a title in black ink: 'Campaign of 1809. From Strasbourg to Vienna'. He glanced through the last pages. His journal stopped on 14 May and he hadn't made any entries since. The last words in his hand read, 'Enclosed a copy of the proclamation. Superb weather, very hot.' Folded in at that page was a celebrated proclamation which the Emperor had had printed on the day before Vienna's capitulation. Henri unfolded it to read it through again. 'Soldiers! Be good to the unfortunate peasants and the citizens who have so great a claim to your goodwill; we should not be proud of our success, but see in it only a token of that divine justice which punishes the ungrateful and the perjured...' He broke off. Not believing a word of this high-sounding declaration, he shook his head and frowned with disgust. A few days before, in a hamlet, he hadn't been able to find so much as an egg and he had noted in his journal, 'Everything the soldiers couldn't take away had been smashed...' He turned the ineffectual proclamation over and wrote on the back, in pencil:

May 22, at night. Vienna.

    At dusk we returned to the ramparts. The horizon was red and still flickering with the fires of the battle, of which we had no reliable news. A reassuring official bulletin did not reassure me, and Mlle K still less. I watch her wilt as time passes and, down there, the danger mounts. How many dead? It's I, the invalid, who must support her. She looks like Juliet before the body of Romeo, who she imagines is dead, 'O happy dagger, this is thy sheath! There rust, and let me die . . .'

Henri scribbled 'check quotation' in the margin. He sighed, as if at the theatre, then started a new paragraph to record the strange behaviour of young M. Staps. Hearing footsteps on the stairs, he thought it was him going up to his garret, but there was a knock at the door. He closed his notebook in exasperation and muttered, 'What does that Illuminato want from me now?' It wasn't the German. In the corridor, a flat candlestick in her hand, the old governess in a turban was standing in front of a man whom Henri did not recognize at first, so out of the ordinary did his presence seem on the landing. Once in his room, Henri was left in no doubt: it was the man who had been hiring out spyglasses on the ramparts, slightly hunchbacked, with a fringe of white hair below a smooth pate and little round glasses perched on the middle of his nose. He spoke a rough, broken French. 'Monzieur, Eyem reeturn your money.'

    He walked with a rolling gait over to the table, on which he threw down a worn leather draw-string purse.

    'My money?' Henri said, hastily turning out his trouser and waistcoat pockets to discover that his florins had disappeared.

    'On the battlement you haf dropped it.'

'But I...'

'Az I am honest...'

'Wait! How did you know my address?'

'Oh, my good sir, it's not that difficult.'

The interloper suddenly spoke in a low, resonant voice without a trace of a foreign accent. Henri stood open-mouthed. The governess had slipped away and shut the door behind her. The man took off his frock coat, unstrapped his fake hump and tore off his wig, saying, with unmistakable glee, 'I am Karl Schulmeister, Monsieur Beyle.'

Henri studied him carefully by the faint light of his candle. The individual masquerading as a hirer-out of spyglasses was thick-set, of average height and ruddy complexion, with deep scars on his forehead. Schulmeister! The whole world knew him, but how many could actually recognize him? Through years of spying for the Emperor, he had refined the art of disguise to such a degree that the Austrians had let him escape every time they had run him to earth. Schulmeister! A thousand stories were told about his exploits. Once, he'd inveigled his way into the Archduke's camp dressed as a tobacconist. Another time he'd left a besieged town by taking the place of a dead man in a coffin. And on another occasion, disguised as a German prince, he had reviewed a parade of Austrian battalions and even attended a council of war alongside Francis II. Napoleon had entrusted him with the policing of Vienna, as in 1805, and Henri asked him, in amazement, 'With the task His Majesty has given you, do you still find time for fancy dress?'

'No doubt I have a taste for it, Monsieur Beyle, and then this idiosyncrasy of mine does come in very useful.'

'What good does it do you hiring out spyglasses on the bastions?'

'I listen to rumours, I remember the dishonest things people say, I gather information. Poor morale can wreak havoc in times of war, you know.'

'Are you saying that with reference to me?'

'No, no, Monsieur Beyle.'

'Am I then so important as to deserve a visit from you? Do you wish to recruit me into your services?'

'Not exactly. Did you know that the young Mlle Krauss' father is a close relative of the Archduke?'

'You are wasting your time.'

'I never do that, Monsieur Beyle.'

'Mlle Anna Krauss thinks only of Colonel Lejeune . . .'

Henri instantly regretted having said too much, but he hurried on, hoping that he could play down his disclosure. 'Lejeune, my friend Lejeune, is Marshal Berthier's aide-de-camp.'

'I know. He was born in Strasbourg, like me. He speaks our adversary's language perfectly.'

'So?'

'Nothing . . .'

Schulmeister had returned to the table and was consulting the grey notebook. He read out one or two sentences in a loud voice. '"Out of prudence, I note nothing but observations upon myself. Nothing political."'

He closed the notebook and turned to Henri. 'Why *out of prudence*, Monsieur Beyle?'

'Because I don't want to reveal any military information, even the most minor detail, to anyone who might chance upon my journal.'

'Of course!' said Schulmeister, looking at the last notes

Henri had scribbled on the back of the imperial proclamation. He asked, 'Who is this Staps whose behaviour you call strange?'

'A lodger in this house.'

Henri had to describe how he had caught the young man unawares, his incantations in front of a statuette, the butcher's knife he held like a sword.

'Put your frock coat on, Monsieur Beyle, and show me the way to the room of this fanatic.'

'At this hour?'

'Yes.'

'...ound to be asleep.'

'...hen, we'll wake him up.'

'...now, what I really think is that he's just not right ...d ...'

'...g your candle.'

...i gave in. He led Schulmeister to the top floor and ...d the young German's door. The policeman entered wit...t announcing himself, took the candle from Henri and saw that the little room was empty.

'He lives at night, does he, your Staps?' he asked Henri.

'He is not my Staps and I'm not spying on him.'

'If he intrigues you, then he intrigues me.'

The statuette was still in its place. The two men observed more closely. It was of Joan of Arc in armour.

'What does it mean?' said Schulmeister. 'Joan of Arc! What sense is there in that?'

*

The last quarter of the moon was waning and the stars were hidden by the smoke from the fires. Lying on his back in the grass, Cuirassier Fayolle was not asleep. He had eaten dutifully, without appetite, from the mess tin he shared with Brunel and another two cuirassiers, and then he had lain down, acutely aware of every sound: a horse's neigh, a muffled conversation, the crackling of wood in the bivouac fire, the metallic clang of a cuirass as it was thrown on the ground. Fayolle was asking himself questions: something which hardly came naturally. Action suited him because one flung oneself into it without a thought in one's head, but afterwards, this so-called rest, what a curse! He had experienced most of the sensations of war. He knew how to plunge his blade with a jerk of the wrist into a man's chest – the crack of breaking ribs, the spurt of blood as one wrenched out the sword with a sharp tug; how to avoid an enemy soldier's eyes as one disembowelled him; how to hamstring a horse when one was dismounted; how to stand the sight of a comrade being blown to a pulp by a white-hot missile; how to protect oneself and parry sword cuts; how to be on one's guard; how to forget one's exhaustion to charge a hundred times into a throng of cavalrymen. And yet, the death of his general tormented him. The ghost of Bayreuth had been right about Espagne, even if the canister shot that tore his heart to shreds had been only too real. Is what will happen written? Can an unbeliever believe that? And what about him, Fayolle, what would his fate be? Could he steer it, and in which direction? Would he still be alive tomorrow night? And Brunel, next to him, grumbling in his sleep? And Verzieux – where was he at this hour, and in what shape? Fayolle didn't give a damn about ghosts but he kept a hand on his loaded carbine. He thought of the young Austrian peasant girl he'd killed by accident in the little house in Essling. He'd had his fun with her corpse while it was still supple, but Trooper Pacotte, his stooge, had had his throat cut by the guerrillas of the Landwehr and there had been no other witnesses to the affair. What bloody nonsense, thought the cuirassier. Murder, that was his trade. He killed – cleanly or messily – as he had been trained to do. He had a talent for it. How many Austrians had he sabred during the day? He hadn't counted. Ten? Thirty? More? Less? They didn't stop him sleeping – he couldn't even picture their faces – but the girl haunted him. He'd been wrong to look into her eyes and see the fear there. All the same, it wasn't as if it was the first time he'd come face to face with others' fear! He loved that. The terror that comes before certain death – it excited him. What power! The only power. Fayolle had felt it himself at Nuestra Señora del Pilar, facing a monk stabbing at him in a frenzy, but he had escaped with a slash across the face. Wounded, he'd managed to strangle the friar and strip him of his sackcloth habit to make into a coat. Afterwards he had thrown the body in the Ebro where Spaniards' corpses in sacks floated by the hundred. The girl from Essling had been left on her mattress. Had someone found her? A skirmisher looking for somewhere to take cover who'd have got a shock at the sight of her? Perhaps no one had. Perhaps a shell had burnt the house to the ground. He ought to have buried her and this thought preyed on his mind. He saw her, she grimaced, then the look of terror on her face changed into one of menace and he could not get rid of the image.

He stood up.

At the head of the small valley in which the squadrons were quartered, the first houses of Essling were visible, their roofs standing out against the backdrop of a lurid red sky. Without a helmet or cuirass, his straight sabre slapping against his leg, Fayolle set off like a sleepwalker in their direction. As he skirted the plain, moving from thicket to thicket, he encountered the sort of vultures who always appeared on the nights of battles: civilian touts whose job was to take the wounded back to the ambulances and whose sideline was to strip the dead for their own profit. Two of them were working up a sweat over the stiff body of a hussar whose boots they were pulling off. Next to him, on top of his pelisse and dolman, they had put a watch, a belt, ten florins and a locket. A third, squatting down, held the locket close to the lantern which he had set on the ground. 'Whooah!' he said. 'She's a pretty one, his intended!'

'And now she's fancy free,' said his crony, busy trying to get a boot off.

'Pity there's no address or name.'

'Maybe on the back of the portrait.'

'Good idea, Fat Louis . . .'

With a knife, the ambulanceman tried to prise the portrait away from the locket. Others walked past with armfuls of clothes. One bright spark had strung his haul of helmets and shakos on a stick, like a ratcatcher in the countryside, and the plumes, horsehair crests and tassels hung down like those animals' tails. Further on, Fayolle ran into a sentry who put the barrel of his rifle against his chest. 'Where are you off to, eh?'

'I need to walk,' Fayolle said.

'Can't get some shut-eye? You're the lucky one! I go to sleep standing up, like a bloody horse!'

'Lucky?'

'Yes, and you'll keep it that way if you steer clear of the

plain. The Austrians are thirty paces away. See that fire over there, on the left of the hedge? Well, that's them.'

'Thanks.'

'Lucky devil,' the sentry muttered again as he watched Fayolle receding into the distance towards the village.

He walked on in the darkness, stumbling several times; thistles scratched at his trousers and his espadrilles were soaked when he trod in a puddle. When he came into Essling, he couldn't distinguish the sleeping from the dead. Boudet's voltigeurs were sprawled, dog-tired, in the streets, against the low walls, one on top of the other, all blurring into one in their state of collapse. Fayolle tripped over the gaiters of a soldier who half-sat up and cursed him. Nothing seemed important any more. He made for the house which he had visited twice before. He had no trouble recognizing it, but the troop had taken up position there and barricaded it with mounds of sacks and broken furniture. The girl hadn't been burnt, then, her house hadn't been shelled. Someone must have found her dead and tied up. What had become of her body? He looked up at the first-floor window. The pane was broken, the shutter hanging off, and a voltigeur was leaning on the windowsill, smoking a pipe. Fayolle felt compelled to enter the house, but instinctively he held back. Standing in the street, he didn't dare move a muscle.

*

No one was sleeping soundly except Lasalle, most probably, who preferred the life of the camps to that of the salons and could take his rest in the worst conditions; he'd wrap himself up in his greatcoat, lie down and instantly start snoring and dreaming of the heroic exploits he was impatient to perform. The others – officers and other ranks – were on edge, anxious, their faces drawn, their brows furrowed. Some vigilant generals had already made their battalions stand to for next to no reason: skirmishes, isolated outbursts of firing caused by the proximity of the Austrian encampments and the pitch darkness, made it impossible to tell the different uniforms apart. Everyone thought that they would get their rest after the battle, either stretched out on the ground or under it.

Sitting on a drum in Essling's fortified granary, a plank across his knees, Colonel Lejeune was writing to Mlle Krauss. He pondered as he dipped his quill pen made from a crow's feather into the little inkwell he always carried with him for drawing. He was telling Anna nothing of the horrors and dangers: he spoke only of her, of Vienna's theatres, which they'd visit, of the pictures he planned to paint, of Paris above all, of the renowned Joly, that hair-dresser at the height of fashion who would twist her hair into a chignon à la Nina, of the presents he'd give her – jewellery or the shoes from chez Cop, so delicate they'd tear if you walked in them. They'd stroll along the avenues and amongst the pavilions of the Tivoli Gardens, in the glow of the red lanterns that hung from the trees. Glow, red: these words did not conjure up the Tivoli Gardens in Lejeune's mind; they were prompted by the fires sur-rounded him. The thing was, he wanted to be light-hearted, but he couldn't bring it off, or only imperfectly, and that must make itself felt: his sentences came out too dry and too terse, as if driven by anxiety. There is nothing lyrical about war, he thought, or if so, then only at a distance. After all, he had almost died at least three times in the course of that savage day. In his mind's eye, Aspern in flames took the place of Tivoli's peaceful gardens and Masséna that of the hair stylists whose artistry fashion rewarded by making them wealthy men.

'Lejeune!'

'Your Excellency?'

'Lejeune,' asked Berthier, 'what stage have the repairs to the large bridge reached?'

'Périgord is on the spot. He will inform us when the troops on the right bank can cross the Danube.'

'Let's go and have a look,' continued Berthier who, until that moment, had been discussing the situation with Marshal Lannes.

They had taken a tally of their losses, and so knew that Molitor had lost half his division – three thousand men strewn across the streets of Aspern and the surrounding fields – not counting the wounded who would be of no use in the next day's fighting, in three or four hours at the most, when the opposing sides would meet at dawn and, exhausted, launch themselves into the fray again. Together, Berthier, Lannes, their aides-de-camp and equerries stood up and, in procession, led their horses at a walk along the Danube which was faintly lit up by the flames still engulfing parts of the two villages. Lejeune had not finished his letter and he dried the ink with a handful of sand. The wind had risen and was driving the smoke towards Lobau, making their eyes smart. As they drew near to the rear of Aspern, they heard firing.

'I'm going there!' said Lannes, wheeling his horse.

He disappeared into the tall, dark wheat which lay between him and Aspern. His aide-de-camp, Marbot, automatically followed; then, after several strides, he took the lead because he knew the way and its hazards better. The others continued towards the island and the small bridge. The marshal and captain rode forward slowly and cautiously. In its last crescent the moon was weak and the night so thick they couldn't see a thing. A headwind carrying with it a smell of burning irritated the horses and ruffled the feathers on the marshal's tricorn. To relieve his horse and test out the ground with his boots, Marbot dismounted and led his mount by the bridle.

'You're right,' said Lannes, 'this is no time to break a leg!'

'Your Excellency, we could find a barouche for you to direct our attacks from.'

'Fine idea! I'm fond of my legs the way they are, you know.'

And he in turn dismounted to walk beside the captain whom he had held in high esteem for such a number of years.

'What do you think of the day we had of it yesterday?'

'We have seen worse, Your Excellency.'

'Possibly, but the truth is that we didn't manage to break the Austrian centre.'

'We held our ground.'

'One against three: yes, we held our ground, but that's not enough.'

'By dawn tomorrow, we will have received fresh troops and Davout's army. Whilst the Austrians have no hope of being reinforced.'

'Their Army of Italy . . .'

'It's still a long way off.'

'We have to carry the day tomorrow, Marbot, no matter what the cost!'

'If you say so, then that's how it will be.'

'Oh, don't flatter me!'

'I have seen you on the attack a hundred times, and the army loves you.'

'I offer them up to cannon and bayonets and they love me! Sometimes I don't understand any more.'

'Your Excellency, this is the first time that I have heard you expressing doubts.'

'Is it now? In Spain, I had to keep my doubts to myself.'

'Here we are . . .'

There were no sentries posted on that side of Masséna's bivouacs and the two men passed noiselessly between the soldiers drowsing on the ground. Near a fire, they saw Masséna's tall, stooped silhouette and, next to it, that of Bessières. As Marbot was walking in front, Marshal Bessières recognized him first by his civilian hat: since he'd been wounded in the forehead in Spain, Marbot hadn't been able to wear Lannes's aides-de-camps' customary fur cap. Thinking that he had come on his own, Bessières snapped at him, 'Captain, since you are here for information, I will give you a piece. Go back and tell your master that I will not forget his insults!'

Lannes, who had a fierce temper, pushed aside his aide-de-camp and strode into the light of the bivouac fire.

'Monsieur,' he said to Bessières, barely containing his anger, 'Captain Marbot knows how to risk his life and take a punishing! I demand that you speak to him in a more civil tone! He has been wounded ten times while others have been parading in front of the enemy!'

Bessières raised his voice, which was not characteristic. 'What, I parade about, do I? And you? I didn't see you at close quarters with the uhlans!'

'Some people fight, others prefer to spy and denounce!'

The allusion was crude but unmistakable. Lannes was reviving their old animosity. When Bessières had taken Murat's side against Lannes's, he had revealed that Lannes, as commander of the Consular Guard, had overspent their equipping budget by two hundred thousand francs. Napoleon had instantly withdrawn Lannes's command, and Murat had married Caroline. On that night, outside Aspern which was still in flames, the marshals' hatred for one another knew no bounds.

'That's too much!' shouted Bessières. 'You will give me satisfaction!'

With his arms crossed, Masséna was waiting for the quarrel to wear itself out, but Bessières had drawn his sword, Lannes had swiftly followed suit and they were on the verge of fighting a duel. Masséna stepped between them. 'Enough!'

'He has insulted me!' Bessières said, enraged.

'Traitor!' roared Lannes.

'In the face of the enemy? You're going to tear each other's guts out in the face of the enemy? Break up: that's an order! You're under my jurisdiction here! Sheathe your swords!'

They obeyed, despite themselves.

Without a word, and trembling with rage, Bessières turned on his heel to rejoin his horsemen. Masséna took Lannes by the arm. 'Do you hear?'

'I don't hear a thing!' said Lannes, scowling.

'Listen, you ass!'

In the still of the night, fifes were playing a rhythmical refrain which Lannes had no difficulty recognizing. He felt shivers run down his spine.

'Your men are playing the "Marseillaise"?' he asked Masséna.

'No. It's the Austrians stationed on the plain. The music carries a long way.'

They fell silent in order to listen to the former anthem of the Army of the Rhine, which had been spread through all insurgent France by the volunteers from Marseilles, which had accompanied the Revolution and its soldiers at every step until the emergence of the Empire, when it was forbidden by decree as a vulgar, seditious chant. Lannes and Masséna avoided each other's eyes. They remembered their former exhilaration. They were dukes and marshals now, they possessed as much land and money as the nobility before them, but the 'Marseillaise' had roused them to arms in the past; at the sound of it, they had left their provinces to go and fight, and how many times had they sung its verses at the tops of their voices to give themselves courage? Lannes couldn't help mouthing the words to the refrain the enemy was playing, either as a provocation or because they believed that it was their turn now to wage a war of liberation against despotism. Masséna and Lannes thought of the same things, they relived the same scenes, they felt the same emotions, but they didn't exchange a word. They listened with grave expressions, absorbed and deeply moved. They had been young and poor and patriotic. They had loved those martial verses. And here they were, flung back at them by their adversaries as an insult or an appeal to their consciences.

*

Death rattles, wailing, moaning, sobbing, crying and screaming: there was nothing nostalgic about the song of the wounded on the island of Lobau. The medical orderlies, their uniforms cobbled together from mismatching jackets and trousers, had long since ceased to feel anything as they chased the swarms of flies away from the open wounds with palm leaves. His long apron and forearms running with blood, Dr Percy had lost his bonhomie. In the little hut of branches and reeds which had been renamed an ambulance, his assistants were laying out on the table the men they'd fished out from the mass of naked and near dead. The doctor's helpers, whom he'd obtained by bitterly protesting his predicament, had, for the most part, never studied surgery. So, since he couldn't treat such a number of maimed and such a variety of wounds on his own, he marked the writhing bodies with chalk to show where they had to saw, and the helpers − not much more than stop gaps, really − sawed. Sometimes they removed limbs right up to the joints. The blood spurted out as they cut into the bare bone; their patients lost consciouness and lay still. A great number died of heart attacks or bled to death in this way, an artery severed through bad luck. 'Cretins! haven't you ever carved a chicken?' the doctor would shout.

Operations couldn't last longer than twenty seconds. There were too many wounded to attend to. Afterwards, the arm or leg was thrown onto a pile of arms and legs. The unqualified orderlies would make a joke of it to stop themselves vomiting or passing out. 'Another leg of lamb,' they'd shout raucously as they tossed away the amputated limb. Percy kept the difficult cases for himself. He tried to knit bones together, to cauterize wounds, to avoid amputation, to alleviate the men's pain − but how could he, with such wretchedly inadequate facilities? At the slightest opportunity, he'd coach the brightest orderlies. 'You see here, Morillon, the fragments of the tibia are riding and exposed...'

'Can they be set, Doctor?'

'They could be, if we had time.'

'There's a mass of them waiting out at the back.'

'I know!'

'So what do we do?'

'We cut, imbecile, we cut! And I loathe that, Morillon!'

With a rag, he wiped his face drenched in sweat. His eyes ached. The wounded man – the condemned man, more like – was entitled to a line of chalk which Percy drew above the knee. He was lifted onto the table where, only a little while before, Austrian peasants would have been drinking their soup, and an assistant began sawing, his tongue poking out of his mouth as he concentrated on following the line. Percy was already leaning over a hussar, recognizable by his moustache, his side-whiskers and his queue.

'Gangrene is setting in,' muttered the doctor. 'Forceps!'

A tall, clumsy lad held out a repellent pair of forceps, a handkerchief over his nose. Percy used them to tear away the burnt flesh. 'If we only had some Peruvian bark,' he fumed. 'I'd steep it in lemon juice, use that to soak a pad of tow, and then we could wash all this, relieve the pain and save a man's life!'

'Not this one's, Doctor, he's gone,' said Morillon, a bloodstained carpenter's saw in his hand.

'So much the better for him! On to the next one!'

With a corner of his apron, Percy dug out the maggots that had worked their way into the next man's wound. He was delirious, his eyes turned up in their sockets.

'Done for! Next!'

Two assistants, one holding him under the arms, the other by the legs, hoisted Private Paradis onto the surgeon's table.

'What's he got, this lad, apart from where it's swollen, there?'

'We don't know, Doctor.'

'Where does he come from?'

'He was in the batch we picked up near Aspern cemetery.'

'But he hasn't even been wounded!'

'He had pieces of flesh all over his face and sleeve. They thought he'd taken a cannonball but it came off when we scrubbed him down.'

'Well, then, one his comrades must have been blown to bits and caught him full in the face. At any rate, his head must have taken a knock.'

Percy bent down towards this impostor amongst the ranks of the wounded. 'Can you talk? Can you hear me?'

Paradis didn't move but mumbled his name and rank: 'Private Paradis, Voltigeur, Second Infantry of the Line, General Molitor's 3rd Division, under the command of Marshal Masséna . . .'

'Don't worry, I'm not going to send you back there, you're in no fit state to hold a musket.' Turning to Morillon, he ordered, 'He's a strong lad, go and get him dressed, we've got work for him.'

The doctor and his assistant set Paradis back on his feet and the voltigeur in his drawers meekly followed Morillon. Outside, the wounded considered by Percy to be condemned to death, because of the lack of medicine and equipment, were sprawled on stacks of straw bales with a chalk cross on their foreheads; that way they wouldn't be confused with the new arrivals or inadvertently brought back to the surgeon's table. The dying men probably wouldn't see the dawn; they were lost to the battle and to life. Only a few paces away, under a screen of elms, the ambulance touts had set up a sort of boutique where they sold on, for their own profit, the greatcoats, knapsacks, cartridge pouches and clothes which they had scavenged from the Austrian and French corpses strewn over the plain.

'Fat Louis,' Morillon said to a hulking lout wearing a cap, 'you're going to kit out this strapping lad.'

'Has he got any sous?'

'Dr Percy's orders.'

Fat Louis sighed. His trade was tolerated, but if he refused to obey the doctor, he could be forbidden to sell any soldiers' effects he recovered. He complied reluctantly and Paradis found himself rigged out in green breeches with yellow stripes, a pair of boots that were too big, a shirt with a torn right sleeve and a light-cavalry waistcoat which he had difficulty buttoning up. Morillon handed him over to a team of canteen workers who were responsible for cooking the wounded men's broth.

*

The fare was not so coarse at the Emperor's table, set up in his bivouac at the head of the small bridge. Cooks' boys were turning chickens on spits over a fire of brushwood and the skins sizzled as they turned a golden brown, filling the air with a delicious smell. M. Constant had set out his trestle tables, tablecloths and lanterns under a copse, so that the guests couldn't see the convoy of unfortunates being carried back to Dr Percy, who, if they didn't die first, would presently have one of their limbs sawn off. Dinner could be enjoyed in peace, and the cannon forgotten for a moment. Lannes was sitting to the right of the Emperor, who had invited him to coax him out of his bad humour. The marshal had recounted his altercation, bending the truth to show himself in a better light, and Napoleon had summoned Bessières, given him a sharp lecture and then dismissed him. Bessières had been the offended party, but he became the one who had given offence because His Majesty had decided so, and because he loved to perpetuate this sort of injustice to toughen up his entourage, doling out kisses and slaps for no good reason other than it pleased him. Instead of reconciling the two marshals, he was stirring up their animosity and driving them further apart, because he needed to feel in every circumstance that he was the supreme judge and the sole recourse, and because his dukes could never be too friendly lest one day they combine against him.

These considerations were beyond Marshal Lannes, who had been plunged into gloom by his latest quarrel and whilst he normally devoured chickens by the dozen, was only picking at a brown drumstick. He preferred to mull over melancholy thoughts. He took delight in it. He dreamed he was elsewhere, with his wife in one of his houses or riding safely through Gascony, his fortune secure, peace having been declared. The Emperor spat some bones out onto the grass and noted his marshal's lugubrious mood. 'Aren't you hungry, Jean?'

'I have no appetite, sire . . .'

'You're sulking like a little girl who's been given a scolding! *Basta!* Tomorrow Bessières will obey you and we will win this damn shambles of a battle!'

174

The Emperor tore the carcass of his chicken apart with his hands, sunk his teeth into it and, with his mouth full, having wiped his lips on his sleeve and his fingers on the tablecloth, he explained to Berthier, Lannes and his headquarters staff the plan of action they were going to follow. 'With the troops who are going to cross the large bridge, Berthier, how many men will we have at our disposal?'

'Roughly sixty thousand, sire, not forgetting Davout's thirty thousand, who ought to have reached Ebersdorf by now.'

'Davout! Get someone to hurry him up! Cannon?'

'Five hundred pieces.'

'*Bene!* Lannes, you will rout the Austrian centre with Claparède's, Tharreau's and Saint-Hilaire's divisions. Bessières, Oudinot, Lasalle and the light cavalry and Nansouty will wait for your breakthrough before they surge into the breach, and then they'll turn back on the enemy's wings massed in front of the villages . . .'

The Emperor gestured to Constant, who draped his frock coat over his shoulders because it was growing cold. Caulaincourt poured him a glass of Chambertin and he continued, 'Supported by Legrand, Carra-Saint-Cyr and the skirmishers of my Guard, Masséna will recover a stronger position in Aspern. We'll keep Molitor's voltigeurs in reserve, they've deserved it. Boudet will defend Essling.'

The Emperor drank and, getting to his feet, dismissed his guests. Lannes went off by himself, his tricorn under his arm. He was no more tired than he had been hungry. He walked across the little bridge jammed with wounded, and reached the stone house where he had spent the previous night in Rosalie's arms, but tonight the hunting lodge was empty. The girl had gone back over the bridge before it had broken, early the previous day. He would have liked to have left her a present: that little cross of chased silver, set with diamonds, which he had worn round his neck since Spain. It took his mind back to Saragossa, a few months before, when a Spanish chaplain guarding the shrine of Nuestra Señora del Pilar had offered him a fortune if he spared their lives. Almost five million francs worth: gold crowns, a topaz pectoral, a cross of the order of Calatrava in enamelled gold, portraits, the little cross ... He undid his jacket and shirt, grasped the piece of jewellery with his right hand and snapped the chain with a sharp tug. Walking towards the sandy riverbank, he threw it with all his might into the Danube, which was still rising. Then he stood for a long time beside the roaring torrent.

*

On the same bank of the Lobau, about a kilometre to the west, in the brushwood where the main pontoon bridge came out, Lejeune and his friend Périgord were waiting for the repairs to be finished. Pontoneers and sailors of the Guard had been working continuously, and several had drowned in spite of the precautions and their own experience. The truth was that materials were in short supply and, instead of constructing the bridge anew, they were simply patching it together. Berthier's two aides-de-camp observed with distress the river's unrelenting savagery, its eddies and waves rolling at the speed of a tidal bore, and the uprooted tree trunks smashing into the fragile edifice. Breakwaters should really have been erected upstream: barricades of piles and chains, like dykes, to break the current and hold back – or at least slow down – the trees and the terrible triangular craft that the Austrians were still launching against the bridge. These projectiles were even deadlier at night, despite the lanterns hung from poles, and the torches. By the time they saw a floating island covered in foliage or one of the trees transformed by the speed of the current into battering rams, it was almost always too late. They had trouble knocking them off course and they were constantly returning to sections which they had only just finished repairing. The work dragged on interminably.

Suddenly, Lejeune made out strange, moving shapes which seemed to be struggling in the dark, choppy waters. He wondered what the Archduke's strategists had come up with this time, but then he recognized an entire herd of stags which had been driven from the forests by the flooding and were floating downstream, their heads and antlers above the water. Some of the animals became entangled in the ropes, others were washed up on the island and every soldier thought to himself as he saw them, 'Here's some meat coming our way, just in the nick of time...' A large stag had managed to right itself as it clambered out of the reeds and, soaked to the skin, shook itself a few paces away from Lejeune, as trusting as a farm animal. Soldiers from some regiment or other – they were only in shirt sleeves, but armed with bayonets which they held like knives – instantly surrounded it. Périgord and Lejeune walked over to the cluster of men. The stag was watching them, a tear at the corner of its eye, as it realized that its death was imminent.

'It's very strange,' commented Périgord. 'I've seen this a hundred times out hunting. A stag that has been run to ground will draw itself up to its full height, strike a haughty pose and shed a tear to make the hunter take pity on it.'

'You have a sense of how things should be done, Edmond,' said Lejeune, 'try to at least give this creature a dignified death.'

'You're right, my dear friend. These beggars only know how to kill men.'

Périgord pushed his way through the circle of soldiers, 'The animal is out of breath, gentlemen, but leave it to me. I can take this in hand so that the meat won't be spoiled.'

With a single, well-aimed sword cut, Périgord opened the stag's throat. It trembled on its thin legs and then collapsed, its tongue hanging out and its eyes opened wide, with that tear still at one corner.

The soldiers seized hold of their prey and cut it into quarters which they were going to grill. They were hungry. Lejeune turned on his heel and, after wiping his sword on the grass, his friend followed. An unkempt sergeant-major ran up to report, 'That's it! The bridge has been made fast.'

'*Molto bene!*' shouted Périgord, imitating the Emperor's voice.

'Thank you,' said Lejeune, who was now able to send a messenger to Vienna with his letter to Anna.

'Are you coming, Louis-François? Let's go and inform His Majesty.'

They mounted their horses which their grooms were holding a little way off in a clearing reserved for the officers. The latter weren't singing any more, as on the day before. Lying on the ground in their greatcoats, they gazed at the starless sky and the last sliver of a crescent moon. Some of them stroked the grass distractedly, as if it was a cat's back or a woman's hair. Half asleep, they dreamt of civilian life.

*

In his bivouac, with his hands behind his back, the Emperor was bent over the maps which Coulaincourt had weighed down with pebbles to prevent them blowing away. He was pondering the coming battle. Fortune, it seemed, was on his side. Against the same Austrians, worn out by a day's fighting, he was going to send new, alert troops. He would launch them all into an attack against the enemy's weakest and most depleted point, the centre, as he had announced to his headquarters staff over dinner. When Lejeune and Périgord arrived to report that the bridge was repaired at last, the news didn't even give him pleasure. It was as he had anticipated. From now on, events would unfold according to his plan, which he could modify depending on circumstances and with his customary speed. Napoleon felt strong. He gave orders for the troops on the left bank to cross the Danube and take up position on the approaches to the plain. Caulaincourt and Roustan, his Mameluke, helped him hoist himself into the saddle so that he could witness the march past of the fresh regiments. As they were doing so, a shot rang out and a bullet smashed into the bark of an elm, grazing the Emperor. There was a flurry of panic. An Austrian marksman, hidden at least two hundred metres away, had aimed at the Mameluke's white muslin turban.

'Why are you fretting?' asked the Emperor. 'If you hear the whistle of a bullet, that's because it's missed you!'

Surrounded by his escort, he took the road to the main

bridge. In the middle of this cluster of horsemen in uniforms sewn with gold thread – who, for dramatic effect, he asked to remove their plumed hats and salute the reinforcements – the Emperor watched the arrival of his soldiers. The three divisions of grenadiers led by Oudinot crossed first, then Count Saint-Hilaire's division, the three brigades of cuirassiers and carabineers under Nansouty and the remainder of the Imperial Guard, and finally the artillery. There were more than a hundred cannon and they could see the roadway sinking below water level under the weight of the caissons and powder kegs.

At three o'clock in the morning, the Austrians started their bombardment again. At four o'clock, as day broke, the battle resumed.

Five

THE SECOND DAY

'What peace in death! Like Iphigenia I shall miss the
light of day; but not what it reveals.'

Demi-jour, Jacques Chardonne.

FOG COVERED THE PLAIN. A red sun rising above the
horizon stained the countryside the colour of blood. Aspern
was still burning. Black, acrid smoke fanned by an insistent
wind curled into the air in thick whirls. A few crouching
figures warmed themselves at the campfires. Colonel Sainte-
Croix shook Masséna by the shoulder. The marshal, who
had snatched two hours of sleep on the ground between
trees felled by cannon fire, stood up, threw on his grey
cloak and started yawning and stretching. He looked at his
aide-de-camp, inclining his head because the young man
was barely taller than the Emperor, but slighter in build
and fair-haired and smooth-cheeked like a young woman.
From the look of him, one would never have guessed what
energy he possessed.

'Your Grace,' he said, 'we have just received a delivery
of ammunition and powder.'

'Have it distributed, Sainte-Croix.'

'It's been done.'

'So we're going back in, are we?'

'The 4th of the Line and the 24th Light Infantry are crossing the small bridge and marching to join us.'

'Let's not wait. We have to take advantage of this fog to recapture the church. Tell Molitor to muster the survivors from his division.'

The drummers sounded the assembly and the battalions re-formed, joined by a number of well-schooled horses who cantered up even though they were riderless. Masséna stopped a hussar's chestnut horse, whose rider was probably dying on the plain, mounted it unaided, adjusted the reins to his length and set it prancing in the direction of Aspern. All around soldiers got to their feet, chilled to the bone and dazed from too little, broken sleep, and groped their way over to the stacks of muskets to collect their weapons. Numbed by fatigue and the proximity of death, they seemed like ghosts, silent and noiseless. They fell in behind Masséna as he headed for the start of the main street. It was impossible to see more than ten metres ahead. The church, which had been held overnight by one of Baron Hiller's brigades under the command of Major-General Vacquant, was lost in the smoke and mist. The only sound was the echo of hooves and the tramp of boots. Masséna drew his sword from its scabbard and, with the point, silently indicated the course the remains of Molitor's division was to follow. In columns they passed the houses on the main street and regrouped behind the trees and ruins surrounding the central square.

'Do you see what I see, Sainte-Croix?'

'Yes, Your Grace.'

'Those scum have demolished the wall round the cemetery and the close! We can only attack them out in the open! What do you make of it?'

'We have to wait for Legrand and Carra-Saint-Cyr's troops, at least to have the advantage of numbers.'

'And by then the fog will have lifted! No! The fog is our protection. Let's attack!'

A thousand half-awake voltigeurs broke into a run, heading for the church that been transformed into a stronghold. In the thick fog, with bayonets levelled, they tripped over corpses from the day before, and stumbled in holes dug by the enemy shells.

The Austrians had anticipated the attack and they opened fire from every angle, even from the charred remnants of the bell tower. Again and again, soldiers crumpled face first onto the ground. Between the tombs of the cemetery and the rubble of its low wall, the voltigeurs glimpsed a major on horseback waving a standard fringed with gold. A tightly packed troop of Austrians dashed out to surround him, and with a shout, charged forward to run the French through. Everything is permitted in hand to hand combat. Some held their muskets like sledgehammers, others like scythes or larding needles as they tore one another's guts out, roaring at the top of their voices. Others stood back for a second to observe their opponents, then hurled themselves forward. Any soldiers that fell were instantly pinned to the ground, and everyone splashed and floundered in human entrails, oblivious to the sound of death rattles, killing so as not to be killed, colliding at full pelt, tearing at flesh with fingernails and teeth, blinded by earth thrown in their eyes and, in the fog that enveloped them all, never realizing the danger they were in until it was too late.

Masséna consulted his aide-de-camp's watch, as Sainte-Croix fumed with impatience. 'Our men are losing ground, Your Grace!'

He pointed to a tattered band who were falling back, carrying or dragging wounded men smeared with blood. 'Let me go forward, Your Grace!' Sainte-Croix urged.

'Your Grace, Your Grace! Stop making my ears ache with your *Your Grace*! I'm the Duke of what, exactly, eh? An Italian hamlet, a symbol?' In a mocking tone, he added, 'I don't call you Your Excellency the Marquis the whole time, do I now, my little Sainte-Croix?'

Sainte-Croix gripped the pommel of his sword so hard his knuckles went white. His father had indeed been a marquis and Louis XVI's ambassador in Constantinople, but although his family had intended him for a diplomatic career, Sainte-Croix had always felt drawn to military life. He had been employed very young by Talleyrand before enrolling, by special favour, in one of the regiments the Emperor had formed of émigrés and former nobility. Masséna had singled him out and taken him onto his staff.

'You should keep an eye on those nerves of yours, Sainte-Croix, if you want to take command. You saw a hundred voltigeurs falling back, did you? Well, so did I.'

'I could lead them back into battle, if you'd only give the order!'

'So could I, Sainte-Croix.'

Masséna explained to the young colonel that the point was to wear down the Austrians, who were as exhausted by the previous day's fighting as they were, while waiting for the fresh regiments to arrive. Sainte-Croix was twenty-seven, and more impetuous than experienced, but he learnt quickly. He had a real gift for soldiering. The stories of the *Iliad* had thrilled him as a child. For many years he had wanted to rival Hector, Priam and Achilles, imagining their javelin fights under the ochre ramparts of Troy when the gods became the accomplices of those ferocious, magnificent giants, fleet-footed despite the weight of their armour and greaves. On this morning he thought he saw Achilles in his wolfskin coat and helmet adorned with boar's tusks, that glorious brigand whose lies the goddess Athena admired. Then Sainte-Croix heard drums and he looked around. Red plumes were emerging from the fog. It was Carra-Saint-Cyr's fusiliers arriving.

*

Lejeune had the unpleasant feeling that he was vanishing into a grey cloud. He no longer recognized the road from Lobau to Essling, ridden a hundred times the day before; hedges and trees loomed up in front of his horse at the last moment and he had lost all his bearings. He walked his mount forward, guiding himself by the noises closest to him. A rustling to his left, probably in the direction of the plain swamped by fog, put him on his guard. He drew his sword and reined in his horse. A blurred shape stirred within his reach. He called out in French and German, but, getting no answer, he assumed it was a threat and rode hard at the vague shape, slashing all about him with his sabre. It was only a large bush, shaken by the wind. Covered in leaves and twigs which he'd hacked off, Lejeune felt relieved and ridiculous. Eventually he saw a gleam of light and cautiously headed towards it, without slackening his grip on his sword. The light disappeared as he rode closer. In the fog, which was starting to break up into wisps, he came across a party of cuirassiers trampling on their night's fire to smother it.

'Soldiers,' Lejeune said, 'I have to go to Essling, by order of the Emperor! Show me the quickest way.'

'You're too far forward on the plain,' a captain said, his cheeks grimed with stubble. 'I'll give you an escort. My men could find their way round here blindfold.'

Captain Saint-Didier grumbled as he buckled his belt. Despite orders, bivouac fires were still flickering a hundred metres away.

'Brunel! Fayolle! You, and you two over there! Go and impress upon those imbeciles that every fire has to be put out!'

'I'll go with them,' said Lejeune.

'As you wish, Colonel. Then they'll take you to Essling . . . Fayolle! Put on your breastplate!'

'Thinks he's invulnerable, Captain,' Cuirassier Brunel said, as he jumped on his horse.

'That's enough of that nonsense!' growled Saint-Didier, adding in a quieter voice for Lejeune's benefit, 'I can't blame them, the general's death has shaken them badly . . .'

Fayolle strapped on his breastplate and Lejeune watched him. This was the fellow he'd had words – and even come to blows – with when he'd had tried to loot Anna's house. The cuirassier hadn't recognized him. Fayolle picked up his carbine mechanically and heaved himself into the saddle. The six horsemen set off towards the camp fires. When they were fairly close and the silhouettes could be seen more clearly, they recognized, with a start, the brown uniforms of the Landwehr. A group was eating beans straight from the pot, while others were polishing their muskets with handfuls of leaves. The Austrians hadn't time to realize that they were surrounded by French troopers and, thinking they were outnumbered, they stood up and held out their hands to show that they were unarmed. Before Lejeune could give an order, Fayolle had spurred his horse and hurled himself into the Austrians. With his carbine he blew out one man's brains and then, bellowing with rage, he sliced off another's raised hand with a sweep of his sabre.

'Stop that madman!' ordered Lejeune.

'He's taking revenge for our general,' said Brunel, with an angelic, heavily ironic smile.

Lejeune urged his horse alongside Fayolle's and as Fayolle was about to plunge his sabre into an Austrian curled up in a ball on the ground he caught his wrist from behind and twisted it. The two men came face to face, panting heavily, and Fayolle whispered, 'We're not at a ball now, my little colonel!'

'Calm down or I'll kill you!'

With his left hand, Lejeune pointed his horse pistol at the cuirassier's throat.

'You want to break my jaw again?'

'I can't wait.'

'Go on then, you're the one with the epaulettes!'

'Fool!'

'Sooner or later: it makes no difference to me.'

'Fool!'

Fayolle shouldered himself free and his horse shied away to the side. During this brief altercation, the cuirassiers had rounded up their defenceless prisoners. Three of them had managed to get away during the quarrel, but the others had meekly given themselves up, relieved that their fighting had come to an end.

'What shall we do with these birds, Colonel?' asked Brunel, who had dismounted to try the beans in the pot.

'Take them to Staff Headquarters.'

'What about you? Aren't we taking you to the village?'

'I don't need a whole troop. He knows the way.'

Lejeune pointed to Fayolle who was catching his breath, slumped over the neck of his horse.

Entrusting the prisoners to the cuirassiers, Lejeune followed Cuirassier Fayolle as he led his horse through the sheets of mist. At the foot of a hill they passed the immaculate battalions of the Young Guard's skirmishers, muskets slung over their shoulders, white gaiters, shakos topped with a long white and red plume, and then a division of the Army of Germany climbing in silence towards the plain. They heard the crack of the artillery train drivers' whips and saw their light blue jackets and the gunners' red woollen epaulettes as they hauled dozens of cannon towards the front. Finally they rode alongside the interminable columns of infantry under Tharreau and Claparède's command. Fayolle halted to give way to a stream of chasseurs à cheval going to join Bessières's cavalry. The fog was thinning and the burnt houses on the outskirts of Essling were now clearly visible.

'That's as far as I go, sir,' said Fayolle, without looking at Lejeune.

'Thank you. This evening we'll be celebrating victory, I promise you that.'

'Oh, that won't do me any good. I'm just one of the herd . . .'

'Come now!'

'When I see that village all smashed to pieces, I get a strange feeling.'

'Are you afraid?'

'It's not normal fear, sir. It's not really fear, I don't know what it is, it's like fate has got something bad in store.'

'What did you do before this?'

'Nothing, or not very much. Rag-and-bone man. But whether it's a towing hook or a sabre, it's still dirty work for three sous. Look, there's Marshal Lannes coming out of Essling.'

Fayolle wheeled his horse. Lannes was riding towards them with Generals Claparède, Saint-Hilaire, Tharreau and Curial.

*

Standing firmly in his dusty boots in front of the tileworks which housed his headquarters staff, the Emperor crossed his arms. He smiled at the clearing fog. It felt as if he were controlling the elements, since this bad weather was like having another ally. In the past he'd been able to use winter, rivers, mountain ranges and valleys to fall like lightning on his enemies. Today, thanks to the fog still veiling the countryside, his army would be able to burst out en masse against the Austrians on the slope between the villages. Lejeune had delivered Marshal Lannes's orders and the masses of infantry could be seen manoeuvring in squares on the sloping bank. The steel of the raised swords and bayonets, the golden braid of the generals' uniforms and the eagles on the regimental standards glinted in the rising sun. The drums rolled, each regiment's drummers answering those of the next, their patterns blending, merging and swelling into one continuous, rhythmical clap of thunder. The squadrons followed in the second file, formed up at the bottom of the shallow valleys: the blue lancers of Warsaw, hussars, Gardes du Corps of Saxony and of Naples, chasseurs of Westphalia. At the sight of this spectacle, Napoleon thought that there was no longer such a thing as troops from Baden, Gascony, Italy, Germany or Lorraine, only a single well-ordered force gathering itself to sweep away the Archduke's weakened troops in the fury of its onslaught.

A short while before, a patrol of cuirassiers had brought in a group of Landwehr, with their strange hats festooned with leaves, whom they had taken prisoner. The Emperor had questioned them and General Rapp, an Alsatian who spoke their language, had translated. They had pointed out their units, named them and spoken of their tiredness, their weaknesses, their lack of conviction. Lannes, therefore, was going to launch twenty thousand infantrymen at a point in their front line between the Hohenzollern guard and the reserve cavalry commanded by Liechtenstein, that prince whom the Emperor would have liked as ambassador in Paris. Berthier passed on the latest information he'd received. Aspern's church had at last been captured and Masséna was consolidating his position. Riding up from Lobau, Périgord confirmed that Davout's thirty thousand men had arrived and were marching towards Ebersdorf on the opposite bank of the Danube. They would cross the main bridge in an hour. Everything seemed to be following the plans of attack drawn up overnight. Bessières's six thousand cavalry were going to swarm into the breach opened by Lannes, while Masséna, Boudet and Davout simultaneously advanced from the villages to attack the enemy's flanks. We should have victory, the Emperor reckoned, before midday.

Knowing the influence he had on his men, and the ways to exploit it, Napoleon decided to ride along the columns and show himself. The sight of him would rouse their spirits and redouble their courage. He had his most docile grey horse brought round, climbed up a little stepladder which had been unfolded beside it, and swung himself into the saddle.

'Sire,' said Berthier, 'our troops are on the march. Why not rather stay here, where we can take in the full sweep of the battlefield?'

'My job is to cast a spell over them! I must be everywhere. I hold those fellows by their heart-strings.'

'Sire, for pity's sake, keep out of the range of the cannon!'

'Do you hear cannon? I don't. They growled at dawn to wake us, but since then they've kept silent. Do you see that star?'

'No, sire, I see no star.'

'Up there, not far from the Great Bear ...'

'No, I assure you.'

'Well then, as long as I'm the only one to see it, Berthier, I will carry on my own way and I will not suffer any remarks! Let's be off! I saw this star of mine when I set out for Italy with you. I saw it in Egypt, at Marengo, at Austerlitz, at Friedland ...'

'Sire ...'

'You are getting on my nerves, Berthier, fussing around me like an old maid! If I were going to die today, I would know!'

He rode off, loosely holding the reins and followed at a short distance by his officers. The Emperor held in his clenched fist a stone scarab which he had carried with him everywhere since Egypt, an amulet he'd picked up in a pharaoh's tomb. He felt fortune on his side. He knew that a battle was like a mass, that it demanded the same ceremony. The cheering of the troops going off to die took the place of canticles and gunpowder that of incense. He hastily made two signs of the cross, as Corsicans do when they take a important decision. An electrifying clamour greeted him as he reached the grenadiers of the Old Guard, to the rear and the left of the tileworks. Seeing him, General Dorsenne raised his tricorn and shouted, 'Present arms!' but his 'grumblers' waved their bearskins or shakos on the tips of their bayonets and bellowed the Emperor's name.

*

In the centre of the troops deployed on the edge of the plain, Marshal Lannes was giving his generals their instructions. 'The weather is brightening, gentlemen. Go and take up your commands. Oudinot and his grenadiers on the left of the front line, Claparède and Tharreau in the centre and you, Saint-Hilaire, on the right, in front of Essling.'

'Aren't we waiting for the Army of the Rhine?'

'It's already here. Davout will arrive at any moment to support us.'

Count Saint-Hilaire had the profile of a Roman coin, with short hair combed onto his forehead and a high, embroidered collar tightly buttoned up to his chin. Ramrod-straight in the saddle and firmly reining in his temperamental horse, he returned to his chasseurs, a cohort in freakish uniforms identifiable only by their green woollen epaulettes. He halted in front of the line of drummers and, noticing one who looked to him like a child, he questioned the drum-major, a colossus made even more imposing by his plumed bearskin whose sparkling uniform was thick with garlands and braid from his collar to the tops of his boots. 'How old is that boy?'

'Twelve, General.'

'And what of it?' growled the young lad.

'What of it? I think you have time to get yourself killed. Are you in such a hurry?'

'I was at Eylau before and I beat the charge at Ratisbon and I didn't get a scratch.'

'Neither did I,' laughed Saint-Hilaire, although he was lying, having forgotten the wound he'd received on the Pratzen plateau at Austerlitz.

From his saddle he looked down at the little fellow and his drum, almost as large as he was, supported by a round leather apron.

'Your name?'

'Louison.'

'Not your first name, your family name.'

'Everyone calls me Louison, sir.'

'Well, then, take your drumsticks from your shoulder strap, Louison, and play as you did at Ratisbon!'

The child obeyed. The drum-major raised his malacca cane with its silver pommel and the others began drumming in time with the little boy.

'Quick march!' ordered Saint-Hilaire.

'Quick march!' shouted General Tharreau in the distance to his men.

'Quick march!' shouted Claparède.

The army advanced into the green wheat. The fog was thinning into strips and the Austrians caught sight of Lannes's infantry as it was marching on them. The Marshal galloped forward and fell into a trot beside Saint-Hilaire. He raised his sword and the division charged, preceded by Louison who beat his drum like a madman, convinced that he too had something of a marshal about him.

Surprised by the fierceness and suddenness of the attack, the Hohenzollern soldiers tried to retaliate but the chasseurs strode over their dead comrades and rushed forward with levelled bayonets. Under the onslaught, the Austrian front lines fell back and kept on falling back. Behind the throng of infantrymen, they could see the mouths of a hundred cannon aiming at them from the crest of the slope.

In the cruellest heart of the battle, Lannes shed all his doubts. He became nothing more than a fighter. He shouted himself hoarse, gesticulating among the men whom he kept on urging forward. Leading by example, he dazzled them with his bravery, he swept them along, he parried blows, he even had a decoration torn from his chest. One moment they saw him launch his highly strung horse against some gunners, knock them to the ground and sabreing them furiously. The next, he was ignoring the whistling bullets to charge an enemy square, pick up an intricately patterned yellow flag and run a lieutenant through with its gilt spike. Saint-Hilaire rode to his aid, burying his sword in the back of a white-uniformed grenadier. Side by side they flung themselves into the fray, terrifying the enemy and inflaming their soldiers to such a degree that the Austrians, who had at first retreated methodically, started to panic, and their fear showed in the disorder of their withdrawal and the breaches that opened up as they scattered over the trampled crops.

'We are winning, Saint-Hilaire,' Lannes said, panting, and he gestured to a scene unfolding in the rear of the Austrian army. A hundred metres from them, officers were beating their runaways with sticks to make them return to the ranks.

'The Emperor was right, Your Excellency,' replied Saint-Hilaire, still on his guard.

'The Emperor was right,' repeated Lannes, looking all around him.

And then they redoubled their murderous rage, taking lethal risks, killing and yet coming through unscathed, as if they were invulnerable. Suddenly Liechtenstein's cavalry burst out on their right with sabres drawn to relieve their routed compatriots, but the chasseurs met them with a violent hail of fire. Then the cuirassiers sent by Bessières rode forward to engage and repulse them. For a long time the air was thick with the metallic clatter of cuirasses being struck by sabres. Like Eckmühl! thought Lannes. Their cavalry's only good for covering their defeated infantry. My friend Pouzet, my brother, my master, would say that either they have too much cause to be afraid or too little to believe in! We'll be celebrating this in Vienna tonight! He thought of the beautiful Rosalie, of clean sheets, of a lavish supper, of being able to sleep without nightmares. He thought also of the Duchess of Montebello, who had stayed behind in France. He saw her face, her smile; he

murmured, 'Ah! Louise-Antoinette...' Then he brandished his sword to continue the massacre.

*

Major-General Berthier had sent Lejeune to tell Davout to
speed up his march. The colonel had taken his orderly
officer with him some of the way. 'Follow me onto the
right bank and then cut along to Vienna to deliver this
letter to Mlle Krauss.'

'Gladly, Colonel,' said the orderly officer, delighted to
be given such a simple assignment so far from the battle.

He slipped the letter under his dolman and rode ahead
of his officer onto the main bridge.

'Not so fast, hothead!'

Lejeune's voice was drowned out by the noise of the
river. His orderly officer had too much of a head start to
hear. He was riding at a brisk trot and the colonel repeat-
edly thought that the imbecile was going to topple over
into the rushing waters, taking the horse and letter with
him, because the Danube was lashing the long bridge and
making it lurch from side to side. But no, he had almost
reached the other bank. He turned in his saddle, raised his
gloved hand to salute the colonel, who saluted back, and
then dug both spurs into his horse's flanks to set off on the
road to Vienna, past the troops of the Army of the Rhine.
On the horizon, above the last, thin strips of mist, Lejeune
caught sight of the tall spire of St Stephen's Cathedral and
his spirits soared: at last his letter was going to reach Anna.
He swung his gaze back to the right bank, along which the
interminable columns of Davout's men, an artillery train
and wagons of munitions and supplies were making their

way. Sent on ahead as scouts, some chasseurs à cheval in
dark green uniforms, with black fur caps as round as
bowling balls pulled down over their foreheads, were
stepping onto the bridge. With a squeeze of his knees,
Lejeune urged his horse into a walk to go and meet them
without skidding on the sodden and, in places, loose boards
of the roadway. Since the day before, the pontoneers and
sappers had organized themselves so as to check the progress of the beams, tree trunks and burning rafts the
Austrians were still launching into the current. They
patched up the bridge as soon as it was damaged and
Lejeune paid no attention to this now routine work. He
had almost reached the middle of the bridge when he was
startled by shouting. Opposite him, the troopers had halted
and were looking upstream.

The yelling was coming from a team of carpenters who
had climbed into one of the pontoons. They were nailing
the boards and strengthening the mooring ropes. Lejeune
dismounted and leant over. 'What is it?'

'They're chucking houses at us now, to break up the
bridge!'

'Houses?'

'That's right, Colonel!'

'See for yourself,' said an officer of engineers with a
thick moustache and a shirt open to the waist. He passed
his field glass to Lejeune, pointing at a spot parallel to
Aspern's blackened belfry. Lejeune scanned the Danube.
He saw figures in white uniforms scurrying about a wooded
islet. As he looked, they became clearer. The men were
bustling around a large water mill whose wheels they had
just removed. Others were forming a chain to carry large

stones. The officer of engineers had climbed up onto the bridge beside Lejeune. 'Their plan is simple, Colonel,' he explained. 'I've worked it out and it makes me shudder . . .'

'Tell me.'

'They coated the mill with tar a while ago, and now they're going to rope it onto two boats ballasted with stones. Do you see?'

'Go on . . .'

'They'll float the mill into the current and then bloody well set it alight. What can we do about that, eh?'

'Are you sure?'

'I wish I wasn't!'

'You saw them tarring this mill from here?'

'Of course! It was pale wood before and now it's black! Besides, we've known for hours what they're up to and they've been sending down burning rafts which we've had a hell of a job overturning. But this one's too big, we don't stand a chance.'

'I hope you're mistaken,' said Lejeune.

'Hoping doesn't cost a thing, Colonel. I'd love to be wrong, course I would!'

He wasn't. Obsessed by this mill as tall as a three-storey house, Lejeune studied the terrible manoeuvre. The Austrians were pushing their structure into the river; it began to float. Grenadiers accompanied it out into the middle of the Danube in skiffs to prevent it running aground on either bank. They were carrying torches wrapped in tow, which they lit with tinderboxes and threw at the base of the incendiary. The mill caught fire in a second and was carried downstream by the seething current.

The helplessness of the French increased their panic: how were they to going to stop this hellish device? Transformed into a floating inferno, the mill was approaching the large bridge, picking up speed. The barriers the engineers had rigged up to divert the burning rafts, with chains stretched across the river, wouldn't be strong enough to turn aside the colossal projectile, yet even so they all resumed their posts in the roped-together skiffs and hunched over the poles, boathooks and tree trunks pointed upstream like buffers. Each of them waited anxiously for the moment of impact and wondered if they would survive.

Lejeune slapped the crupper of his horse to send it back to the island. The chasseurs had retreated helplessly to the right bank and Davout's columns of soldiers, horrified by the spectacle, had rested their muskets on the ground. The burning mill grew larger as it came closer, listing from side to side in the choppy waters without toppling over. As it drew level with the skiffs and the chains, parts of its timber frame broke off and crashed into the water, sizzling and giving off a thick smoke, but the bulk of it stayed upright and increased its speed. When it crashed into the chains, it tore them loose and flung the skiffs and their crews against its blazing timbers. The skiffs burst into flames and were lost in the swirling waters. A soldier was catapulted against the burning tar, but no one could hear his hoarse screams and he, in turn, sank into the Danube. Now nothing impeded the burning mill's course. Some pontoneers, seeing there was no time to climb onto the roadway and get away before the collision, dived into the river and the waves battered them against the hulls of the pontoons. Lejeune felt someone grab his arm. It was the moustachioed officer pulling him back and he ran towards the Lobau. Behind him he heard a huge crash and the bridge shuddered. The officer and Lejeune were thrown flat on their stomachs on the drenched boards. Sparks rained down around them, and were extinguished by the great waves thrown up by the impact. A number of sappers, their uniforms on fire, fell into the water and drowned. When he pulled himself up onto his elbows, Lejeune saw the extent of the catastrophe: the large bridge had broken open and its two halves were drifting away from the banks. The shattered mill was still burning and the mooring ropes, the beams and the roadway were catching fire.

*

Two young men were walking along the Jordangasse. They were both almost the same tender age and wore dark woollen frock coats and top hats. The oldest, who must have been twenty, toyed with his cane to give himself a nonchalant air. The other, Friedrich Staps, had not gone back to his room in the Krauss household that night and so didn't know that it had been visited by Schulmeister, the police officer, and that his underhand manner, his mocking remarks, his air of secrecy and the statuette of Joan of Arc had aroused the suspicions of Henri Beyle, the French lodger on the floor below. When they finally reached his lodgings, instead of saying goodbye, Ernst hurried Friedrich on, murmuring without looking at him, 'Keep walking as if we're out for a harmless stroll. Don't turn around . . .' Friedrich obeyed because his friend had sensed some danger but he didn't dare ask him the grounds for his distrust until they reached the nearby Judenplatz. They pretended to look into a tailor's window. 'What have I to be afraid of?'

'There was a Berline opposite your front door.'

'There may have been.'

'I've got a sixth sense for the law.'

'The police? Are you sure? No one knows me in Vienna.'

'Let's be on our guard. Our comrades will put you up, don't set foot in that house again. Did you leave your things there?'

'Oh, yes . . .'

He was thinking mainly of his statuette, since he had kept his knife with him.

'Never mind,' said Ernst.

'It can't be helped,' sighed young Staps, but the exploits he was going to perform demanded sacrifices on his part.

The previous evening, Staps had met Ernst von der Sahala in the quiet salon of a Viennese café. They had recognized each other immediately – by a sense of affinity – without needing to introduce themselves.

'How is our brother, Pastor Wiener?' Ernst had asked.

'May God bless him for having recommended me to you!'

They were both German and Lutheran, but Ernst was a member of the Illuminati who, like other sects of the time – Colonel Oudet's Philadelphians, the Concordists, the Black Knights – declared themselves tyrannicides and called for the death of Napoleon, the oppressor of peoples. The two boys had talked for a long time without showing any outward emotion, their voices rendered inaudible to the neighbouring tables by the playing of a violin. Then they had wandered along the ramparts, admiring the countryside lit up by the fires of the battle. Staps had spoken of his mission. He told how he had disappeared from his home one morning, leaving a note for his father: 'I'm going to do

what God has ordered me'. He believed he was chosen. He
had heard voices. He had passionately read Wieland's
Oberon, the naive poem inspired by the Middle Ages in
which a dwarf, the elf king, helped Huon of Bordeaux in
his expedition to Babylon. Thanks to a magic horn and
bowl, Huon won the hand of the Caliph's daughter, after
stealing hairs from her father's beard and three of his
molars. Above all, he had read Schiller, the sentimental
Schiller, inhuman in his nobility, and he had been transported by the *Maid of Orleans*. He had become Joan of Arc.
Like her, he would liberate Germany and Austria from the
Ogre's yoke. And so he bought a knife.

Eight o'clock in the morning sounded from the clock
towers. The two boys walked through the streets of the old
town, arm in arm, singing softly as if they were a little
drunk. 'In war,' Ernst had said, 'patrols never challenge
people if they're out carousing on a spree.' They passed the
Dominican church and ran into a police patrol, who made
fun of them. Finally Ernst led his new follower into a
covered passageway which brought them to a paved courtyard. Ernst headed straight for one of the doors and
knocked several times according to a code. It opened and
they entered a corridor and then a long room weakly lit by
two candles. At the end of a table, a thin, old man dressed
in black was reading the Bible.

'Pastor,' Ernst said to him, 'we must give this brother
shelter.'

'He can leave his bags here. Martha will take him up to
the rooms on the third floor.'

'He has no bags. We'll have to get him what he needs.'

'What he needs?' the old pastor said. 'Hear what the
Prophet Jeremiah tells us . . .' He took his Bible and read in

a quavering voice: ' "For this is the day of the Lord God of Hosts, a day of vengeance, that he may avenge him of his adversaries: and the sword shall devour, and it shall be satiate and made drunk with their blood. The nations have heard of thy shame, O daughter of Egypt, and thy cry hath filled the land: for the mighty man hath stumbled against the mighty, and they are fallen both together." '

'How beautiful that is,' said Ernst.

'How true,' said Friedrich Staps.

*

Napoleon was pale, his skin almost translucent, his face as smooth and expressionless as an unfinished statue. He looked at the sky then lowered his empty eyes to the ground. Standing at the head of the large bridge, which had broken apart moments before and now pitched and rolled like a boat, he was observing the burnt mill; its smoking wreckage would have to be removed before the two halves of the roadway could be coupled together over a span of a hundred metres, and the breach repaired through which the river was rolling like a mountain torrent. Mute, more dumbfounded than upset, the Emperor kept his hands behind his back, but gripped his whip tightly. That morning, the situation had favoured him; the offensive had been taking effect. Lannes was routing the Austrian centre and pursuing his forays deep into their lines, while Masséna and Boudet waited to lead their divisions out of the villages. But on those immense plains the Emperor couldn't apply his usual tactics. Surprise and rapidity: he had tried these when the army surged across from Lobau and they had bought him to the brink of victory. But war was changing. As under the monarchies, battles now were played out between rival artilleries and rival regiments, with masses of troops launched against other masses – always more men, more dead, more canister shot and musketry. The sight of the extra men he needed on the other bank drove him into a fury: Davout's army at a standstill, his cannon, his wagons of powder and supplies, his useless columns of men.

A few paces behind him, ill at ease and anxious, Berthier and a group of officers didn't dare move or speak. They waited, hoping for the dazzling order, the moment of inspiration that would turn their predicament on its head. Lejeune was among them, bareheaded, without his shako, his uniform in disarray. Without looking round, transfixed by this bridge, too long and too fragile, which defied his will, the Emperor called out, 'Bertrand!'

Discreet and devoted, General Count Bertrand stepped up, his hat under his arm, and stood to attention. The Emperor had decided where the bridge was to be thrown across the river, he alone had determined the time needed for it to be built, but he constantly wanted to lay blame on others and Bertrand was in command of the Engineers.

'*Sabotatore!*'

'Sire, I carried out your orders to the letter.'

'Traitor! Look at it, this bridge of yours!'

'In one night, sire, it was not in our power to construct anything better on such a difficult river.'

'Traitor! Traitor!' Rounding on the others, he said, '*Ha agito da traditore!* And you as well! All of you! You betray me!'

No one replied. There was no use. The Emperor had to vent his wrath.

'Bertrand!'

'Sire?'

'How long to repair your sabotage?'

'At least two days, sire . . .'

'Two days!'

Bertrand caught a powerful blow of the whip full in
the face. The Emperor was breathing heavily. He walked
towards his horse and, with an impatient wave, asked
Berthier to follow.

'Did you hear the insolence of that damned Bertrand?'

'Yes, sire,' said Berthier.

'Forty-eight hours! Where is the Archduke?'

'In his camp on the Bisamberg, sire.'

'Hmm . . . He will soon learn of our misfortune.'

'Certainly in an hour or two. And he will seize on it to
send all his reserve troops against us.'

'Unless we persevere with the attack, Berthier! Lannes
is in an excellent position, he has thrown the Hohenzollern
infantry into confusion!'

'But we're going to run short of munitions.'

'Davout can ferry supplies across in boats.'

'In small quantities, sire, and with a high risk of cap-
sizing.'

'Then we'll order the withdrawal.'

'If we withdraw, sire, the Archduke's armies will
regroup.'

'And if we do not withdraw, the Archduke will attack
our poorly protected flanks and it will be a massacre! We
must fall back.'

'Where, sire? Onto the island?'

'Of course! Not into the Danube, you idiot!'

'It's impossible, in the time we have, to take across somewhere near fifty thousand men, and cannon and *matériel*, before the Archduke falls on our rear from the riverbank.'

'Let's first withdraw without haste to last night's positions. Masséna and Boudet will entrench the villages, Lannes will hold the slope. When night has fallen, we will blockade ourselves on the island.'

'So, we have to hold out for ten hours...'

'Yes!'

*

Once again at nine o'clock in the morning, Colonel Lejeune was galloping joylessly through the wheatfields, this time to deliver Marshal Lannes's order to withdraw. He passed a procession of Austrian prisoners marching in the opposite direction, an entire battalion of fusiliers without muskets or caps, their eyes fixed on the ground, some with slash wounds and a perfunctory bandage round their heads or their arms in slings. A few limping stragglers brought up the rear, their gaiters stained with blood. They marched past into the wheat, led like a flock of geese by young Louison, who was improvising a remorseless saraband on his great drum. Despite his heavy heart, Lejeune smiled. It reminded him of Guéhéneuc's adventure after the victory at Eckmühl. The colonel was delivering a message when he came across a regiment of enemy cavalry wandering aimlessly in the dark, who, without further ado, had surrendered. The Emperor had been greatly amused. 'So, Guéhéneuc, you're the fellow who surrounded the Austrian cavalry singlehanded, are you?' But behind that morning's batch of prisoners came Lannes's men, wild-haired, swaggering and dressed in their spoils like bandits. They carried enemy muskets under their arms like firewood and hauled five undamaged cannon with the caissons still coupled, pouches stuffed with cartridges and a flag riddled with bullets.

Lejeune carried on towards the front line which had pushed so far forward that, in the distance, he could see chasseurs à cheval in the hamlet of Breintenlee, on the flank of the firing. Marshal Lannes was sitting on a caisson without wheels, directing the battle by dictating the necessary orders to his aides-de-camp, who ran to deliver them to Saint-Hilaire, Claparède or Tharreau.

When Lejeune dismounted, Lannes frowned and exclaimed, 'Ah! Here comes the colonel, our harbinger of doom!'

'I'm afraid Your Excellency is right.'

'Speak.'

'Your Excellency . . .'

'Speak! I have grown accustomed to terrible news.'

'You must halt the attack.'

'What? Repeat that piece of nonsense!'

'The offensive is suspended.'

'Again! Barely an hour ago your comrade Périgord asked the same of me so that the damage a burning raft had done to that devil of a bridge could be repaired! Is it made of straw, this bridge of yours?'

'Your Excellency . . .'

'Do you know what's been happening, Lejeune? Over there, they formed up the minute we gave them a breathing space and we had to break through them again. And we did. We left some of our lads behind on the field, but we routed the Austrians a second time! And what, we're expected to sit down and watch those Hohenzollern puppets rally round again?'

'The Emperor has ordered a withdrawal to Essling.'

'What?'

'It's more serious this time.'

Lejeune explained the recent events to Lannes. Thrown by the news, the marshal lost all patience. 'We held victory in our grasp! We held it, I tell you! One hour more, with Davout's support, and it would have been all up with the Archduke . . .'

Then he dictated his orders to his aides-de-camp. 'Bessières is to pull the cavalry back to between the villages, Saint-Hilaire and the others are to withdraw in good order, but gradually, so that our about-face isn't obvious. It must look as if we have a new strategy, as if we're hoping for reinforcements to arrive at any moment or allowing the artillery to deploy on the plain. We have to keep the Austrians guessing and not give them anything to cheer about.'

He stood up to watch his officers leave to deliver the painful orders, then noticed that Lejeune hadn't moved. 'Thank you, Colonel. You may return to the Headquarters Staff. If you come through this and one day find yourself telling our story, however far-fetched it may sound, I give you leave to say that you saw Marshal Lannes undone – oh, not in combat of course, but by an order. All it needs is one word to lay a soldier low. What does Masséna think of this?'

'I couldn't say, Your Excellency.'

'It must enrage him as much as me, but he has a longer

fuse and keeps his tongue under a tighter rein. He never lets anything show. Unless he doesn't give a hang . . .'

Lannes took a deep breath and threw out his chest. 'I wish this withdrawal to be a model of its kind. Run and tell His Majesty that.'

Lejeune rode off, leaving Marshal Lannes standing in the wheat. He thought that this was no ordinary battle; their spirits rose and fell too often and it wore their nerves thin. The fighting was beginning to die down. It was already very hot. Lejeune felt like taking a long siesta. How he would have loved Vienna if he had come simply as a traveller. He heard Anna Krauss's German songs echoing in his ears. When the war was over, they'd go to the Opéra together. With high, jerky steps his horse picked its way between the corpses of both armies.

*

Colonel Lejeune's orderly officer was greedily devouring a cold chicken. After he had handed the letter to Mlle Krauss, he had met Henri who had instantly bombarded him with questions. He was a decent lad but something of a braggart who loved to sing his own praises and so he had pretended to be exhausted by the fighting he'd witnessed from a distance, safe on the island of Lobau, until Henri asked him if he was hungry. Then he had brightened up and followed him to the kitchens, his muddy boots treading dirt into the floorboards. A chair was drawn up at the table covered with provisions delivered on the sly from the commissariat. Feeling quite at home, his coat unbuttoned, he plunged his hands into the various dishes, punctuating his sentences with a wave of a gnawed drumstick and charging his glass with a light Viennese white wine so often that the carafe became smeared with greasy fingerprints. 'Yesterday was hard going,' he said, as he chewed and took another drink, 'but the Colonel didn't get a scratch, I swear, and this morning, when I left him on the long bridge, Marshal Davout's army was coming in the nick of time with cannon and wagons of supplies.'

'Supplies which, judging from your appetite, were running awfully low!'

'When it came to that, yes, Monsieur Beyle. It was a close-run thing. All the poaching meant that there was no game left on the island at all.'

'And what about in the field?'

'Everything is proceeding admirably under the inspired command of His Majesty. At least that's what Colonel Lejeune said to me, Monsieur, but he wasn't lying, you could tell that from the confident air he had about him. The Austrians are getting a thrashing, there, that's the truth of it, and our men are flying at them. Victory is within our grasp.'

Anna had entered the room, holding the anodyne letter Louis-François had written her in German, and she was staring fixedly at the ravenous lieutenant, whom she found extremely vulgar. Having paid a visit to check that Henri was taking his potions and that his health was improving, Dr Carino translated the officer's news for her in a low voice. Anna gradually became paler. She wrapped herself up in her embroidered shawl as if it was cold, and crumpled the letter in her clenched fist. Henri observed her out of the corner of his eye and he found it hard to understand why she wasn't in the least overjoyed by the good news. Then he said to himself that the young woman was Austrian, perhaps her father was fighting for the Archduke; she would justifiably be anxious on his behalf, one side's victory would mean the other's rout and, whatever the outcome, the situation was bound to be painful for her. This contradicted the theories Henri was developing, based on his conviction that love surpasses and eclipses family ties just as surely as those of nationality. He reflected on this, barely listening to the orderly officer who was describing dashing exploits under fire while attacking a hare terrine. What if Anna were not in love with Louis-François? In that case, did Henri stand a chance?

'Then,' the orderly continued, gulping down an enormous mouthful of terrine, 'the Emperor ordered the offensive and the whole army came out of a bank of fog . . .'

But that's it, Henri persuaded himself with a smile. She doesn't love him. Anna was looking wretched and she fell into a chair as Carino continued to describe the advance of Napoleon's armies and the flight of the Hohenzollern regiments, which the lieutenant was transforming into wholesale defeat. Anna's eyes welled with tears and the crumpled letter, which she didn't even consider worth picking up, fell to the floor. The doctor put a hand on her shoulder and she burst out sobbing, to the great astonishment of the lieutenant who kept on working his jaw muscles like a cow chewing the cud. He filled a glass to the brim and stood up to offer it the young woman. 'It's given her a shock, the poor lady, a little wine will set her right . . .'

Henri stopped him, took the glass and drank it himself. 'What she needs most is rest.'

'Ah, war! When you haven't had a taste of it, it can really shake you up.'

The lieutenant cut himself a thick slice of terrine and

continued his chatter. 'That's not like the Duke of Monte-bello's mistress. She's an old hand, no doubt about that. She came onto the island and she even asked me, because I happened to be there . . .'

'Thank you, Lieutenant, thank you,' said Henri, to cut him short. He wanted to help Carino take Anna back to her room, but she feverishly waved him away. The doctor apologized for her, raising his eyes to the ceiling. When they had gone out, Henri bent down to pick up Lejeune's letter, which he smoothed out and was unable to read.

'Do you understand German, Lieutenant?'

'Oh, no, Monsieur Beyle, very sorry. I can get by in Spanish, that's not too bad, owing to the spell we put in there with the Colonel during that damned rebellion of theirs, but German, no, I haven't had the time yet.'

Then he bored Henri senseless with his reflections on the difficulties of that particular language.

*

Vincent Paradis's sleep was filled with naive images which were barely dreams, more like pictures and always the same ones, taking him back to his village, the surrounding hills and the badly kept-up courtyard where his father mixed leaves with scraps to make compost. They lived off what grew in the fields and, depending on the year, met their needs. Last year they'd killed a pig. Such a rare event had been a memorable occasion. The neighbours had taken part and they'd quartered the animal and filled the salting tub. The mayor had given them the salt and, since he didn't know how to fill out the registers, he'd also protected them from the gentlemen of the town, especially the one who had it in mind to drain the swamps. In their part of the world, they knew all about monotony and death from natural causes, but then the gendarmes and soldiers had come to pick out the strongest for the war. Like his eldest brother, Vincent had drawn the short straw and his family didn't have a sou to pay someone to take his place. He had baulked at imitating his friend Bruhat, who worked at the tannery and had come up with a way to stay in the country. With a laugh, he'd showed his toothless mouth. 'Oh yes, I pulled them all out by the roots, because, you see, without teeth you can't open cartridges and they don't want anything to do with you!' Vincent had followed the sergeants meekly and full of regret.

'Hey! On your feet, you sluggard!'

Vincent Paradis felt a clog kicking him in the shoulder. Yawning, he opened his eyes and saw Morillon, the medical orderly in charge of the battalion of ambulance men which he had been drafted into the day before on Dr Percy's orders.

Paradis pushed himself off what had been his pillow for the night and realized that it was a dead man, but it didn't shock him because he'd seen a mass of them by then. He simply muttered, 'Sleep in peace, comrade, and who knows, see you soon . . .' Without a musket to lug about, he felt light on his feet and followed Morillon as he had followed the recruiting sergeants before. The ambulance battalion was made up of louts and the scum of big cities who'd do anything for a piece of gold, because Dr Percy paid them out of his own pocket so he could employ them as he wished. They were fanned out in a line behind a wagon with big wheels on which they were putting those who had been wounded in the battle. Two medical orderlies accompanied them to sort the dying into groups: the most seriously wounded would be sent to the ambulance post at the entrance of the little forest, the rest evacuated onto the island. The troop passed through rows of maimed soldiers who had collected on the riverbank. The wind covered them with clouds of dust and they shaded themselves from the fierce sun with leaves they had torn from the clumps of reeds. Some dragged themselves to the Danube to vomit into its waters, others were convulsed by spasms. There were hundreds of them, groaning, screaming, moaning in agony, mumbling incomprehensible sentences and raving deliriously. They insulted the ambulance men, and feebly tried to grab hold of their breeches. They wanted to be finished with it all, one way or another, which was why any weapon that could still do harm had been put out of their reach: every sword, bayonet and knife with which they would gladly have opened their veins, stopped the pain and disappeared, once and for all.

The ambulance men followed the wagon along the riverbank as far as Essling where General Boudet's division, having been forbidden to mount an attack, had set about barricading itself in. The entrenched village now presented a sort of defensive wall towards the plain. Furniture, mattresses, broken caissons and corpses were piled pell-mell up to the first floor of the stone houses which had been blown open by cannonballs and, overnight, the breaches had been blocked with harrows and rubble. The most recent casualties were waiting under the trees lining the main street, on the grass which some of them were soaking with blood. A captain propped himself up against a tree, his left eye covered with a bloodstained handker-chief, and he grimaced as he bit down on his pipe hard enough to split a tooth. Paradis helped lift up a dragoon who had taken a lance thrust in the side of the forehead; one could see where the bone had been cut into. Then a voltigeur, who screamed as he was put in the wagon on the bundles of hay. His shoulder blade was shattered and Morillon, with an expert air, commented, 'A good amount of flesh will have to be cut away to get at those splinters of bone . . .'

'You operate as well, do you, Monsieur Morillon?' Paradis asked, dazzled by such a display of scientific knowledge.

'I assist Dr Percy, you know that!'

'Will this poor lad make it?'

'I'm not a fortune teller! Come on! We haven't got time to waste!'

The din of the battle could be heard again. It seemed to be getting closer. So, the Austrians weren't withdrawing any more. The wounded squeezed onto the wagon which did a half-turn towards the little wood and the Danube. Paradis wiped his red, sticky hands on the grass. His ears rang with the sound of groaning but he was proud of his new assignment. Dr Percy and his assistants would be sure to save a few bodies from the maggots.

Just before the small bridge, where they were going to unload their pitiful cargo, the ambulance men met a procession of skirmishers carrying the body of an officer on a plank who was thrashing around in agony.

'Whooah!' Paradis said. 'That's got to be at least a colonel, with all that gold braid on his chest!'

'Count Saint-Hilaire,' said Morillon, who knew all the generals of the Empire by sight.

Paradis, forgetting the wounded he'd picked up, posted himself in front of the ambulance door. The soldiers laid the officer on Percy's table. 'He's had his left foot taken off by canister shot...'

'I can see that!' Percy said, tearing off what was left of the boot and shouting, 'Lint!'

'None left.'

'A piece of jacket, a rag, some straw, grass, anything!'

Paradis tore off his shirt-tail and handed it to the doctor. The latter used it to wipe his forehead, which was covered in sweat. He was exhausted. He had been amputating constantly for more than a day now. His sight was becoming blurred. With a white-hot cauterizing iron he burnt the wound to kill the nerve endings. Saint-Hilaire opened his mouth wide as if to scream, but made do with a grimace instead. His face drawn with pain, he stiffened and then fell back onto the table as Percy began sawing off his ankle because tetanus had set in. The doctor paused, lifted the patient's eyelid and announced, 'Gentlemen, you can take the general away. He has just died.'

Paradis never found out whether General Saint-Hilare was entitled to an immediate burial or if they waited to take his body back to Vienna, because Morillon sent him and ten other ambulance men to prepare broth for the wounded. They went away grumbling but at least cookhouse fatigue was not dangerous. Fresh supplies were still on the right bank with Davout and no one could fight or survive on an empty stomach, so Percy's battalions had been ordered to help the cooks on the mobile canteens. Teams of men had spent the previous night scouring the ground between the villages for dead horses whose bellies were beginning to swell up. They tied ropes around them and artillery nags had dragged them back to the ambulance, where they formed a hideous mound of muzzles, manes,

hooves and hocks. Paradis and his new workmates were to
cut up the carcasses with blunt swords or cleavers. Then
the quarters of fresh meat would be thrown into a cuirass
from a pile of them that had been salvaged, covered with
muddy water from the Danube and set to boil on a series
of fires. Gunpowder would do for seasoning. Paradis had
started quartering when a band of starving voltigeurs
marched up to him. 'You're not giving all that to men
who're going to die anyway, are you?'

'You've got your rations,' answered Fat Louis, who was
in charge of the apprentice butchers.

'Our mess tins are empty.'

'Well, too bad!'

The voltigeurs surrounded him and threatened him
with their bayonets. 'Shove over!'

'If it's swordplay you're after,' said Fat Louis, raising his
cleaver, 'the Austrians are crying out for your sort!'

'And there's plenty of horses to eat on the plain,' added
Paradis.

'Thanks, my lad, but that's where we've come from.
Shove over!'

The voltigeur bundled Paradis out of the way and sank
his bayonet into the neck of a grey mare. Fat Louis chopped
the bayonet in half with his cleaver. Two soldiers as
scrawny and vicious as wolves grabbed him from behind,
calling him a stinking civvy. He lashed out and they started
fighting. Paradis ran and hid behind the mound of glassy-
eyed horses. The soldiers and ambulance men were throwing entrails in one another's faces, while one sly devil cut
himself off a piece and sank his fangs into the meat.

*

Bessières had taken the Emperor's unwarranted reprimand hard and resolved, from that moment on, not to take the slightest initiative. He would defer absolutely to Lannes's orders, whether he approved or not, without thinking of ways they might be improved, and consequently delay the movements of his troops. He applied all his ingenuity to keeping his cavalry safe, only sending to the front the squadrons he was ordered to send. They were to withdraw? So be it. They were to attack? So be it. He had been kept awake all night, brooding over his anger. He had inspected his troops, worn out two horses and, with his Gascon dragoons, breakfasted on a slice of bread rubbed with garlic. The Emperor disappointed him but he put a brave face on it. They shared a similar history, hated by the Jacobins and despised by the Republic, even though Marshal Bessières's links with the nobility were purely a matter of the education he'd received at the hands of his surgeon father, an abbot who was a relative and the teachers at the Saint-Michel de Cahors school. He understood the Emperor's methods and they cut him to the quick: did so much hatred have to be stirred up for him to rule? Two years earlier, Lannes himself had been mortified when, at the last moment, the Emperor had preferred Bessières to him to go and meet the Tsar at Tilsit. Whims bear little relation to sense, Bessières thought as he studied the plain. Through his spyglass he saw the Austrians redeploying their cannon and pouring canister shot into the unfortunate Saint-Hilaire's battalions, whom Lannes, the pigheaded fool, was mustering to his rear. An isolated shot rang out, sharp and distinct amongst the confused din of the fighting. It came from a company of cuirassiers. Bessières steered his horse in their direction and found two dismounted troopers quarrelling. One of them had blood all over his hand. Captain Saint-Didier, rather than keeping them apart, was helping the taller cuirassier pin the struggling wounded man to the ground.

'An accident?' asked Bessières.

'Your Excellency,' said the captain, 'Cuirassier Brunel tried to kill himself.'

'And I knocked the carbine away,' added Fayolle, holding his friend down with all his weight, one knee on his chest.

'An accident. Get that hand dressed.'

Bessières didn't order any punishment for Cuirassier Brunel, who had snapped under the strain. Suicides, like desertions, were on the rise amongst the army. It was no longer unusual in the middle of a battle for a conscript at the limits of his endurance to creep away into a thicket and blow his brains out. The marshal turned around and rejoined a regiment of black-maned dragoons, disappearing amidst the brass helmets bound in navy-blue calfskin which gleamed in the sun. Brunel pulled himself up on his elbows, gasping for breath. A cuirassier cut strips from his saddle cloth for him to bandage his hand, two fingers of which had been sheared away by the bullet. Captain Saint-Didier took a flask of alcohol from his saddle holster, uncorked it and stuck it between the trooper's lips. 'Drink and then back in the saddle!'

'With his hand mashed up like that?' asked Fayolle.

'He doesn't need his left hand to hold a sword!'

'But he does to hold the bridle.'

'He can just wind it round his wrist!'

Fayolle helped Brunel put his feet back in the stirrups, grumbling, 'The horses can't take any more, either.'

'We'll ride them until they drop!'

'Aah, Captain! If the horses knew how to shoot, I tell you, they'd kill themselves straight off!'

Brunel looked at his comrade. 'You shouldn't have done that.'

'Bah . . .'

Fayolle couldn't think of anything clever to say, but he wouldn't have had time to either, because once again the trumpets were blowing the assembly, once again they drew their swords, once again they set their horses off at a jog-trot towards the Austrian batteries.

As they crested the slope, they found themselves facing lines of cannon ploughing up the green wheat, but when the trumpets summoned them to attack, it was impossible to force their exhausted horses into a gallop. Poorly fed on barley, their strength sapped by endless cavalry charges, none of them could manage more than a brisk trot, the most gruelling pace for cuirassiers. Jolted up and down in the saddle at every stride, their steel backplates and breast-plates cutting into their shoulders, necks and hips, they were even more exposed to the constant fire, because the cannons spat relentlessly, almost like a fusillade, and the roundshot fell like driving rain, ravaging their ranks. Even so, Saint-Didier's troopers charged slowly forward under the hail of fire, their swords drawn. Fayolle thought he was riding to certain death but it was Brunel, his neighbour, who went to hell first. A roundshot took off his head and, as his heart kept beating out of habit, jets of blood came spurting out of the top of his cuirass. Frozen in the saddle with his sword arm stiffly outstretched and his sword dangling from the lanyard round his wrist, the headless trooper rode on to dash himself against the line of artillery.

At the same moment and in the same volley of cannon fire, Fayolle's horse had a hoof sliced off and it span around, whinnying with pain. Fayolle dismounted, paying no attention to the barrage of canister shot. He looked fondly at the worn-out animal; it was standing on three legs and licking his face as if to say farewell. The cuirassier let himself fall full length into the wheat. Flat on his back, arms crossed, forgetting death and its racket, he closed his eyes and fell asleep.

*

Napoleon had halted at the edge of the lethal plain which the Austrians were bombarding remorselessly with two hundred guns. His officers had mangaged to persuade him against riding into Aspern, where he wanted to restore the courage of Masséna's men.

'Don't take pointless risks!'

'The battle is lost if you are killed!'

'You're trembling as much as my horse,' Napoleon had growled, holding the reins too tight, but he had sent an emissary to the village to find out how matters stood.

'Here is Laville, sire . . .'

A young officer in a stylish uniform galloped up. To report more quickly, he jumped the fences round the enclosures and reached the Emperor out of breath. 'The Duke of Rivoli, sire.'

'He's dead?'

'He has retaken Aspern, sire.'

'He'd lost that devil of a village, then, had he?'

'Lost it and retaken it, sire, but the Hessians of the Confederation of the Rhine have been of great service to him.'

'And now?'

'His position appears to be a strong one.'

'I'm not asking what his position appears to be but what he thinks of it!'

'The Duke was sitting on a tree trunk, he was perfectly composed, he assured me that he could hold out for twenty hours if necessary.'

The Emperor made no reply: this young aide-de-camp irritated him. He abruptly wheeled his horse and the little band headed back to the tile factory where the Major-General was waiting and praying that he hadn't been killed. The Emperor asked for his arm to dismount, complaining, as he did so, about his unruly horse. Once on the ground, he said, 'Berthier, send General Rapp to give the Duke of Rivoli the support he needs.'

'He is a general on your headquarters staff, sire.'

'I am aware of that, damn it!'

'With which troops?'

'Put him in command of two battalions of the fusiliers of my Guard.'

Then the Emperor immersed himself in the map which two aides-de-camp held unfolded at eye level. As on the previous day, the front stretched in a semicircle from one village to the other, its arc ending, on both sides, at the Danube. The Austrians had to be prevented from breaking through this deployment, so that they could effect a complete withdrawal onto the Lobau when night fell. The Emperor couldn't hesitate any longer. He had to use the Guard, which had been kept in reserve until then, to strengthen an extremely precarious position. Berthier, who had dictated and signed Rapp's orders, came back to deliver the latest information he had received. 'Boudet has barricaded himself in Essling, sire, and set up firing positions throughout the village, but he is not threatened yet. The Archduke is directing the bulk of his forces against our centre. He is leading the attack in person, with the twelve battalions of Hohenzollern grenadiers . . .'

'Supplies?'

'Davout is sending us what ammunition he can by boat but the oarsmen are having trouble not to be swept downstream, past the island.'

'Lannes?'

'His aide-de-camp will report to Your Majesty himself.'

Berthier pointed at Captain Marbot, who was sitting on a caisson and unravelling strips of tow to dress a thigh wound which was staining his breeches with blood. 'Marbot!' the Emperor said. 'Only the Major-General's dispatch riders are entitled to wear red breeches!'

'I am entitled to on one leg, sire.'

'Your turn comes round often enough!'

'Nothing serious, sire, just a flesh wound.'

'Lannes?'

'He is keeping up the fight and pulling Saint-Hilaire's men back in front of Essling.'

'And facing him?'

'At first the Hungarian grenadiers struck terror into the youngest recruits, who had never seen such strapping and moustachioed fellows, but His Excellency gave them heart by shouting, "We're no worse than at Marengo, and the enemy's no better!"'

The Emperor pulled a face and his blue eyes faded for a moment to grey: like a cat, he had the ability to change their colour according to his mood. Marengo? Lannes's example was a clumsy one. Of course Desaix's infantry had

routed the grenadiers of General Zach, whom the Archduke was leading today, but it had been a very close-run
thing. Kellerman, the son of the victor of Valmy, had
followed up with a decisive cavalry charge, but what if
General Ott's army corps had arrived in time? Napoleon
thought of Davout, who had not arrived in time. What
thread did victories hang by? A delay, a gust of wind, the
whim of a river.

*

'See for yourself, Colonel.'

General Boudet pushed Lejeune into a wooden case-
mate cobbled together from wardrobe uprights and
ammunition boxes. That section of Essling's fortifications
commanded a panoramic view of the plain and, from here,
the enemy's movements could be surveyed without undue
risk. Lejeune looked out as he had been invited. 'We're
soon going to have several regiments on our backs,' Boudet
insisted wearily. 'The Archduke hasn't been able to break
through Lannes's battalions and Bessières's squadrons, so,
with good reason, he is now turning to this village which
he assumes to be less heavily defended. Hours of bombardment and musketry have brought us to our knees. The
men are tired, they're hungry and they're starting to be
afraid.'

Lejeune could see the Hungarian regiments advancing
towards Essling in order of attack. Vast waves of them
were going to break against the barricades of furniture and
stones which were too flimsy to hold for long. Given their
numbers, they would swamp General Boudet's already
decimated division. In the middle of the infantrymen and
the black fur caps, the Archduke himself, flag in hand, was

directing the floodtide as it began to roll towards the village. The soldiers standing mutely on sentry duty shivered or felt despair as they watched this deployment.

'Take the news to His Majesty,' the general ordered Lejeune. 'You have seen, you have understood. If I don't get help very soon, we're all headed for disaster. Once they're in Essling, the Austrians will be able to reach the Danube. Rosenberg's cavalry is pawing the ground behind the wood. If the line is broken here, he'll be able to get through and cut off our rear. The whole army will be caught in a pincer movement.'

'I'm on my way, General, but you?'

'I'm evacuating the village.'

'Where to?'

'To the granary, back there a way, at the end of the avenue of elms. It has thick walls, dormer windows and reinforced sheet-metal doors. I've already had what's left of our munitions and powder taken there and we're going to try to hold out as long as possible. It's a fortress.'

A shell trailing its fuse fell a few metres away from them, then another. A wall collapsed. A roof caught fire. General Boudet passed a hand over his lined face. 'Hurry, Lejeune, it's beginning.'

The colonel remounted, but Boudet held him back. 'Tell His Majesty . . .'

'Yes?'

'What you have observed.'

Lejeune spurred his horse into a full gallop and rode off down the main street. Boudet watched him depart, muttering, 'Tell His Majesty to go to hell . . .'

He called his officers and ordered the drummers to beat an immediate retreat. At this sound, the voltigeurs left their posts, emerging from the church, the houses and from behind the barricades to gather together in a confused throng. The cannonade was getting heavier.

Fifteen hundred men fell back to the granary and prepared to withstand a siege. Muskets pointed out of the dormer windows and windows half shielded by shutters. The doors were wedged open to accommodate the barrels of the cannon which had been hoisted into the ground-floor rooms that morning. A section of infantry took up positions nearby in grassy ditches, folds in the ground and behind the elms. The village was ablaze. The barricades must have already been shattered by roundshot.

There wasn't long to wait. Barely half an hour had passed before the first white uniforms loomed up at the end of the avenue and in the neighbouring fields, running, bent double under their packs. Boudet recognized the regimental colours of Baron d'Aspre's grenadiers. He gave the order to fire. The guns played havoc with the first wave of attackers, but they were coming from all directions, in serried ranks, vast numbers of them, and there wasn't even time to wheel the flaming cannon inside to reload them. Musket fire sprayed from every window, behind the wire grilles and up on the roof; the Austrians were falling, but others were taking their places and running full tilt at the granary's solid walls. Boudet took a musket and laid out an officer in a grey cloak who was yelling as he raised his curved sabre. The man crumpled to the ground, but nothing stopped the soldiers in white, some of whom were working their way along the walls, carrying axes which they sank into the shutters and closed doors. Inside, the voltigeurs were coughing because of the smoke and the lack of air. Some were wounded by ricochets. They squatted down, reloaded, jumped up at the corner of a window, levelled their muskets and aimed blindly into the mass of men as if at a flock of starlings. They'd hit something, obviously, but, unable to see what, they'd crouch down once more, load, stand up, fire, duck down again and so on for an eternity.

Eventually the fighting began to lose its edge. On the third floor, through the gap left by a sheet-metal shutter, Boudet saw intervals opening up between the waves of Austrian attacks. He ordered the ceasefire, and then everyone heard a familiar roll of drums. Boudet smiled, shook a young soldier who was as white as chalk, and roared in his Bordeaux accent, 'Lads! We're going to come through this yet!'

Relieved, they opened the windows to peer out. They saw the green and red plumes of the fusiliers of the Young Guard. The uhlans threw down their lances and unsheathed their more wieldy sabres for hand-to-hand combat. The battle was shifting back to the village. Boudet walked outside, holding a musket, as a plumed officer came out in front of the granary in the centre of a cavalcade. 'Monsieur, General Mouton and four battalions of the Imperial Guard are clearing Essling.'

'Thank you.'

Boudet made his way back to the ruined church on foot, stepping between pools of blood and corpses strewn across the road. Terrible screams rose from the cemetery. He asked what was happening. A lieutenant of the Guard replied that it was Hungarians having their throats cut among the tombs.

'We can't afford to slow ourselves down with prisoners any more.'

'How many of them are there?'

'Seven hundred, General.'

*

On both sides the ammunition was running out. As the firing died down, the impression it gave of a general lull was deceptive, since the two armies clashed just as frequently and lethally with sabres, bayonets and lances, but the engagements had become less fierce. Sharpshooters fired to keep the battle going and the attacks seemed to lack conviction, as if only in self-defence or to hold the front line. The grenadiers around Lannes had run out of cartridges. The marshal felt betrayed by the river in spate. He was walking with his friend Pouzet in a little hollow below the level of the plain, protected from Austrian cavalry by fences, which would break the legs of any horse that tried to jump them. Lannes unbuttoned his coat: the day was drawing on but it was still very hot. He wiped his forehead with the back of his sleeve.

'How long before nightfall?'

'Two or three hours,' answered Pouzet, consulting his fob watch.

'We can't turn it around.'

'Nor can the Archduke.'

'Our men are still dying, but for what? We have been fighting for thirty hours, Pouzet, and I've had enough of it! The noise of war sickens me.'

'Sickens you? What, you haven't been wounded and yet you're moaning? Almost every single one of your officers has been put out of action. Marbot's a lame duck with that bullet in his thigh, Viry's taken one in his shoulder,

Labédoyère's got a canister splinter in his foot, Watteville broke his arm falling off his horse . . .'

'We stun them so as to lead them the more easily to their deaths. That bloody fellow Bonaparte will lead us all down that road!'

'You've said that before. At Arcola, wasn't it?'

'This time I believe it . . .'

'Tonight we'll cross the Danube by boat, and as long as we don't capsize we'll be in Vienna tomorrow.'

'Pouzet!' yelled the marshal. A bullet had struck Pouzet in the middle of the forehead. He fell over as if poleaxed. Some grenadiers ran up and saw that the general had not stood a chance. He had died instantly.

'A stray bullet,' said one of them.

'Stray!' exclaimed the marshal and walked away from his friend's body.

The stupidity of this battle made him quiver with rage. He set off towards the tileworks and then, seeing a ditch, lay down in the grass and stared at the sky. He stayed like that for a long time. Four soldiers carrying a dead officer in a greatcoat passed in front of him. The men stopped to catch their breath: the body was heavy and they had a way to go. They put their load down. A gust of wind blew open the coat and Lannes recognized Pouzet. He jumped to his feet. 'Is this sight going to hound me wherever I go?'

One of the soldiers pulled the coat back over the general's face. Lannes unbuckled his sword and threw it to the ground.

'Aaaaaagh!'

When he had shouted until his voice cracked, he gasped for breath, walked away a few paces and sat down at the edge of a ditch, his legs crossed, his head in his hands so as not to see anything any more. The soldiers carried Pouzet off to the ambulances and the marshal was left on his own. Cannon could be heard firing again.

A small, three-pound roundshot ricocheted and struck Lannes in the knees. He winced, tried to stand up but lost his balance and collapsed onto the grass, swearing, 'Damn it all!' Marbot, who wasn't far away, had seen the accident and limped over as fast as his thigh wound allowed.

'Marbot! Help me stand!'

The aide-de-camp lifted up the marshal but he fell instantly, his shattered knee unable to take his weight. Marbot gave a shout and grenadiers and cuirassiers came running. They managed to carry the marshal away, holding him under the arms and the waist, his dislocated legs hanging limply beneath him. The wounded man didn't complain but the colour was draining from his face. The stray roundshot had hit his left kneecap and lacerated the right leg crossed underneath it. After a few metres his bearers had to stop, as gently as possible, since even the slightest jolt caused him terrible pain. Marbot went on ahead to look for a cart, a stretcher – anything he could find. He caught up with the grenadiers carrying General Pouzet's body. 'Give me his coat, quick! He doesn't need it any more!'

But when he returned to the marshal with the blood-soaked coat, Lannes recognized it and refused in a voice that was still firm, 'That's my friend's coat! Give him back his coat! Drag me along anyhow, I don't care!'

'Go and break off some branches, some leaves,' ordered Marbot, 'make a stretcher!'

The men went to cut branches from a clump of trees with their sabres and they made a rudimentary stretcher. Then Marshal Lannes was carried in a little more comfort past the tileworks to the Guard's ambulance, where Dr Larrey was in charge, assisted by two of his eminent colleagues, Yvan and Berthet. They dressed the marshal's right thigh first, while he requested, 'Larrey, have a look at Marbot's wound as well . . .'

'Yes, Your Excellency.'

'This lad has hardly been attended to. I'm worried about him.'

The three doctors examined Marshal Lannes's wounds and drew aside to decide on their diagnosis and treatment.

'You can barely feel his pulse.'

'The right knee joint hasn't been damaged, mind you.'

'But the left is shattered to the bone . . .'

'And the artery is severed.'

'Gentlemen,' said Larrey, 'it's my opinion that the left leg should be amputated.'

'In this heat?' protested Yvan. 'That makes no sense!'

'Alas!' added Berthet. 'Our esteemed colleague is right. Personally, I would recommend the amputation of both legs as a precautionary measure.'

'You're both mad!'

'Let's amputate!'

'You're mad! I know the marshal, his constitution is strong enough to pull through without amputation!'

'We know the marshal as well, my dear colleague. Have you seen his eyes?'

'What's wrong with them?'

'They're sad. He's losing his strength.'

'Gentlemen,' Dr Larrey said decisively, 'I must remind you that I am in charge of this ambulance and the decision, therefore, rests with me. We will amputate the left leg.'

*

When Edmond de Périgord reached the Old Guard's encampment between the small bridge and the tileworks, he found General Dorsenne reviewing his grenadiers for the umpteenth time. He wanted them to be immaculate, their uniforms pristine. With his expert eye, he noticed specks of dust on a sleeve, a stain on a white cross-strap, an imperfectly waxed moustache, a pair of sagging gaiters. At barracks, he was liable to lift up their waistcoats to check that their shirts were clean. As far as he was concerned, one went to war as if one was going to a ball, elegantly, and he was equally obsessive about his own uniform. He devoted as much care to his appearance as if his entire life was spent gliding through salons full of mirrors. He was a handsome man, so women said, with his black curls, his pale complexion and his delicate features. The Court gossiped about him, each courtier knowing by heart the details of his love affair with the alluring Mme d'Orsay, the wife of the celebrated dandy, about whom Fouché, the Minister of Police, used to tell salacious stories. Périgord, although the younger man, cut a fine figure as well and he had often run into Dorsenne at the theatre or at concerts at the Tuileries. Unlike most military men, both of them wore silk stockings, buckled shoes and even those extravagant uniforms which caught the attention of duchesses as if they were the most natural thing in the world. Both of them had real courage, but they loved to make a show

of it; their posturing was taken for disdain and they grated
on people's nerves.

'General of the Guard, sir,' said Périgord, 'His Majesty
requests you to advance into line.'

'Splendid!' answered Dorsenne, pulling on his gloves.

'You will present a wall of troops to the enemy across
the breadth of the slope, to the right of Marshal Bessières's
cuirassiers.'

'Very good! Consider us there.'

With a lithe movement, Dorsenne mounted the horse
which had been led forward for him, shouted an abrupt
order and the Imperial Guard moved off in step, the band
and eagles leading, as if they were on parade at the
Carrousel. Périgord watched them admiringly and then
headed back to Staff Headquarters to report to Berthier.

The appearance of the Guard's bearskins on the crest of
the slope was enough to make the Austrian cannon hesitate
for a moment, but then they resumed firing. General
Dorsenne deployed his grenadiers in three ranks. He
wheeled his horse to make sure that they were standing as
near elbow to elbow as possible and, in so doing, had
unconcernedly turned his back on the Archduke's cannon
and infantry. Whenever a roundshot knocked over one of
his men, with arms crossed, he ordered, 'Close up!' and the
grenadiers, kicking the body of their fallen comrade out of
the way, closed their ranks.

This happened twenty times, perhaps even a hundred,
and each time they closed ranks. When one of the standard
bearers had his head blown off by roundshot, a shower of
gold coins fell to the ground – the fellow having decided to
hide his savings in his stock – but no one dared bend down

to pick up a handful for fear of being reprimanded. His closest neighbours glanced longingly, all the same, at the ground where the coins gleamed. Roundshots continued to whistle through the air and wreak havoc amongst the Guard.

'Close up!'

Irritated at not being able to outflank the French, the Archduke ordered that the bombardment be stepped up. Formed up in a square under the hail of roundshot, the drummers played beside the motionless grenadiers presenting their arms. Dozens of them had already keeled over into the wheat, and the remainder kept on closing ranks.

Dorsenne eventually found that his defensive wall of men was spread too thin and drew his soldiers back to a single line facing the enemy. One incident alone came close to undoing this display of heroism designed to cow the Austrians. A number of fusiliers and chasseurs à pied formerly under Lannes's command were fleeing headlong across the plain before Rosenberg's infantry. They held up their wounded as they ran, many having tossed aside their knapsacks so that they could escape quicker. Reaching the bastion of the Guard, these survivors came between the grenadiers and the Austrian batteries, so some of the 'grumblers' grabbed them by the neck or the sleeve to drag them out of the way. Reassured by this protection, they fell to their knees, maddened with terror, and rolled around on the ground foaming at the mouth like epileptics. Learning of the battalions' rout, Bessières hurried forward with two of his staff captains to re-form any of the men who had held onto their muskets. 'Where are your officers?'

'On the plain, dead!'

'Let's go and find their bodies! Load your weapons! Form up!'

'Close up!' Dorsenne continued to order a hundred metres away.

A grenadier with shrapnel in his leg dragged himself out of the line of fire. When he fell to the ground, he had snatched up some of the coins the standard bearer, his former neighbour in the line, had hidden in the folds of his stock. He surreptitiously opened his hand, took a close look at his treasure and muttered bitterly that it wasn't worth anything any more. On 1 January 1809, the Emperor had had removed from all coinage the motto which still figured on the coins he had picked up:

UNITY, INDIVISIBILITY OF THE REPUBLIC.

*

Night fell early on this battle without a victor. Napoleon and the officers of his household left the tileworks in procession to return to the imperial tent which had been erected the previous day in a grassy clearing on the island. They walked their horses along a track jammed with empty caissons, dismounted cannon, riderless, panic-stricken horses and slow-moving columns of wounded led by the ambulance men. At the abutment of the small bridge, the Emperor turned pale. First he saw a major of cuirassiers weeping silently. Then he recognized Drs Yvan and Larrey bending over a patient who was being laid on a bed of oak branches and greatcoats. It was Lannes, with Marbot propping up his head. His face was livid, disfigured by pain and running with great beads of sweat. A red cloth was wound tightly round his left thigh. The Emperor asked to be helped to dismount and, in a few strides, he was at the marshal's side. He crouched down by his head. 'Lannes, my friend, do you recognize me?'

The marshal opened his eyes but stayed silent.

'His strength is very depleted, sire,' murmured Larrey.

'But he recognizes me, doesn't he?'

'Yes, I recognize you,' whispered the marshal, 'but in an hour you will have lost your best support . . .'

'*Stupidita!* We'll keep you going. Isn't that right, gentlemen?'

'Yes, sire,' said Larrey obsequiously.

'Since Your Majesty wishes it,' added Yvan.

'You hear them?'

'I hear them . . .'

'In Vienna,' said Napoleon, 'a doctor has designed an artificial leg for an Austrian general . . .'

'Mesler,' said Yvan.

'That's it, Bessler. He'll make you a leg and next week we'll go hunting!'

The Emperor took the marshal in his arms. The wounded man whispered in his ear so that no one else could hear, 'Stop this war as quickly as possible, that's what everyone wants. Don't listen to your entourage. They flatter you, they bow and scrape, but they don't love you. They will betray you. They are already betraying you as it is by always hiding the truth from you . . .'

Dr Yvan intervened, 'Sire, His Excellency the Duke of Montebello is exhausted. He must conserve his strength, he mustn't talk too much.'

The Emperor straightened up, frowned and stood for a moment contemplating the prone figure of Marshal Lannes.

His waistcoat was stained with blood. He turned to Caulaincourt. 'Let's cross to the island.'

'The small bridge is barely passable, sire.'

'*Su, presto, sbrigatevi!* Quick! Hurry! Think of a solution!'

The Emperor couldn't easily cross a small bridge being reinforced by carpenters, whose efforts were hampered by a constant tide of mutilated soldiers. These unfortunates shook with fever and rage as they jostled one another, clambered over bodies, tried to get out of the way, clung to ropes and moorings which sometimes snapped under their weight, and squabbled and cursed one another. Some could be seen diving into the waves or, without hesitating, spurring their horses into the turbulent river. Caulaincourt had one of the pontoons untied and checked to see that it was watertight and undamaged. He picked ten rowers from the strongest of the Seaman of the Guard, and in the twilight the Emperor stood in the middle of this craft as it drifted two hundred metres downstream in the current, and then beached on the Lobau.

He walked through the brushwood and over the strips of sand covered with thousands of dying men. They stretched out their arms towards him as if he had healing powers, but the Emperor stared straight ahead, protected by the escort of officers surrounding him. He reached his tent, a large cotton-drill marquee with sky-blue and white stripes. Constant was waiting for him. He helped him take off his greatcoat and green coat. While he was still changing out of the kerseymere waistcoat stained with Lannes's blood, the Emperor grunted between clenched teeth, 'Write!'

His secretary, sitting on a cushion in the antechamber, dipped his quill in the inkwell.

'Marshal Lannes. His last words. He said to me, "I desire to live so long as I can be of service to you . . ."'

'"Service to you",' repeated his secretary, scribbling away at his portable writing desk.

'"And to our France as well." Add that.'

'I am.'

'"But I believe that within the hour you will have lost the one who has been your best friend . . ."'

Napoleon sniffed. He fell silent. His secretary's quill hung in the air.

'Berthier!'

'He is not on the island yet,' said an aide-de-camp standing at the entrance of the tent.

'And Masséna? Is he dead?'

'I'm not sure, sire.'

'No, it's not Masséna's style. Have him come here immediately!'

Six

THE SECOND NIGHT

IT WAS A MOONLESS NIGHT. Bathed in the pale reddish glow of the last of the fires, the copses and undergrowth on the left bank appeared misshapen and distorted from over the river. The wind had picked up, rustling the leaves in the elms, shaking the bushes and driving heavy black rainclouds across the sky. On the sandy bank of the Lobau, between flattened clumps of reeds, the Emperor was walking with Masséna. The marshal had turned up the collar of his long grey coat and sunk his hands in his pockets. In profile, with his short hair fluttering like feathers about his temples, he looked like a vulture. Despite the roaring of the river, the two men could hear the dull murmur of the plain like an echo, the creaking of wheels, the shouts of soldiers and the noise of clogs and hooves striking the wooden roadway of the little bridge close by. Napoleon was speaking in a numb voice. 'Everyone lies to me.'

'Don't put on that act, it's only the two of us.'

They addressed each other with the familiar 'tu', as they had done during the Italian expeditions under the Directory.

'No one dares tell me the truth,' lamented the Emperor.

'Nonsense!' replied Masséna. 'There's a few of us who

can speak frankly to you. Whether you listen, well, that's another matter!'

'A few: Augereau, you . . .'

'The Duke of Montebello.'

'Jean, of course. I never could scare him. One night, before a battle, I don't remember which, he barged past the sentry into my tent, pulled me out of bed and shouted in my ear, "Are you trying to make a bloody fool of me?" He used to question my orders.'

'Stop talking about him in the past: he's not dead – not yet anyway – and you're already burying him.'

'He's in a parlous state. Larrey admitted as much to me.'

'You don't die from losing a leg. I damn well had one of my eyes put out thanks to you, but has that held me back?'

The Emperor pretended not to hear this allusion to the shoot at which he had blinded Masséna in one eye and blamed it on Berthier's clumsiness. He remained deep in thought, then, in a gruffer voice, he said, 'I'm certain the whole army knew of Lannes's misfortune before I did.'

'The soldiers are fond of him and they're concerned about what happens to him.'

'Your men as well? Were they demoralized when they heard?'

'No, not demoralized, but they were affected. They're brave men.'

'Ah! If only poor Lannes were being treated in Vienna this very minute, in the best possible conditions!'

'Have him ferried across the river in a skiff.'

'You're not serious? In this wind and with that current, he'd be tossed about like a cork – it would be too much for him.'

The Emperor whipped a clump of reeds with his riding crop as he turned the situation over in his mind. A minute or two passed and then, in a firmer voice, he said, 'André, I need to pick your brains.'

'You want to know what I'd do in your place?'

'Berthier advocates that we take cover on the right bank.'

'Idiocy!'

'The major-general thinks we should go so far as to withdraw to the rear of Vienna.'

'The major-general has no business thinking. Especially not wrongheadedly. And then what? While we're at it, why not go back to Saint-Cloud! If we give up this island, we'll be acknowledging the Archduke's victory, but we haven't lost.'

'We haven't won either.'

'We've avoided taking a terrible beating.'

'Fate is hounding me, Masséna.'

'Archduke Charles has not succeeded: we have kept him at bay, his troops are dog-tired, he has almost run out of ammunition . . .'

'I know,' said Napoleon, casting a glance at the river. 'It was General Danube that defeated me.'

'Defeated! Don't be crass! The Army of Italy is going to join up with us. Last week Prince Eugène took Trieste, now he'll march on Vienna with nine divisions, more than fifty thousand men! Lefebvre entered Innsbruck on the nineteenth: as soon as he has finished with the Tyrolese rebels, he'll bring us twenty-five thousand Bavarians . . .'

'So, we should dig ourselves in on the island?'

'We've got enough time tonight to have our troops brought over, if we hurry.'

'Can you guarantee me an orderly retreat?'
'Yes.'
'That's the spirit! Return to your post.'

*

The silence woke Fayolle. Opening his eyes, he realized that the fighting must have stopped when night fell. The cuirassier remained flat on his back, too dazed to sit up and take off his heavy breastplate. Even if he had pulled himself upright, in the pitch dark he wouldn't have been able to see the thousands of bodies covering the plain, each marking the spot where they'd rot and be torn to pieces by crows. He felt his face with his hand, bent one of his legs and then the other: he wasn't wounded, everything seemed to be in order. The wheat still standing swayed in the cool wind and a smell of gunpowder, dung and blood hung in the air. Suddenly Fayolle heard gnawing: something had taken a fancy to his torn espadrilles. He shook his foot. Some sort of rodent with thick fur was attacking the rope sole. The animal ran off. He didn't know what it was called: coming from the slums of Paris, all he knew were rats. He took a deep breath, relishing the strange, self-absorbed feeling of peace that had come over him. Fayolle had always been alone. By turns a porter, a rag-and-bone man and a fortune teller on the Pont Neuf, he had lived a full life by the age of thirty-five, but not a good one. The Revolution hadn't made it any easier. He hadn't even been able to make something out of Barras's reign, though it was a time when every sort of swindle was encouraged. In those days immediately after the Terror, he had set up a stall in the Passage du Perron to sell on stolen goods: soap, sugar, pipe stems, English pencils. Afterwards he'd hung around the Palais Royal, where girls solicited in their hundreds in the arcades and wooden galleries built onto them as extensions. On the first floor of one restaurant, the ceiling of the oriental salon opened up and naked goddesses descended from heaven on a gilded chariot, whilst in the adjoining establishment, *hetairae* massaged their clients in baths of wine. People had told him this, because, with his foxskin cap and hangdog expression, he never stood a chance of being allowed in himself. Instead he made do with watching, hungrily, the girls who advertised themselves with erotic engravings or lifted up their skirts. Some, to appeal to the customer's sense of compassion, walked about with children they'd rented, while others called down to passers-by from above the Café des Aveugles, in black hats with gold tassels and satin ballet pumps. They were sublime but they didn't give credit. They gave themselves names out of poems: Betsy the mulatto, Sophie Beau Corps or Lolotte, Fanchon, Sophie Pouppe, the Sultana. Chonchon des Allures ran a gaming house. Venus was a heroine because she had rebuffed the advances of the Count of Artois.

Fayolle had imagined that his cuirassier's blue uniform with red facings would stand him in good stead with the ladies, or at least give him some impunity in his thieving, but no: he had never got anything except by force or as the spoils of war. He thought back to the pretty nun he'd raped during the sack of Burgos, and the tigress in Castille who'd scratched his face and whom he'd left to the mercy of a brutal Polish lancer. Above all, he thought of the peasant girl in Essling, of her haunting eyes staring back at him from the other side. He shivered. Was it terror or cold? The wind was turning icy. He made an effort to pick up his brown coat. As he propped himself up on one elbow, he heard the creak of cartwheels.

Screwing up his eyes, Fayolle strained to make out shapes in the dark. The glint of bivouac fires in the far distance, towards both the Bisamberg and the Danube, allowed him roughly to guess where the armies were encamped. Who was coming? Austrians? French? What were they doing? What was the cart for? They were coming in his direction, because the noise of the wheels was growing louder and merging with the muffled sound of men's voices and the clatter of metal, but none of this made him any the wiser. Unsure what to do, he lay back down, and concentrated on keeping still. The cart was lumbering towards him. It could only be a few metres away now. Through half-shut eyes, Fayolle glimpsed silhouettes bending over with lanterns. In the faint light he recognized an Austrian grenadier's busby, a branch of leaves sticking up from it like a plume. He held his breath and played dead. Feet trampled through the wheat and stopped beside him. A hand undid his iron breastplate. He felt a man's breath near his face.

'Hey, there's a good crop over here . . .'

Hearing these words spoken in French, Fayolle caught the thief by the wrist, making him scream, 'Aaagh! This one's woken up! Help me!'

'Keep your voice down,' said one of his accomplices.

Fayolle sat up, leaning on both hands. Two ambulance men stared at him wide-eyed.

'Not dead, eh?' Fat Louis asked him.

'He doesn't even look badly wounded,' added Paradis, who was wearing an Austrian busby.

'What the hell are you up to?' growled Fayolle in an ugly voice.

'Calm down, friend!'

'Well, you see,' explained Paradis, 'we're collecting the cuirasses, that's our orders. Mustn't leave anything behind.'

'Apart from the dead,' Fayolle said scornfully.

'Oh, no one's said anything to us about the dead. Besides, there's too many of those.'

Fayolle stood up, took off his cuirass and threw it into the cart.

'You can keep it,' said Fat Louis, 'seeing as you're alive.'

The cuirassier wrapped himself in his Spanish coat. His eyes were growing accustomed to the dark and he could see dozens of lanterns scouring the plain. Paradis, Fat Louis and other ambulance men were beating the ground with sticks; whenever they struck the iron of a breastplate, they bent down, unfastened it and stacked it on the cart.

'Look, this one's an officer, at least . . .'

At these words of Paradis's, Fayolle walked straight over to him.

'Do you know him?' asked Paradis, lowering the lantern over a man's face.

'It used to be Captain Saint-Didier.'

'He can't have been that old . . .'

'Take off his cuirass and keep your mouth shut.'

'Right you are, let's pretend I haven't said a word.'

When Paradis had finished, Fayolle snatched the lantern out of his hands and crouched down over the captain. He'd been shot through the neck. He looked as if he was asleep with his eyes open. His right hand still held a loaded pistol which he hadn't had time to use. Fayolle prised open the frozen fingers and tucked the weapon into his belt.

*

In a clearing on the island of Lobau, Marshal Lannes was lying on a dozen cavalrymen's coats. Captain Marbot hadn't left his side for a minute, watching over him like a wet-nurse, anticipating his needs and comforting him more by his attentive presence than by anything he said. Lannes babbled and flew into rages, his mind wandering. He thought that he was still on the battlefield and gave incoherent orders. 'Marbot . . .'

'Your Grace?'

'Marbot, if Rosenberg's cavalry take Essling from the rear, from the forest, Boudet is done for.'

'There's no need to be alarmed.'

'There's every need! Send Pouzet to the fortified granary, no, not Pouzet, he has been wounded, better make it Saint-Hilaire. Has that fool Davout sent ammunition across by boat? No? What's he waiting for?'

'You should rest, Your Grace.'

'This is not the time!'

Lannes gripped his aide-de-camp by the arm. 'Marbot, where is my horse?'

'He has lost a shoe,' lied the captain. 'We're taking care of it.'

Marbot answered each feverish question in such a soothing voice that eventually the marshal grew exasperated.

'Why are you talking to me as if I am a three-year-old? I'm wounded, I know that, but it's not as if it's the first time! I've already died once, at Saint-Jean d'Acre – don't you remember? A bullet in the nape of the neck, that's not just some trifle! And at Governolo, Aboukir, Pultusk . . . At Arcola I was hit three times. I survived.'

'You are immortal, Your Grace.'

'If you put it like that . . .'

Lannes shook his head from side to side and tried to moisten his parched lips with his tongue.

'Give me something to drink, Marbot, I'm thirsty, and then let's launch the grenadiers against Liechtenstein: it's him or us. Do you understand what's at stake here? Oudinot will come up in support ... Oh, but how black the sun is, my friend, how ill these clouds serve us, you can't see more than ten metres ...'

Soldiers brought him a water-bottle drawn from the Danube; there was no drinking water left in the canteen workers' tanks. Lannes drank a mouthful and spat it out. 'That's not water, that's mud! We're like sailors here, Marbot, surrounded by water we can't drink ...'

'I'll find you some clean water, Your Grace.'

The Marshal had left his valet on the island guarding his portmanteau. Marbot went and asked him for one of the Marshal's shirts of the finest material. He tied its openings with string, like a goatskin, went back to the riverbank, dipped the bag into the muddy water, and tied it to a low branch above a water bottle. The Marshal drank the cold water which had been filtered through the shirt with a sigh of relief.

'Thank you,' Lannes said, 'thank you, Captain. Why the deuce are you only a captain? I'll see to it as soon as victory is ours. What would I do without you, eh? Without you and Pouzet, I'd already be dead, that's the truth of it, isn't it? Do you remember our first meeting?'

'Yes, Your Grace, it was the day before the victory at Friedland. I had recently married.'

'You had been wounded at Eylau ...'

'Yes, in the arm, by a bayonet thrust. A roundshot had torn a hole in my hat.'

'You were serving under Augereau. He entrusted you to me, just as he did last year . . .'

'I joined up with you at Bayonne . . .'

'We were leaving for Spain to command the Army of the Ebro. You knew the country and I did not . . . Burgos, Madrid, Tudela . . .'

'Where we swept the enemy aside with our first onslaught.'

'Ah yes . . . Our first onslaught . . . A wretched country, all the same! I came very close to losing you, Marbot.'

'I remember, Your Grace. A bullet grazed my heart before lodging in my ribs, a bullet as flat as a coin. It had teeth like the cog of a watch and was engraved with a cross like the Host.'

'Alberquerque was one of my aides-de-camp by then, wasn't he? At any rate, we brought him back from Spain, I think . . . Where is he? Why isn't he at your side?'

'He can't be far away, Your Grace.'

But he was: Alberquerque was a long way away and Marbot knew it. A roundshot had shattered the small of his back that evening and he had fallen to the ground, stone dead. Lannes spoke in an almost inaudible voice, 'Tell Alberuquerque to pass this on to Bessières. It is imperative he send in his cuirassiers. We must be sprung from this trap, no matter what the cost!'

'It will be done.'

Lannes continued to move his lips, without any discernible words emerging. Then he closed his eyes and his cheek fell back on the coat which had been put under his head as a pillow. Marbot felt a surge of panic. 'Is that it? Is he dead?'

'No, no, Captain,' a surgeon's assistant, whom Larrey

had appointed to stay by the marshal, reassured him. 'He is asleep.'

*

Not far away, near the imperial tent, Lejeune was assessing the fresh dangers of that night. He feared two things: the island being flooded by the Danube in spate and the Austrians suddenly deciding to bombard them from the riverbank above Aspern. He was unburdening himself to Périgord, who was more sceptical and considerably more confident of their position.

'I have studied the bark of the willows and maples, Edmond, and I can assure you that you can see signs of a previous flood.'

'You're a gardener now, are you, my dear friend?'

'I'm serious! Every island is vulnerable to flooding.'

'Except the Île de la Cité in Paris.'

'Stop joking! I'd be only too glad if you were right, but I can't help seeing this as a possible threat.'

'What, that our wounded would be drowned?'

'And our retreat jeopardized. We'd all be stuck here. On the other hand, if the Archduke Charles . . .'

'Your Austrian cannon don't frighten me, Louis-François. Are you blind? And deaf as well, for good measure? If the Archduke had wanted he could have driven us into the Danube, but he broke off the battle at exactly the same time as us.'

'If he were in his place, the Emperor wouldn't have thought twice.'

'No, but that's what the Archduke is doing: he's thinking twice.'

Berthier had had the same thoughts as Lejeune. He had

ordered a blackout on the island and had campfires lit on the strip of ground between the villages, to create the impression of an army settling in for the night and ensure their escape. The Emperor had approved the measure. Lejeune and Périgord, therefore, were walking in pitch darkness, their hands stretched out in front of them so as not to bump into a tree. Suddenly Lejeune felt the tips of his fingers touching a jowly face and heard a man ask him in a thick Italian accent, 'Have you quite finished pawing my chin?'

'May it please Your Majesty to forgive me . . .'

'*Coglione!* You are forgiven, now lead us to the bank!'

The elms and willows were swaying and their leaves shook in the wind. Sighs and groans of agony could be heard from the thousands of wounded choking the river-banks or stretched out on the grass. Lejeune and Périgord walked ahead of the group made up of the Emperor, Berthier and the officers of his household.

'The boat is ready, sire,' said Berthier, holding onto Caulaincourt's shoulder as he walked in front of him, feeling his way with the tips of his cavalry boots.

'*Perfetto!*'

'I have personally chosen fourteen rowers, two pilots, two swimmers . . .'

'Swimmers? *Perche?*'

'In case the boat capsizes, sire . . .'

'It will not overturn!'

'It will not overturn, as you say, but one has to allow for every eventuality, even the worst . . .'

'I detest the worst, Berthier, you damn ass!'

'Yes, sire.'

Walking in single file, Napoleon and his staff reached

the windswept riverbank without falling or crashing into anything. The boat was waiting. The Emperor took out his fob watch and sounded it. 'Eleven o'clock.'

The river could only vaguely be seen by the light of the new moon, but the noise of it made any sort of conversation hard. Waves broke against the island's sloping banks, throwing up a fine spray like rain, the waters rolled like a torrent and the wind whistled in their ears.

'Berthier!' shouted the Emperor. 'I'm going to dictate the order for retreat!'

'Lejeune!' yelled Berthier.

Périgord had managed to light a torch by sheltering under a copse. In its yellow, trembling light, Lejeune laid his sabretache across his knees like a desk, and, with the paper and inked quill he'd been handed by the secretary who was in attendance, he took down the order, improvising when he couldn't understand something above the roar of the river and the wind. At midnight, the Emperor dictated, Masséna and Bessières were to withdraw onto Lobau with all the troops. Once the entire army had reached this refuge, the little bridge was to be destroyed and the pontoons and trestles brought over on wagons to repair the main bridge.

When Lejeune had finished, Berthier signed the document and it was dried with a handful of sand. Then Napoleon climbed down the bank to the large boat; the brawny rowers who were holding it steady took him under both arms and helped him aboard. Périgord handed his torch to one of the pilots. Berthier, Lejeune and the others staying behind watched the Emperor draw away from the island. For a moment, they could see his expressionless face and his tail-coat flapping in the wind. When the boat had pulled away a few arms' length, the torch guttered and died in a gust of wind and the Emperor disappeared into pitch darkness, as if swallowed up by the Danube.

*

It was Lejeune's job to take the Emperor's order for retreat to Masséna, but he no longer had a mount. His mare had twisted a leg during their last gallop, and since his orderly officer was still kicking his heels on the right bank after returning from Vienna, he had had no choice but to leave the horse with Périgord's valet – even though the fellow hadn't the first idea of what treatment she needed. Time was short. The Colonel caught sight of a sapper leading a Hungarian hussar's mount by the bridle.

'I need that animal.'

'It's not mine, it's the lieutenant's.'

'I'm borrowing it!'

'I don't know if the lieutenant will agree...'

'Where is he?'

'On the main bridge which is being repaired.'

'There's no time for that! Anyway, this horse has been stolen.'

'No, it hasn't! It's been captured.'

'I'll bring it back within the hour.'

'I can't take that responsibility...'

'If I don't bring it back, I'll pay for it.'

'What proof have I got?'

Exasperated by this slow-witted sapper, Lejeune thrust the letter addressed to Masséna and signed by the major-general under his nose. Dumbfounded, the man let go of the reins. Before he could change his mind, Lejeune leapt

into the red, fur-covered saddle fringed with gold braid
and, taking a guess at the right direction, rode back against
the tide of wounded still crossing onto the island. The
closer he got to the little bridge, the more heavily congested
the road became, but Lejeune urged his horse into the
crowd, not hesitating to knock over fusiliers with bandaged
heads, soldiers without arms, the mutilated and the lame
who shook their fists at him and lashed out at his boots.
The crush on the little bridge was tragic. The fugitives
formed a tightly packed crowd that was inching forward
only a step at a time.

'Make room! Make room!' yelled the colonel.

The mass of bodies flooded round him, forcing him
backwards. He persevered, shoving the crippled away from
his horse's neck and even raising his whip, although he
couldn't bring himself to strike the survivors of the battle.
They looked up at him blankly or with hard, threatening
eyes.

'By order of the Emperor!'

'By order of the Emperor,' repeated a sergeant of
dragoons, grinding his teeth, and he held up the stump
of his left arm bandaged in a piece of linen.

After what seemed an eternity, Lejeune completed his
ordeal and once on the left bank galloped down the slope
and across the blackened countryside. Hurrying from one
bivouac fire to the next, he headed for Aspern where
Masséna should have been encamped, but how to be sure?
The sombre bulks of the first houses loomed up, then a
lane, but his horse couldn't get through the rubble of
shattered walls and he rode on to the next lane to cut
through to the church square. Seeing a sentry lighting a

pipe, he made straight for him to get information. The sentry had heard him coming and, before the colonel said a word, he asked, '*Wer da?*'

The man was an Austrian, shouting, 'Who goes there?' Instead of turning tail and losing himself in the night, thereby earning himself a musket shot, Lejeune's sensible instinct was to reply in the same language that he was a headquarters staff officer: '*Stabsoffizier!*'

A second figure, a major in Baron Hiller's regiment, stepped out of the lane and asked him the time in German. Without wasting time taking out his watch, Lejeune replied that it was midnight, '*Mitternacht* . . .'

The sentry had leaned his musket against a low wall and the major was walking towards him; Lejeune wheeled his horse and fled through a thicket of trees. He heard bullets whistle through the air. He roamed at a slow trot along a sunken road, straining to catch any sound, passing campfires that were alight but deserted, and then plunged into a wood which led him back to the oxbow of the Danube. He was riding between two trees when a man seized his horse by the bit and another grabbed him by the arm and tried to pull him off his saddle. They weren't wearing shakos, but by the remnants of their uniforms and their cross-straps, Lejeune thought he recognized French voltigeurs and shouted, 'Colonel Lejeune! On the Emperor's service!'

The two voltigeurs apologized. 'We couldn't tell . . .'

'You've got a Hungarian horse there, so, you know, we said, "This is a good catch."'

'Where is Marshal Masséna?'

'We're not too sure.'

'Meaning?'

'We saw him with the general not an hour ago.'

'Which general is that?'

'Molitor.'

'And where did you see them?'

'Over there, by the edge of this wood.'

'Are you on patrol?'

'Something like that.'

'Don't go too near the village, the Austrians are setting up there.'

'We know.'

'Thank you!'

Lejeune rode deeper into the wood, several times almost being shot to pieces by French patrols because of his Hungarian horse. Finally a non-commissioned officer directed him towards Masséna's temporary camp, pitched by reed beds that bordered an expanse of marshy ground – a natural defence which they knew the enemy wouldn't be able to breach. A great number of fires and torches indicated an important bivouac and by their flickering light Lejeune recognized Sainte-Croix's thin silhouette surrounded by officers wrapped up in their coats. Lejeune took the last part of his journey on foot, until he stumbled over a body lying on the ground. A voice yelled, 'Hey! Who's walking on my legs?'

'Your Excellency?'

Masséna had been drowsing for an hour or two while he waited for the order to retreat. He stood up, shook himself, cursed the cold and damp and, by the light of a torch held by a half-asleep skirmisher, read the Emperor's message. He folded it in two, slipped it into a pocket of his long coat, adjusted his tricorn hat, thanked Lejeune and set off, without any noticeable urgency, towards the group of officers chatting by the fire.

*

Fayolle had accompanied the cart and its cargo of cuirasses as far as Essling. The fusiliers of the Young Guard were striking tinderboxes to light fires they'd made of planks and branches, as if they were settling in for the night, but they kept their muskets slung over their shoulders and their knapsacks on their backs. Everywhere corpses were tossed pell-mell into heaps: uhlans, voltigeurs, Austrians, French, Hungarians, Bavarians, stripped of their boots and uniforms, naked, mutilated, horrifying. Some had been half-burned.

Fayolle sat down on a bench in the small ransacked garden of a low house, next to a hussar whose eyes were closed but who wasn't snoring. Cartridge papers fluttered on the grass.

'Know where there's any powder?'

The hussar didn't reply. Fayolle shook him by the shoulder and the trooper slumped forward; he was dead; someone must have thought he was asleep for him still to have a uniform. Fayolle searched him, took the powder and bullets from the bag slung over his shoulder and stared at his elegant soft leather boots. He smiled. The battle was over but at last he had found some boots that would fit. He pulled them off. He took off his espadrilles and put them on. Then he squatted down by the nearest fire, in which chairs and branches were burning. He stretched out his hands, glad for the warmth. Behind him, someone called out, 'Hey, you there!'

He looked round to be confronted with the suspicious stare of a grenadier of the Guard, hands on hips, immaculate in his white gaiters.

'Are you French? Where've you come from? What regiment? Are those hussar's boots you're wearing?'

'Stow it, can't you, you and your damn jaw!'

'Deserter, are you?'

'If I'd deserted, you sap, I'd be a long way from here by now.'

'That's true enough. So who are you?'

'Cuirassier Fayolle. My squadron was cut to pieces by the cannon. I fell off my horse, got knocked senseless and I woke up when those vultures from the ambulances were trying to pick me clean.'

'Can't stay round here. We're clearing out.'

'Don't try and tell me what's good for me, eh . . .'

Troopers riding four abreast walked their horses between the blazing fires on the square. The French battalions followed, in disarray, and in turn disappeared down the main street. The army was leaving Essling. The grenadier let Fayolle be with a shrug of his shoulders; he spat on the ground and added that he'd warned him. Fayolle went and sat down by another fire. He took Captain Saint-Didier's pistol out of his belt, cleaned it because the powder had got wet, loaded it with the hussar's fresh powder, and slid a bullet into the barrel. Weapon in hand, he stood up, proud of his new boots, and walked along the main street under the elms. Most of the houses had been destroyed or were on the verge of collapse, their roofs shattered by roundshot, and plumes of smoke rose from the fires still smouldering in some of them. The peasant girl's house, which he'd entered two days ago with his dead friend Pacotte, was barely standing, an entire section of the wall facing the garden having given way. Fayolle wanted to go in but he needed a torch. Retracing his steps, he picked up a stick and lit it at one of the dummy campfires. It didn't give much light, but it couldn't be helped. Holding this firebrand, he stepped through one of the breaches in the wall. The staircase seemed to be intact, at least intact enough to risk it. He walked through the gloom of the first floor as if he had lived there for a long time and pushed open the door of the room at the back of the house. He saw the shape of a body on the mattress. His heart beat like a drummer of the Guard. He bent over with his light and looked at the body: probably a skirmisher, stripped of his uniform but recognizable by his sideburns. What if the peasant girl of the other night had never existed? He put his torch down on the bed, which caught fire; then he pressed Captain Saint-Didier's pistol to his temple and blew his brains out.

*

Rounding a final clump of elms, the cart piled with armour halted in the tall grass and Paradis and his colleagues suddenly saw the spectacle of the French army in retreat. Below them, the smoke of hundreds of flares rose above a meadow which fell away towards the start of the little bridge and was hidden by a thick wood from the villages and the plain. On a rise, in front of his commissioned officers, Masséna was directing the evacuation with his riding crop as if he were staging an opera. The order of the regiments drawn up in line succeeded the chaotic throng of the wounded. The men were in rags, they stank, they were caked with dirt and almost fully bearded, but they were happy to be alive, to have two arms and two legs and eyes to remember what they'd seen and voices to put it into words. They knew how lucky they were and rosaries could be seen looped round some of the officers' wrists. They smiled with exhaustion: it was over. The hooves of Oudinot's horses drummed on the boards of the mended bridge, then came the shattered remains of Saint-Hilaire's division and Molitor's voltigeurs, a flash of yellow at the tips of their green plumes, a sergeant at their head who had tied the regimental colours to his musket and was holding it up like a standard. At that distance, the ambulance men of course could barely make out the colours, but Paradis swore he could see them, from having seen them too many times already. General Molitor stepped forward and saluted Masséna, who doffed his feathered hat, and then fell in at the rear of the two thousand men of his who had been spared. Behind them marched the other voltigeurs, fusiliers and chasseurs à pied who had been regrouped by Carra-Saint-Cyr and Legrand; the latter, a powerfully built man, was wearing his huge tricorn, which had had a half moon taken out of its brim by a cannonball. Not a murmur, only jingling and the thud of boots on the earth and then on the wooden roadway. One by one the battalions disappeared under the black trees of Lobau.

'Shove over, you rogues!'

'Who's calling who a rogue?'

An artillery train was coming out of the wood behind the ambulance men, its teams of horses foaming at the mouth as they hauled the heavy guns which lurched violently at every rut. A mounted gunner with a great red plume sticking up from his shako and a moustache as stiff as a bottlebrush was shouting himself hoarse at the head of the convoy. The drivers in sky-blue jackets blackened with gunpowder lashed the cruppers of their terrified animals.

'Shove over!'

'When it suits me,' shouted Fat Louis, and he slapped the lead horse's nostrils with the flat of his hand, making it rear. The gunner almost fell off and cursed as he struggled to recover his balance. The rest of the artillerymen rushed forward to surround Fat Louis; as he drew a knife from his belt, the gunner brought his musket to his shoulder and took aim at him.

'All right,' Fat Louis said, putting his knife away.

The ambulance men pushed their cart into the brambles to watch the cannon and empty caissons hurtle down the slope. A wheel came off on a patch of scree and one of the caissons rolled over. The drivers set their backs to the shaft to lift it upright.

'That's what comes of being in a hurry,' muttered Fat Louis.

The cart set off down the slope, but away from the regiments flooding towards the bottom corner of the field. Fat Louis steered it to the rear of the hut where Dr Percy, who had moved to the island, had had his ambulances. A throng of requisitioned vehicles, from barouches to hay carts, were waiting to cross the little bridge, all carrying the same odds and ends of cuirasses and muskets. Paradis went to wait by a mound and watch the troops' withdrawal. When he realized that he was leaning against a pile of arms and legs amputated by Percy and his assistants, he leapt up, his legs unsteady beneath him, rushed to the riverbank, fell on his knees and vomited. Afterwards, revolted, he wiped his lips with a handful of leaves and started chewing a blade of grass to get rid of the bad taste. As he walked back to the convoy, a mass of cavalry appeared on the brow of a hill. The re-formed squadrons were arriving. Bessières broke away from them, urged his horse forward to stop in front of Masséna and, steady in the saddle, flung two Austrian standards down on the grass. The cavalry, meanwhile, filed between the flares, which made their weapons and the facings of their uniforms gleam, and, on that night, the onlookers forgot how patched up and improvised those uniforms were. At their head came the 1st Division of heavy cavalry, led by Count de Nansouty, with brass combs jutting out of the black fur of their helmets, then the shining white breeches of the dragoons and the caribineers' scarlet lapels . . .

'This is it, here comes the rain!' said Paradis.

Large drops began to beat down and burst on the iron cuirasses piled on the cart.

*

At three o'clock in the morning, a sudden gust of wind blew open his casement window and Henri immediately got out of bed. His teeth chattering, he pulled his nightcap down over his ears and slipped on a coat over his nightshirt. It was raining hard. As he was going to shut the window, he heard a muffled report: he put his head out to look at the street. The police Berline was still opposite the house, but another Berline with a team of drenched horses had pulled up beside it, blocking its doors. Who had fired? Had it even been a shot? Henri was no longer cold, his curiosity was too great for him to complain. People stampeding down the stairs, doors creaking, a sound of faint whispering: he was desperate to find out what was afoot, and quickly got dressed in the dark. When he leant out of the window again, he could see figures diving into the second carriage; he thought he recognized Anna's profile under a hood and the more fragile figures of her sisters and the governess. Men in broad-brimmed hats dripping with rain helped them climb in and then one of them leaped into the coachman's seat and cracked the whip. The carriage flew off. Henri ran out of his room, tore down the main staircase and landed on the ground floor. He started with fright when he saw someone lying in wait for him in the dark, but no one was there, only his own reflection in a mirror. He thought himself grotesque in this outfit he'd thrown on in haste: frock coat, overcoat on top, long johns tucked into boots and, worst of all, his hair spilling out from under a nightcap, which he tore off and stuffed in one of his pockets. He flung both doors of the carriage entrance open but didn't dare venture out into the downpour. Water streamed between the cobblestones and drenched him as it fell in torrents from the roofs. He thought of the soldiers on the plain which would be a quagmire by now, then of the scene he had just witnessed, and sneezed. He walked back towards the kitchens and checked the time on the clock. Calling out, he climbed the stairs and pushed open the bedroom doors: the beds hadn't even been slept in. Anna and her family's flight had been carefully planned, but who had she gone with and where to?

Downstairs, in the hall, people were walking about. Voices and the tread of boots echoed on the stairs. Henri hadn't time to shut himself in the first drawing room before he was surrounded by a swarm of gendarmes.

'Who are you?' barked a sergeant in a soaking uniform.

'I could ask you the same question.'

'Oh, sir is a wily bird, is he?'

'Leave Commissary Beyle in peace, he has nothing to do with this.'

Schulmeister was climbing the stairs as his gendarmes jostled one another to let him past. He shook himself and handed his cape to the policeman following him, who was one of those Henri had seen in front of the Berline on the Jordangasse. He recognized the one behind as well, who was holding a sort of compress to his arm; a bullet fired through the coach window had torn his frock coat and given him a flesh wound.

'Can you give me an explanation, Monsieur Schulmeister?'

'There's no one left in the house?'

'A desert.'

The chief of police dismissed the gendarmes and led Henri into his room. One of his agents lit the candle while the other closed the window with his good hand.

'Mlle Krauss has gone to join her lover, Monsieur Beyle.'

'Lejeune?'

'Another colonel.'

'Périgord? I don't believe it!'

'Nor do I.'

'Well, tell me who, for God's sake!'

'An Austrian officer, Monsieur Beyle, some sort of field marshal to the Prince von Hohenzollern.'

Henri fell into the only chair in the room, sneezed again and sat there dumbfounded, feverish tears glistening in his eyes.

'You saw nothing?'

'Nothing, Monsieur Schulmeister.'

'I know, you never see anything . . .'

'Who took Anna away?'

'Partisans, they say, troublemakers like M. Staps who are making things difficult for us! What's that?'

'The bells of St Stephen's,' said Henri, sniffling.

'They sound as if they're raising the alarm . . . Do you mind?' Schulmeister pointed at the window.

'What difference does it make?' replied Henri. 'I'm already ill. Open it, open it . . .' And he blew his nose hard enough to make the windowpanes rattle.

The bells of Vienna were pealing out, answering one another from church to church, and, beyond the ramparts, merging with those of the suburbs, perhaps even with those of every village within a ten-league radius. Despite the rain people were coming out onto the streets and shouting.

'What are the Viennese saying, Monsieur Schulmeister?'

'They're saying, "We have won," Monsieur Beyle.'

'Who is this "we"?'

'Let's go and find out.'

They put on hats, capes and overcoats and set off through the streets like looters on the prowl. Townspeople clustered in little groups and talking animatedly. Schulmeister asked Henri to take the cockade off his dripping top hat and they mingled with Vienna's inhabitants who were spreading calamitous news in a state of high excitment:

'The French are trapped on the island of Lobau!'

'They're being decimated by the Archduke's canister shot!'

'The Emperor has been taken prisoner!'

'No, no, he has been killed!'

'Bonaparte is dead!'

Schulmeister took a list which was being handed round and looked at it under the light of a lantern hanging in the porch of a house.

'What does that piece of paper say?'

'That fifty thousand French are dead, Monsieur Beyle. These are their names, well, some of them . . .'

The bells rang out, deafening.

*

The rumours going around Vienna were unfounded. The Emperor was at Schönbrunn, in conversation with Davout. He had caught up with the Army of the Rhine before the rain started and been met by cheering. Then the Marshal had accompanied him in his barouche, with a squadron of chasseur à cheval as escort. He gritted his teeth for the entire journey, but at the palace, in the Lacquer Saloon, he started to analyse the situation at the top of his voice. 'Tonight I have no love of rivers!'

Napoleon seized the back of a little gilt chair and smashed it against a pedestal table, storming, 'Davout, I hate the Danube as much as your soldiers hate you!'

'In that case, sire, I pity the Danube.'

Bald, with bushy sideburns curling over his cheeks and round glasses perched on the tip of his nose on account of his chronic short sight, Marshal Davout, the Duke of Averstadt, knew that he was hated for his extreme severity and his foul language. He treated his officers like valets, but he had never been defeated and he was a rigorous tactician. This Burgundian aristocrat, a fervent republican at the start of the Revolution, had proved exceptionally loyal to the Empire. He remained calm, which made Napoleon even more furious.

'There was nothing in it! You would have come out on Lannes's right and we would have had victory!'

'Most probably.'

'Like Austerlitz!'

'Everything was in readiness.'

'If that ass Berthier had managed to repair the main bridge overnight, this morning we would have routed Charles's stupefied troops!'

'Without any difficulty, sire: the Austrians are at the end of their tether. I would have crossed the Danube with my fresh divisions and we would have crushed them like beetles.'

'Beetles! That's it! Like beetles!'

The Emperor took a pinch of snuff and stuffed it into his nose.

'What do you suggest, Davout?'

'God damn it! We could dine, sire. I'm dying of hunger and I wouldn't refuse a battery of plump Austrian chickens!'

*

The island was filling up. Thousands of soldiers were slipping like shadows under the cover of the tall trees, the luckiest finding a tree trunk to lean against, sliding down onto the mossy ground and falling asleep, their feet in puddles of water. This billet threw the commissariat into a panic, since they'd never manage to feed such a number: the provisions Davout was sending across in skiffs – when, that is, they reached the island – were devoured the minute they were unloaded. The wounded now lay groaning under large awnings or against a wall of carts. The ambulance men had set out barrels to catch the rainwater and fashioned drainpipes out of reeds to channel the water that collected in pockets on the canvas stretched between the tree branches. They tried to heat their revolting horse broth under cover and kept the horses' heads and guts in tubs for the Austrian prisoners, crammed together on the sandy tip of the island, who would eat them raw. From time to time a medical orderly on his rounds of the prone bodies picked up a dead man, dragged him, amidst general indifference, to one or other beach and pushed him into the water.

Across the river, in the meadow, the flames had long since been put out by the downpour, but Masséna still hadn't moved. Stiff-backed, as immobile as a statue sunk in the mud, the rain streaming down his face, he was making sure that the entire army entrusted to him by the Emperor got off the left bank and took refuge in the forests on the island.

'Only the Old Guard is left, Your Grace,' said Sainte-Croix, the plumes of his tricorn drooping pitifully.

'It's scarcely daybreak. We have succeeded.'

'Here come the last of them . . .'

General Dorsenne was arriving at the head of a battalion of grey ghosts, wrapped in greatcoats made leaden by the rain. They floundered and skidded down the hill, still trying to keep step and, as they lifted their feet, clods of mud clung to the soles of their boots. The rain-soaked standards were wound round the flag poles. Muted clarinets played an imperial march, but the drums were silent, covered with aprons so that the rain didn't stretch their skins. Dorsenne halted beside Masséna, and Sainte-Croix had to help him dismount because he had been wounded in the head and seemed very weak. His gloves were tied round his forehead as a bandage.

'It's only a splinter,' he said.

'Hurry up and get it looked at!' Masséna roared. 'Lannes, Espagne, Saint-Hilaire: enough is enough!'

'I will when my grenadiers and chasseurs have passed.'

'You stubborn ass!'

'Marshal, I am hardly entitled to faint before the last act. It would set a very poor example.'

Masséna took him by the arm as they watched the grenadiers step onto the little bridge buffeted by the Danube.

'I'm bringing back more than half,' Dorsenne explained.

'Sainte-Croix,' said Massena, 'take the general to Dr Yvan.'

'Or Larrey,' said Dorsenne, alarmingly pale.

'Oh no, you poor man! Larrey would be quite capable of amputating your head! He's like Dr Guillotine, you know: anything that sticks out, he cuts off.'

They took their leave of one another on this piece of banter. Masséna ordered his officers, 'Your turn now, gentlemen. I will follow.'

The officers were on the island when a salvo rang out in the vicinity of Aspern. Masséna smiled. 'The beggars are waking up!'

But no. It was nothing of consequence, only a few Austrian soldiers emptying their muskets into a deserted bivouac. The Archduke was unaware of the true extent of the damage suffered by the main bridge and afraid that the sappers would quickly finish their repairs and allow the French reinforcements to cross to the right bank, as on the previous day. Anxious and uncertain, he had brought the greater part of his troops back to their former positions. It hadn't even crossed his mind to attack. His army had been bled dry.

All alone, on foot, slowly and without looking back, Marshal Masséna was the last to cross the little bridge. The Seamen of the Guard and sappers were already preparing to dismantle it. Long, narrow, open-sided carts were waiting to take the pontoons to the other side of the Lobau to restore the main bridge, which was fifteen boats short. At six o'clock in the morning, the battle of Essling had come to an end. More than forty thousand dead covered the fields.

Seven

AFTER THE HECATOMB

COLONEL LEJEUNE spent two gruelling days on the island of Lobau, waiting impatiently for the bridge to be restored and, once Hiller's men had taken up position in the abandoned villages, expecting to be bombarded. The Austrians were fortifying the riverbank and it was likely that they would bring up cannon. He drank rainwater and tried the horse broth (which Masséna found delicious), but thought only of Mlle Krauss, not knowing that she had fled. As soon as the main bridge was rebuilt, the Colonel gained permission to leave for Vienna. He paid too high a price for a hussar's horse and hurried to the Jordangasse, where he found only disappointment and bitterness. His first response was anger, a fit of mad rage unassuaged by the speeches which Henri had prepared, clearly foreseeing his friend's fury and grief. Lejeune burst into the room of the faithless one, the deceiver, the conceited hussy, the she-devil – he accused Anna of every conceivable failing – and tore her clothes out of the wardrobes, ripped them to pieces and trampled them on the floor, crying that he had been betrayed and unable to bear the idea that he had been duped and made to look ridiculous. When he had destroyed the contents of three trunks and several wardrobes, he lit a fire of his drawings – Henri was only able to save one –

then lay on his bed fully dressed, barely breathing, staring at the painted wooden ceiling. He stayed like that for several hours. In his concern, Henri took the opportunity of Dr Carino's daily visit to ask him to treat the Colonel. Lejeune sent the doctor packing.

'My condition, Monsieur, is not the sort to be cured by your potions!'

Henri, meanwhile, continued to take his medicine and, exposed to Lejeune's distress, he began to recover: the greater suffering of another can sometimes make one forget one's own, and often the body heals more easily than the mind. He was helped by Périgord, who had returned to take up his quarters in the pink house, and brought with him his fat valet and his silver-gilt cartridge pouch containing the essentials of a dressing-case, from a tongue-scraper to pots of rouge. Together Périgord and Henri sought ways to revive their friend's good humour, trying to drag him with them to the Opéra and scouring the booksellers for rare editions on the Venetian painters. Périgord even bribed one of the cooks from Schönbrunn who came at night to prepare irresistible ragouts, which simmered for hours over a low heat, but Lejeune resisted them. He had lost his appetite. He didn't want music or entertainment or literature. He refused to go to taverns, to take the air in the Prater, to visit the zoo, to eat an ice at the Bastion café. One morning, Périgord and Henri entered his room with a resolute look on their faces.

'My dear friend,' said Périgord, 'we are taking you to Baden.'

'Why?'

'To invigorate you, to give you something new to think

about and to restore – even if only partially – your natural good spirits.'

'Edmond, I couldn't care a rap about any of that! What on earth is that scent you've doused yourself with?'

'Don't you like it? This scent, if you're capable of grasping the notion, is popular with women. It attracts them like a magic spell. You should try it.'

'Leave me in peace, both of you!'

'Oh, no, you don't!' said Henri, losing his temper. 'For three whole days now you've been wasting away here and making us sick with worry!'

'I'm not making anybody sick with worry. I have ceased to exist.'

'Louis-François, that's enough!' Périgord said. 'Tomorrow we're going to Baden.'

'*Bon voyage!*' muttered Lejeune.

'With you.'

'No, you're not. Besides, we have to take part in the Saturday parade at Schönbrunn tomorrow, with the Major-General.'

'I have spoken to Marshal Berthier about you,' Périgord said, 'and he has given me permission to take you to Baden for the good of your health.'

'What did you tell him?'

'The truth!'

'You madman!'

'You're the one who's gone mad, Louis-François. Now, obey orders.'

Taking the waters at Baden was Henri's idea, which had come to him from talking to Baron Peyrusse, Paymaster of the General Treasury of the Crown. The latter had described his brief stay in the small valley four miles from Vienna. You rented a house for a bundle of florins. The waters? You splashed about in pinewood tanks of mineral water with twenty other people, and, above all, men bathed side by side with young girls in wet blouses which would arouse the fancies of even the least fanciful. If Lejeune could fall in love with a young Austrian girl who would replace Anna in his affections, then his recovery would be swift.

*

Dr Corvisart, who had a high forehead and white curls fringing the back of his head, had installed himself in the Emperor's office.

'It's a recurrence of your old eczema, sire.'

'On my neck?'

'Hardly reason enough to have brought me here from Paris.'

'German doctors are all nonentities!'

'I'll jot down the ingredients of your usual ointment to give to His Majesty's chemists.'

'Jot them down, Corvisart, jot them down!'

The Emperor had himself dressed by his valets while Dr Corvisart wrote out the formula for the preparation which had previously succeeded in clearing up Napoleon's recurrent eczema: fifteen grammes of sabadilla in powder form, ninety grammes of olive oil, ninety grammes of pure alcohol. It had worked perfectly since the Consulate.

'Monsieur Constant?'

The head valet appeared at the door of the Lacquer Salon, bowed, and announced, 'His Excellency the Prince of Neuchâtel.'

'Let him come in if he has good news. If it's bad, tell

him to go about his business! Bad news is what brings on
my eczema, isn't that so, Corvisart?'

'Perhaps, sire.'

'The news is good,' said Berthier, entering the salon.
'Your Majesty will be gratified.'

'Well, then, speak: gratify My Majesty!'

The Emperor sat down and stretched out his white
stockinged feet. His shoemaker, who was kneeling by his
chair, slid on his boots.

Berthier summarized their situation in light of the
information he had received that morning.

'Marmont and MacDonald's divisions have effected their
junction near the Semmering Pass. The Army of Italy is, at
this moment, marching on the road to Vienna.'

'Archduke John?'

'He was unable to check their advance and is withdrawing towards Hungary with a reduced force.'

'Archduke Charles?'

'He isn't moving.'

'What a fool he is!'

'Indeed, sire. However, our comparative setback seems
to have given fresh heart to our enemies in Europe . . .'

'You see, Corvisart,' the Emperor said to his doctor, 'this
good-for-nothing wants to make me ill!'

'No, sire, he seeks merely to concentrate your thoughts.'

'Well?' the Emperor asked his major-general.

'Russians are demonstrating against us in Moravia, but
Tsar Alexander assures you of his friendship.'

'Of course he does! He has no desire to see the Austrians
marching back into Poland! He deluges me with fine words
and yet doesn't send me a single Cossack! What about
Paris? What is Paris saying?'

'Rumours of defeat have been circulating, even at Court, and your sister Caroline has had palpitations. The Bourse is down.'

'Bankers! All dullards! And Fouché?'

'The Duke of Otranto has taken the situation in hand and put a stop to any wavering.'

'That fox! What an excellent barometer! Have his powers extended. If he doesn't betray me, it is because he knows where his interests lie!'

'Contrary to our fears,' continued Berthier, 'the English are no longer threatening to invade Holland . . .'

'And the Pope?'

'He has excommunicated you, sire.'

'Oh yes! I'd forgotten. Who is in command of our gendarmerie in Rome?'

'General Radet.'

'Is he trustworthy?'

'It was he who reorganized our gendarmerie, sire. He has been effective in Naples and Tuscany.'

'Where is that swine of a Pope?'

'In the Quirinal, sire.'

'Have Radet abduct him and put him under arrest!'

'Have him arrested?'

'And do it far away from Rome – in Florence, for example. His insolence irritates me and any moment now my eczema will start making me itch, eh, Corvisart? Don't look like that, Berthier! This isn't religion, this is politics.' Looking at his boots, Napoleon said to his shoemaker, 'Have you seen the leather? Even polished, it's still cracking.'

'You need new boots, sire.'

'How much would that cost?'

'Eighteen francs, or thereabouts, Your Majesty.'

'Too expensive! Berthier, is everything ready for the review?'

'The troops await you.'

'Do we have an audience?'

'A large one. The Viennese love parades and they are curious to see you.'

'*Subito!*'

So for more than an hour, in the full heat of the day, Napoleon sat on his white horse, dressed in the uniform of a Colonel of Grenadiers – waistcoat, blue jacket and red facings – with every eye fixed on him at the centre of his entire Headquarters Staff. The Imperial Guard marched past in perfect order and to music. The men were rested, washed and clean shaven, the brass of their uniforms polished until it shone, not a single button or trim was missing, and the crowd applauded the standards. The Emperor wanted to show that, far from having brought his army to its knees, the murderous fighting on the banks of the Danube had been merely a setback. Such a display was sure to impress the inhabitants of Vienna and restore the soldiers' morale. When it came to an end, Napoleon dismounted and walked across the main courtyard back to the palace. As he did so, a young man burst out of the crowd which the gendarmes were scarcely restraining. Berthier blocked his path.

'What do you want?'

'To see the Emperor.'

'If you have a petition for him, give it to me, I will see that it is read.'

'I want to talk to him, and to him alone.'

'That's impossible. Goodbye, young man.'

The major-general signalled to the gendarmes to push
the lad back into the cheering crowd and then he rejoined
the Emperor inside Schönbrunn. The young man's agitation, however, did not subside. He broke away from the
crowd once more and, striding across the paved courtyard,
managed to get closer to the palace. This time, the colonel
of the gendarmerie intervened in person to ask him to
move along, but, alarmed by the overwrought look on his
face, he had him seized by his men. The lad put up a
struggle and, as his green frock coat fell open, the officer
glimpsed the handle of a knife; he took it from him and
ordered that he be taken to one of the Emperor's orderly
officers. It was the Alsatian, Rapp, and they began speaking
to one another in German.

'Are you Austrian?'

'German.'

'What did you want to do with this knife?'

'Kill Napoleon.'

'Do you realize the enormity of what you are confessing
to?'

'I heed the voice of God.'

'What is your name?'

'Friedrich Staps.'

'You are very pale!'

'That is because I have failed in my mission.'

'Why did you want to kill His Majesty?'

'I can only tell him that.'

When he was informed of this incident, the Emperor
agreed to receive Staps. He was astonished by how young
he was and laughed very hard.

'Why, he's only a little boy!'

'He is seventeen, sire,' said General Rapp.

'He looks twelve! Does he speak French?'

'Barely,' he said.

'You will translate, Rapp.' Turning to Staps, he asked, 'Why stab me?'

'Because you are ruining my country.'

'No doubt your father was killed in battle?'

'No.'

'Have I harmed you personally?'

'As you have all Germans.'

'You are an Illuminato!'

'I am in perfect health.'

'Who indoctrinated you?'

'No one.'

'Berthier,' the Emperor said, turning to his major-general, 'have good Corvisart come in . . .'

The doctor entered and was informed of the situation. He examined the young man, felt his pulse and pronounced, 'No excessive perturbation, the heartbeat is normal: your assassin is in good health . . .'

'I told you so!' Staps said triumphantly.

'Monsieur,' said the Emperor, 'ask my forgiveness and you will be free to go. This is nothing but childishness.'

'I will not apologize.'

'*Inferno!* You were going to commit a crime.'

'To kill you would not be a crime but a public service.'

'If I pardon you, will you go home?'

'I will try again.'

Napoleon tapped the parquet floor with his boot. The cross-examination was beginning to bore him. He lowered his eyes so as not to look at young Staps any more and, changing his tone, he said in a curt voice to the others present, 'Take this angelic-looking halfwit away!'

Patrick Rambaud

These words amounted to a death sentence. Friedrich Staps didn't struggle as his hands were bound. Gendarmes pushed him towards one door as the Emperor left by another.

*

Life in Vienna returned to how it had been before the battle – or something close to that. Daru had requisitioned a number of palaces to set up more adequate hospitals. The wounded had been evacuated from the island and they lay between white sheets, with a branch in one hand as a fan to drive away the flies. A tariff for wounds had been fixed: forty francs for two amputated limbs, twenty francs for a single limb, ten francs for any other wounds resulting in a disability. Paymaster Peyrusse helped, by his own count, 10,700 wounded on these terms.

Since Dr Percy was still short of personnel, despite complaining continually, and since the wounded were so numerous that they required teams of nurses, assistants, canteen workers, washerwomen and laundrywomen, General Molitor had given him permission to keep Voltigeur Paradis on in his service: 'This man is unfit for combat,' Percy had said, 'and what he has been through has left him slightly unhinged, but he's got two arms and two legs, he's a sturdy lad and I need his sort. He'll be of more use to me than to you.' Molitor, therefore, had made no bones about signing the transfer; besides, he was hoping for the arrival of a fresh draft of conscripts to restore his division to its full strength. So, while he was carrying a pail of slops, Paradis saw his Emperor for the first time from close up – close enough to touch him. He was visiting the Albertina Palace, which had been turned into a hospital, in order to

286

decorate some brave double amputees, who wept with emotion at the occasion.

It had not been possible to bring the most seriously wounded back to Vienna and so the villagers of Ebersdorf had given them lodgings on the other side of the river to Lobau. Marshal Lannes had had both legs amputated. He was staying in a brewer's house, on the first floor, in a room above a stable. For four days it was thought that he would recover; he talked about prosthetic limbs and dreamt of the future, imagining ways to command an army when one had lost both one's legs – in a barrel, he'd say, like Admiral Nelson. The heat was extreme and the temperature rose to thirty degrees. His wounds became infected. His room stank. One valet abandoned the marshal, unable to bear the stench, another fell ill and only Marbot, the faithful Marbot, remained by his marshal's bedside. He forgot to take proper care of his own wounds and his thigh became swollen and inflamed. He watched over him day and night. He became privy to all his secrets and hopes. He helped, as best he could, Dr Yvan and Dr Franck, a surgeon at the Austrian court who had volunteered his services to his French colleagues. Nothing had any effect. Marshal Lannes suffered terrible delirium, he no longer slept, he was convinced that he was still on the Marchfeld plain and he shouted imaginary orders, seeing battalions advancing through the fog and hearing the guns. Soon he stopped recognizing those close to him and he confused Marbot with his friend Pouzet, who had already been buried. Napoleon and Berthier came to visit every day, a handkerchief over their mouths so as not to breathe in that terrible stench of rotting flesh. The Emperor had given up speaking. Lannes looked at him as if he was a stranger. In one week, he only uttered a single lucid sentence in Napoleon's presence. 'You will never be more powerful than you are now, but you might well be more loved . . .'

*

The Viennese cannot do without music for long. A week after the battle, the theatre on the Wien was packed to the rafters. The four rows of boxes were occupied by French officers, more often than not in the company of beautiful Austrian women in very low-cut, flounced dresses, who fluttered fans made of feathers in front of their bare, ample bosoms. On this particular evening there was a performance of Molière's *Don Juan*, in a version adapted for the opera. Sganarelle entered singing and the sets changed on the open stage. The trees in the garden, which looked real, pivoted to turn into pink marble columns, a bush swivelled to reveal caryatids, the grass rolled up to become a Turkish carpet, the sky changed colour, enormous chandeliers fell from the flies, the walls of the stage slid back on rails and an entire staircase unfolded. A great chorus in dominos invaded the vast stage for a masked ball and Doña Elvira sang the invitation she had received from Don Juan. The spectators joined in, beating time with the music, leaping to their feet, bursting into wild cheers, giving ovations and demanding encores of any aria they liked. Henri Beyle and Louis-François Lejeune, in full-dress uniform, enjoyed this quintessentially Viennese spectacle. The Colonel hadn't forgotten Anna while taking the waters at Baden, but his resentment became less acute and some of the young blondes there had managed to distract him. In their box, the two friends exchanged rapid comments on the singing and the sets. They found Mme Campi, who was playing the Commendatore's daughter, far too thin and lamentably ugly, but they thought her voice charming.

'Pass me your spyglass, won't you?' asked Henri.

Lejeune handed him the telescope he had used in Essling to study the movements of the Austrian army. Henri raised it to his eye, then passed it back to the Colonel.

'Look, she's the third chorus girl from the left.'

'Sweet,' Lejeune commented as he looked at her. 'You've got good taste.'

'Sweet, when it comes to Valentina, is perhaps not exactly the right word. Pretty, yes, effervescent, yes, playful, often witty.'

'Will you introduce me?'

'Nothing could be simpler, Louis-François. We'll go backstage.'

Henri didn't dare explain that Valentina could talk the hind leg off a donkey, and that she was an intrusive and, in every sense, extreme personality – but, with all her faults, wasn't she exactly what Louis-François needed? The opposite of Anna Krauss, that is. She made one's head swim. *Don Juan* continued, its connection with Molière growing steadily more tenuous. In the last act, as the Commendatore's statue sank beneath the ground, Don Juan was seized by a swarm of horned demons. Vesuvius appeared on stage in mid-eruption, expertly rendered waves of lava pouring out of it and lapping against the proscenium arch. With mocking laughter, the demons threw the protagonist into the crater and the curtain fell. Henri led Lejeune towards the dressing-rooms. As they walked along the corridors backstage, they passed half-dressed actresses swooning with pleasure at their admirers' compliments.

'We could be in the foyer of the Théâtre des Variétés,' said
the Colonel, at last breaking into a smile, and it was true
that they would have been squeezing past exactly the same
crowd of playwrights, nymphs and carping or gossiping
journalists if they had been in Paris. Henri knew the way.
Valentina shared her dressing-room with some other chorus
girls who were taking off their make-up. She was only
wearing a tunic and was enchanted when Louis-François
kissed her hand.

'We are taking you to supper in the Prater,' said Henri.

'What a wonderful idea!' she said, her eyes riveted on
the officer, whom she asked in a bantering tone, 'So, were
you in that awful battle?'

'Yes, Mademoiselle.'

'Will you tell me all about it? You couldn't see a thing
from the ramparts!'

'Certainly, as long as you'll agree to pose for me.'

'Louis-François is an excellent painter,' Henri explained,
as Valentina looked surprised.

She batted her eyelashes.

'Painter and soldier,' added Lejeune.

'How marvellous! I will pose for you, General.'

'Colonel.'

'But your uniform is surely a general's, at the very least!'

'He designed it himself,' Henri pointed out.

'Will you design costumes for me?'

They waited outside while Valentina chose a walking-
out dress. A group of people were talking next to them and
they caught snatches of their conversation.

'An Illuminato, I swear!' a fat gentleman in a black
frock coat was saying.

'But he was so young!' a singer said in a quavering voice.

'Nevertheless, he tried to assassinate the Emperor.'

'Tried to, that's very true, but he didn't succeed!'

'The intention sufficed.'

'All the same, to have him shot for such a madcap attempt!'

'His Majesty wished to spare him.'

'Oh, come now!'

'No, no, he did. I have it from General Rapp, who was there. The boy was intractable, he insulted the Emperor. How could he be expected to be pardoned after that?'

'All Vienna is whispering that he will become a hero.'

'Alas, that cannot be ruled out.'

'The Emperor will be accused of brutality.'

'His life was at stake, and ours too.'

'What was his name, this hero of yours who thought himself another Joan of Arc?'

'Stabs or Staps.'

Henri started when he heard the name. At supper he was the most solemn of the three. Valentina amused Louis-François and they decided to see each other again.

*

The island of Lobau was unrecognizable. In a matter of days the thickets and reeds of Masséna's entrenched camp had been transformed into a hidden city with streets lined with street-lamps, solid fortifications, and canals clear enough for boats bringing flour and ammunition to draw water. In one corner was a mill. In another, ovens where bread was baking. Herds of oxen had been penned in a fenced-off clearing. The army had seized quantities of wine from the neighbouring abbeys and the cellars of the Viennese bourgeoisie to keep the troops and the workers happy, since twelve thousand Seaman of the Guard and as many engineers and carpenters had started building three large bridges on stilts, which were protected from floating objects by a stockade of piles upstream. The Austrians were clearly visible on the Essling bank, but they couldn't themselves see the heavy guns trained on them. Every morning, after inspecting the works, Colonel Sainte-Croix rode hard to Schönbrunn to report to the Emperor on their progress. The sentries and chamberlains had learnt to recognize him and they respected him; he became a familiar figure and used to enter the Lacquer Salon without knocking.

On 30 May, at seven o'clock in the morning, Sainte-Croix found the Emperor drinking his usual glass of water.

'Do you want some?' said the Emperor, pointing to the carafe. 'Schönbrunn's spring is cold and very delicious.'

'I can well believe Your Majesty, but I prefer a glass of good wine.'

'*D'accordo!* Constant! Monsieur Constant, send the Colonel two hundred bottles of Bordeaux and the same of champagne.'

Then the Emperor and his new favourite climbed into his Berline, which took them to Ebersdorf, opposite the bridges. Napoleon would usually stop in the village for a few minutes to visit Marshal Lannes, whose health had continued to fail and whose death throes had become agonizingly drawn out. On that morning, Marbot had left the dying man's bedside. He was waiting in front of the stables, leaning on a cane because of the pain his thigh caused him. The Emperor saw him as he stepped out of his Berline.

'The marshal?'

'He died this morning, sire, at five o'clock. In my arms. His head fell back on my shoulder.'

The Emperor went up to the first floor and stayed by the body for an hour, in that stinking room. Then he congratulated Marbot on his loyalty and asked him to have the marshal embalmed before sending him home to France. Deep in thought, he followed Sainte-Croix who was showing him the latest works. He remained silent. He didn't open his mouth again until they entered Masséna's tent. The Duke of Rivoli had one leg bandaged and received him from his armchair.

'What? You as well? What on earth happened to you? The battle has ended, as far as I'm aware!'

'I fell in a hole which was hidden by a thicket and I've had a slight limp ever since. The bones are fragile at my age, sire.'

'Take your crutches and follow me.'

'My doctor has to change the dressing every hour, sire. Let's not go too far.'

Masséna hobbled along behind the Emperor and Sainte-Croix, as the latter explained the capabilities of the landing craft he was having built.

'Each craft, sire, can hold three hundred men. At the bows, as you can see, there is a shutter behind which the men can shelter and, as soon as they beach, the shutter folds down and becomes a gangway by means of which they can leap onto the bank.'

After visiting a number of workshops and making a tour of the fortifications, the Emperor wished to walk along the sandy bank of the island, where his soldiers had got into the habit of bathing under the amused gaze of the

Austrians. To eliminate any risk, Napoleon and the Marshal put on sergeants' greatcoats.

'We attack in a month,' said the Emperor. 'We will have a hundred and fifty thousand men, twenty thousand horse, five hundred cannon. Berthier has assured me of this. What's that, over there, at the far end of the plain?'

'The hutments of the Archduke's camp.'

'They're as far away as that, are they?'

With a twig, the Emperor drew a map in the sand.

'In the first days of July, we cross in strength. MacDonald and the Army of Italy, Marmont and the Army of Dalmatia, Lefebvre's Bavarians, Bernadotte's Saxons. Your divisions, Masséna, will make for between the villages...'

He raised his head to survey the plain.

'I tell you this, Masséna, and you too, Sainte-Croix. Over there, where the Archduke has pitched his camp, that will be his tomb! What's the name of the plateau behind him?'

'Wagram, sire.'

HISTORICAL NOTES

IN 1809

Darwin – *born 12 February*	Napoleon – *40*
Gerard de Nerval – *1 year old*	Wellington – *40*
George Sand – *5*	Espagne – *40*
Victor Hugo – *7*	Lannes – *40*
Alexandre Dumas – *7*	Chateaubriand – *41*
Balzac – *10*	Francis II of Austria – *41*
Vigny – *12*	Bessières – *41*
Lamartine – *19*	Benjamin Constant – *42*
Schopenhauer – *21*	Daru – *42*
Stendhal – *26*	Saint-Hilaire – *43*
Sainte-Croix – *27*	Larrey – *43*
Louis-François Lejeune – *34*	Madame de Staël – *43*
Marbot – *27*	Fouché – *46*
Antoine de Lasalle – *34*	Cherubini – *49*
Dorsenne – *36*	Masséna – *51*
Caulaincourt – *36*	Talleyrand – *55*
Duroc – *27*	Percy – *55*
Walter Scott – *38*	Berthier – *56*
Archduke Charles – *38*	Goethe – *60*
Davout – *39*	Goya – *63*
Beethoven – *39*	Sade – *69*
Hegel – *39*	Haydn – *77*
Tsar Alexander – *39*	

At the end of the 1820s, Walter Scott was greatly admired by French writers and there was a vogue for the historical novel in France. Vigny had a success with *Cinq-Mars*, which went through fourteen editions in his lifetime, Hugo was contemplating *Notre-Dame de Paris*, and Balzac published an involved novel about the Chouans. His work attracted only three hundred readers and the critics pilloried it, finding it confused, pretentious, obscure and lacking in style. But Balzac persevered. In 1831, after *La Peau de Chagrin*, he returned to his historical novel, which he revised and completed, and at the same time announced another work, *Scènes de la Vie Militaire*, which was to include *La Bataille*. He claimed to be working on this book at Aix but the Marchioness de Castries, with whom he was in love, took up too much of his time. He didn't, however, abandon his plan. In December 1834, he spoke of it again with assurance. He promised a portrait of Paris at the start of the fifteenth century, a story from the reign of Louis XIII and, once again, his *La Bataille*, this time specifying its period by adding, *Vue de l'Empire, 1809*.

Which battle? Wagram? No. Essling. The year before he had revealed his intention in a letter to Mme Hanska.

In it I undertake to initiate you into all the horrors, all the beauties, of a battlefield. My battle is Essling – Essling with all its consequences. What I have to do is make a man sitting quite coolly in his armchair behold the country, the inequalities of the ground, the masses of troops, the strategic events, the Danube, the bridges; he must admire the details and the whole of this conflict, hear the artillery, interest himself in every movement on this military chessboard, see everything, and feel, in each joint of that great body, Napoleon, whom I shall not show, or of whom I shall give only a passing glimpse as he crosses the Danube in a boat at the end of the day! Not a single woman: only cannon, horses, two armies, uniforms. On the first page the cannon roars; on the last it falls silent. You read through the smoke, and, when you have shut the book, you must have intuitively seen everything and be able to recall the battle as if you had been an eyewitness.

In 1835 Balzac was in Vienna. He had gone to present the manuscript of *Séraphîta* to Eveline Hanska. He took this opportunity to hire a carriage and visit Essling, the Marchfeld plain, the plateau of Wagram and the island of Lobau. Prince Schwarzenfeld accompanied him onto the battlefield. He took notes. Then he returned home to write *Le Lys dans la vallée*. Jostled by a thousand characters and a thousand subjects, Balzac was never to give us his version of *La Bataille*.

Why did Balzac choose this little-known battle? Possibly because, at Essling, the nature of war changed. Louis Madelin, the historian of the Empire, emphasizes this: 'This battle ushered in the era of the great hecatombs which, from then on, were to mark the campaigns of the Emperor.' More than forty thousand killed in approximately thirty hours. Twenty-seven thousand Austrians and sixteen thousand French – the equivalent of a death every three seconds – quite apart from almost eleven thousand disabled in the Grande Armée. And then Essling was also the first reversal Napoleon suffered when he was in personal command, which both damaged his prestige and gave heart to his enemies. After Essling, nationalist movements began to develop throughout Europe.

To understand the battle and what was at stake, I consulted the historians first. I soon realized that the specialists lack objectivity. When it comes to Napoleon, few of them remain dispassionate: Jean Savant hates him, Elie Faure reveres him, Madelin celebrates him, Bainville is fond of him, Taine fights against him and so on. So then I turned to eye-witnesses. Balzac had access to these, since, for the most part, they were still alive and could tell their stories. Fortunately they left memoirs and other written accounts. They too have strong opinions, favourable or otherwise, about Napoleon, but they give us a mass of details which I wouldn't have dared invent and, in combination with the more anecdotal historians, they provided me with the ideal subject matter. Lucas-Dubreton, for instance, tells the story of the standard bearer of the Guard who was decapitated by a cannon ball: gold coins, his savings which he'd hidden in his stock, rained down on the ground. I owe the broth made from dead horses and seasoned with gunpowder to the memoirs of Constant, the Emperor's valet. The clothes are authentic, as are the songs, the decor, the topography, the weather, the portraits of the principal protagonists, their strengths and weaknesses. I tried not to judge the soldiers. Dorsenne, for example. If Thiébault's *Mémoires* are to be believed, he was a complete imbecile, but Thiébault wasn't at Essling and the examples he gives do not apply to this battle. What's more he exaggerates, one can tell.

A historical novel is the staging of actual events. To achieve this, I had to introduce fictional characters alongside the Marshals and the Emperor. They contribute to the rhythm and help to reconstruct the battle. I invented as little as possible, but it was often necessary to work up a detail or a sentence into an entire scene.

A historian, Alexander Dumas said, defends a point of view and chooses the heroes who will help him to do so. Only the novelist, he added, is impartial: he does not judge, he shows.

Here, arranged by subject, is the list of books which helped me bring the battle of Essling to life as faithfully as possible. For those which I consulted at the Service historique des armées, fort de Vincennes, I have given the reference number preceded by a V for Vincennes.

[*Publisher's Note*. We have for convenience numbered those works that have been translated into English, and listed them on page 308.]

1. On the campaign of 1809 and its course.

Martin, Henri, *Histoire de France populaire*, tome V, Paris: Furne, Jouvet et Cie (undated). Fast-moving, precise, vivid and inspired, Henri Martin gives an incomparable overview.

Cadet-Gassicourt, *Voyage en Autriche, en Moravie et en Bavière fait à la suite de l'armée française pendant la campagne de 1809*, Paris: L'Huillier, 1818. This rare and precious book was composed shortly after the Empire by the pharmacist in ordinary to Napoleon. An occasionally acid account, Cadet-Gassicourt (or Cadet de Gassicourt) is the forerunner of occupational medicine.

Tranié et Carmigniani, *Napoléon et l'Autriche, la campagne de 1809*: Copernic, 1979. This large illustrated history has been indispensable. The text is clear and teems with details. It contains a multitude of photographs, pictures, sketches, portraits and plates of uniforms which helped me to imagine the battle. Moreover the daily plans of operations saved me from making a considerable number of mistakes about the movement of troops.

Pelet, *Mémoires sur la guerre de 1809*, tome 3, V. 72905. Military account by an eye-witness.

Marbot, *Mémoires*, tome 1, Mercure de France, 1983. One of the best memoirists, with an abundance of details and anecdotes. I owe him most of the information about Marshal Lannes at Essling, his wound and his death. I also owe him the figure of Sainte-Croix, to whom he devotes almost an entire chapter. [1]

Lejeune, *Mémoires, de Valmy à Wagram*, V. 40518. Here again I have invented very little. He was a real person who lived in the circumstances I have described. He was a great painter and a liaison officer on the General Staff, which allowed him to cover the length and breadth of the battlefield. The stags swept downstream by the current, the Austrian sentry who shoots at him in Chapter 6 – all this is true. What is invented is his friendship with Stendhal (who was in Vienna, serving under Count Daru) and his thwarted love for Anne Krauss (who did not exist). Louis-François Lejeune wrote as well as he painted and his *Mémoires* are a pleasure.

Masséna, *Mémoires*, tome VI, V. 6835. The Marshal speaks of himself in the third person, like Julius Caesar, and always paints himself in the most flattering light. He is irreplaceable when describing the topography of a battlefield. Thanks to him I walked along the sunken lanes and through the copses of willows and elms, I learnt the thickness of the walls of Essling's granary, the layout of the houses, etc. The story of his equerry killed by a roundshot as he was helping adjust his stirrup is true (and appears in Marbot as well).

Renemont, *Campagne de 1809*, V. 55192. Technical.

Camon, *La Guerre napoléonienne*, V. 66363/1. Technical.

Napier, *Campagne de 1809*, V. 730999, vol. 3. Technical.

Brunon, 'Essling', *Revue Historique des armées*, V. Titre III, ch II, 1959/I. In this I learnt that, due to a shortage of oats, the horses were fed barley and that on the second day they charged at a trot.

Baron Peyrusse, *Lettres inédites*, Perrin, 1894.

2. *On the army.*

Masson, *Cavaliers de Napoléon*, V. 24811. A classic. All the regiments, all the uniforms, all the officers.

Lucas-Dubreton, *Soldats de Napoléon*, V. 61835. Another classic, full of details and revealing anecdotes.

Coignet, *Les Cahiers du capitaine Coignet*, Hachette, 1883 and *Souvenirs d'un vieux grognard*, V. 21980. On the Imperial Guard. A celebrated work. [3]

Pils, *Journal de marche d'un grenadier*, V. 20291.

Parquin, *Souvenirs et campagnes*, V. 41352. [4]

Chevalier, *Souvenirs des guerres napoléoniennes*, V. 17804.

Brice, *Les Femmes et les armées de la Révolution et de l'Empire*. V. 4354.

Masson, *Jadis*, tome 2, V. 9989.

Caziot, *Historique du corps des pontonniers*, V. 37488.

Chardigny, *Les Maréchaux de Napoléon*, Flammarion, 1846. Very thorough.

Zieseniss, *Berthier*, Belfond, 1985.

Histoire et dictionnaire du Consulat et de l'Empire, Fierro, Palluel-Guillard and Tulard, 'Bouquins', Robert Laffont, 1995.

In Hachette's 'Vie Quotidienne' collection, one can consult the three volumes concerning the Empire, composed at different periods by Messrs Robiquet [5], Baldet and Tulard.

3. On the period and Vienna.

D'Alméras, *La Vie Parisienne sous le Consulat et l'Empire*, Albin Michel, 7th Edition (undated).

Bertaut, *La Vie à Paris sous le 1er Empire*, Calmann-Levy, 1949

Kralik, *Histoire de Vienne*, Payot, 1932.

Mme de Staël, *De l'Allemagne*, tome 1, Garnier-Flammarion, 1968. [6]

Grueber, *Sous les aigles autrichiennes*, V. 3523.

Brion, *La Vie quotidienne à Vienne au temps de Mozart et de Schubert*, Hachette, 1986. Any book by Marcel Brion is always a great event and deserves to be read as closely as possible. He led me out onto the now vanished ramparts of the old town and into the taverns on the banks of the Danube. Thanks to him I learnt that Haydn was in Vienna, where he died soon after Essling.

Vienne, Guides Gallimard. Describes the flora and fauna of the island of Lobau.

4. On military medicine.

Percy, *Journal de campagne*, V. 31488.

Larrey, *Mémoires de chirurgie militaire*, vol. 3, V. 71126 and *Clinique chirurgicale*, 4 vols, V. 71125.

Roos, *Souvenirs d'un médecin de la grande armée*, Perrin, 1913.

Toute l'Histoire de Napoléon, vol. 8, *Napoléon et les médecins*: periodical printed at Caen, January 1952. In which I came across the preparation Doctor Corvisart used to treat the Emperor's eczema.

5. *On Napoleon.*

Constant, *Mémoires intimes de Napoléon 1er*, Mercure de France, 1967. The indispensable work. Constant, the Emperor's valet, allowed me to visit Schönbrunn. The numerous and comprehensive notes at the end of this edition are enthralling: they are the work of M. Maurice Dernelle of the Academie d'histoire, for whose erudition I am grateful.

Stendhal, *Vie de Napoléon*, Payot, 1969. Written with panache and no fondness for its subject. [7]

Bainville, *Napoléon*, Fayard, 1931. [8]

Godechot, *Napoléon*, Albin Michel, 1969. Well-constructed series of studies, arranged by subject and including period accounts. Contains the story of Friedrich Staps and his complete cross-examination, recorded by General Rapp (c.f. his *Mémoires*, V. 73242). I have brought the date of the assassination attempt forward in the novel; it actually took place in October 1809. I kept Staps because he is a good representative of the mystical opposition to the Empire which subsequently was to grow stronger. The Emperor would have kept the kitchen knife with which Staps wanted to kill him. The details of the cross-examination appear in the May/June 1922 issue of *Etudes napoléoniennes*.

Ludwig, *Napoléon*, Payot 1929. [9]

Savant, *Tel fut Napoléon*, Fasquelle, 1953. This text was reprinted in an illustrated book entitled *Napoléon*, Henri Veyrier, 1974, and accompanied by a multitude of illustrations, pictures and portraits. For Jean Savant, Napoleon is an entirely negative figure and he gathers together every sort of evidence to this effect. Almost too much.

G. Lenotre, *Napoléon, croquis de l'épopée*, and *En suivant l'Empereur, 'La petite histoire'*, Grasset, 1932 and 1935. The first of these was republished in the 'Cahiers Rouges'. Incomparable. *Mon bon maître*. In homage I have borrowed his description of the Emperor's tricorn which he discovered in a bill of the hatmaker Poupard.

Bouhler, *Napoléon*, Grasset, 1942.

Mauguin, *Napoléon et la superstition, anecdotes et curiosités*, Carrière, Rodez, 1946.

Bertaut, *Napoléon ignoré*, Sfelt, 1951. Describes his superstitions, his horses, his moods.

Brice, *Le Secret de Napoléon*, Payot, 1936. [10]

Frugier, *Napoléon, essai médico-psychologique*, Albatros, 1985.

Emerson, *Representative Men*, 'Essays & Lectures', The Library of America, 1983. The American philosopher devotes his sixth chapter to Napoleon, or The Man of the World. A portrait that is all the more interesting for its unexpectedness.

Taine, *Les Origines de la France contemporaine*, Hachette, 1907, tome 11. An acid portrait. [11]

Faure, Elie, *Napoléon*, 'L'Herne', La Table Ronde, 1964. Reflective and full of admiration. [12]

6. *On Stendhal.*

Œuvres intimes I, 'La Pléiade', 1981. Contains, as an appendix, extracts from the *Journal* of Félix Faure in 1809 from which I have stolen the scene of Molière's *Don Juan* performed as an opera. The production took place on 12 August, and not at the end of May as in the novel. The words I have put in the mouth of my Henri Beyle are, as far as possible, genuinely his own. Similarly, with Napoleon, Masséna and Lannes, I have allowed myself to repeat what, according to witnesses, they actually said.

Correspondance I, 'La Pléiade', 1968.

Stendhal, *De l'amour*, Gallimard, 'Folio', 1980. [13]

Crouzet, *Stendhal ou Monsieur Moi-Même*, Flammarion, 1990.

English Translations

Numbers in square brackets correspond to those in the list above. Where no translator is stated the translation is anonymous. All are out of print save the first.

Marbot, Jean-Baptiste Antoine Marcellin, Baron de, *The memoirs of Baron de Marbot*, tr. Arthur John Butler (London: Longmans Green, 1892; facs. ed. London: Greenhill, 1988). [1]

Lejeune, Baron de, *Memoirs of Baron Lejeune*, tr. Mrs Arthur Bell (2 vols: London: Longmans Green, 1897). [2]

Coignet, Jean Roch, *The narrative of Captain Coignet, soldier of the Empire, 1776–1850*, tr. M. Carey (London: Chatto and Windus, 1897).

    Also *The note books of Captain Coignet* (London: Peter Davies, 1928).

    (Both are translations of *Les cahiers*.) [3]

Parquin, Denis Charles, *Napoleon's army: the military memoirs of Charles Parquin*, ed. B. T. Jones (London: Longman, 1969; repr. London: Lionel Leventhal, 1987). [4]

Robiquet, Jean, *Daily Life in France under Napoleon*, tr. Violet M. MacDonald (London: Allen and Unwin, 1962). [5]

Staël-Holstein, Anne Louis Germaine de, Baroness, *Germany*, tr. O. W. Wight (New York, 1871). [6]

Stendhal, *A Life of Napoleon* (London: Rodale Press, 1956). [7]

Bainville, Jacques, *Napoleon*, tr. Hamish Miles (London: Jonathan Cape, 1932). [8]

Ludwig, Emil, *Napoleon*, tr. Eden and Cedar Paul (London: Allen and Unwin, 1927). [9]

Brice, Léon Raoul Marie, *The riddle of Napoleon*, tr. Basil Creighton (London: Putman, 1937). [10]

Taine, Hippolyte Adolphe, *The origins of contemporary France*, tr. John Durand (Chicago and London: University of Chicago, 1974). [11]

Faure, Élie, *Napoleon*, tr. Jeffery E. Jeffery (London: Constable and Co., 1924). [12]

Stendhal, *Love*, tr. Gilbert and Suzanne Sale (Harmondsworth: Penguin, 1975). (The most recent of several translations.) [13]

DE PROFUNDIS!

Finally, here is what became of the historical figures who feature most prominently in the novel.

Louis-François Lejeune, General and Baron, retired in 1813 after an extremely eventful military career to devote himself to painting. He became the director of the Ecole des beaux-arts in Toulouse and died in that town in February 1848, aged seventy-three. He introduced lithography to France.

André Masséna was created Prince of Essling and, still suffering from a leg injury, gave orders from a barouche at the Battle of Wagram. After an unsuccessful campaign in Spain, he was disgraced. Appointed Governor of Paris immediately after Waterloo, he died there from a chest illness, eight years after the Battle of Essling.

Louis-Alexandre Berthier, Prince of Neuchâtel and of Wagram, fell from a window of Bamberg Castle in Bavaria in 1815. Suicide? He was very depressed by Napoleon's return from Elba. Assassination? Did someone want to prevent him rejoining Napoleon?

Jean-Marie-Pierre-François Dorsenne died three years after the Battle of Essling as a result of his head wound.

Jean Bessières was killed by a roundshot during the Saxony campaign in May 1813, as was Lasalle at Wagram.

Charles-Marie-Robert, Count of Escorche de Sainte-Croix, was cut in two by a roundshot in Portugal, a year after Essling. He was twenty-eight.

Jean Boudet committed suicide in Bohemia in September 1809. The Emperor had unjustly reprimanded him for his conduct at Essling.

Jean-Baptiste Marbot, General and Baron, became tutor to Louis Philippe's son. He died a peer of France under the Second Empire aged seventy-two.

Twenty-one years after the Battle of Essling, Henri Beyle published *Le Rouge et Le Noir* under the name Stendhal.

NAPOLEON'S MAJOR BATTLES

Date	Battle	Napoleon's opponents
15–17 November 1796	Arcola	Austrians
2 July 1798	Alexandria	Egyptians
21 July 1798	Pyramids	Egyptians
18 March to 20 May 1799	Siege of Acre	Ottoman and British – Napoleon defeated for the first time
14 June 1800	Marengo	Austrians
17 October 1805	Ulm	Austrians
2 December 1805	Austerlitz	Austrians
14 October 1806	Jena	Prussians
7–8 February 1807	Eylau	Russians
21–22 May 1809	Aspern-Essling	Austrians – Napoleon defeated
5–6 July 1809	Wagram	Austrians
7 September 1812	Borodino	Russians
26–28 November 1812	Berezina	Russians

| 16–19 October 1813 | Leipzig, 'The Battle of the Nations' | Allies – Napoleon defeated |
| 18 June 1815 | Waterloo | Allies – Napoleon defeated for the last time |

Aspern-Essling, 21–22 May 1809; Day Two

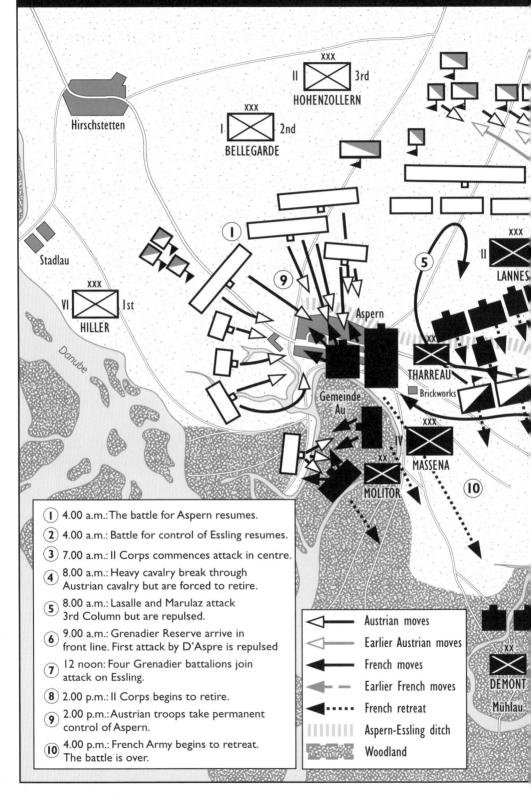

Hirschstetten

XXX
II | 3rd
HOHENZOLLERN

XXX
I. | 2nd
BELLEGARDE

Stadlau

Danube

XXX
VI | 1st
HILLER

①

⑨

Aspern

⑤

XXX
II |
LANNES

XX
THARREAU

Brickworks

Gemeinde
Au

XXX
IV |
MASSENA

XX
MOLITOR

⑩

XX
DEMONT

Mühlau

① 4.00 a.m.: The battle for Aspern resumes.

② 4.00 a.m.: Battle for control of Essling resumes.

③ 7.00 a.m.: II Corps commences attack in centre.

④ 8.00 a.m.: Heavy cavalry break through
Austrian cavalry but are forced to retire.

⑤ 8.00 a.m.: Lasalle and Marulaz attack
3rd Column but are repulsed.

⑥ 9.00 a.m.: Grenadier Reserve arrive in
front line. First attack by D'Aspre is repulsed

⑦ 12 noon: Four Grenadier battalions join
attack on Essling.

⑧ 2.00 p.m.: II Corps begins to retire.

⑨ 2.00 p.m.: Austrian troops take permanent
control of Aspern.

⑩ 4.00 p.m.: French Army begins to retreat.
The battle is over.

	Austrian moves
	Earlier Austrian moves
	French moves
	Earlier French moves
	French retreat
	Aspern-Essling ditch
	Woodland